Viking Warrior

Book 2 in the

Dragon Heart Series

By

Griff Hosker

Viking Warrior

Published by Sword Books Ltd 2014
Copyright © Griff Hosker First Edition

SWORD BOOKS

HOME OF EPIC HISTORICAL FICTION

A CIP catalogue record for this title is available from the British
Library.

Ireland before the Vikings

Chapter 1

I stood at the stern of '*Wolf*'. She was my ship, a drekar. She was not a large ship; she only seated fourteen rowers on each side. Sometimes warriors who did not know me derided her by calling her a threttanessa. I did not mind. They were speaking the truth, she was only small. The *'Ran'* which was Jarl Erik's boat had twenty oars on each side and my step father's ship, *'Man'* had fifty warriors on board, twenty-five on each side. The truth was that we did not decide on her size; the gods did. We used the longest and best pieces of timber for Prince Butar's boat. That was as it should be. We had to use whatever was left over for my boat and so it ended the size that it did. Olaf the Toothless had built her, knowing that she would be mine someday. He and Ragnar had been oathsworn and he looked after me whenever he could. It did not stop me from suffering his blows and his comments when I did not meet his standards but I normally deserved such treatment.

Her sea trials had been forced on us too when we used her on the raid to the mainland. It proved a godsend for we worked out all the smaller problems so that now she flew across the water. I was proud of her because the crew were all handpicked; they were Ulfheonar. They were the sea wolves who each wore a wolf cloak taken from the body of a wolf they had killed. We had all sworn an oath of brotherhood and we were feared by all who fought us. Many warriors feared me because I was Dragon Heart and I had the sword which was touched by the gods. My blade had been struck by lightning and was considered the most powerful blade on the island of our people, Manau.

This was the first time I had captained my ship and I was proud. Yet the pride was tinged with more than a little anger. We were sailing west and we were not raiders. We were heading for Hibernia to recover the family who had been stolen from our land by the pirates who lived there. My mother, Prince Butar's wife, had been murdered by them when they raided our town of Hrams-a. Tadgh, a Saxon who had come from our village on the Dunum, led them and I had sworn to kill him myself. He had always hated me. When we had been children he and his friends had mercilessly picked on me because I was different. I had a Saxon father and a mother who had been stolen from her people in the west. My childhood had been a torment until I had been captured and enslaved. Ironically that improved the quality of my life.

The warriors who sailed with us on our three ships were not singing. That was always a sign that they were not happy. All of us knew someone who had been enslaved by the Hibernian Norse. Renegade

Norse pirates were despised by true warriors and the Hibernians were known to have no honour. All of the men who rowed were determined to bring back all of the captives. My wife, Erika, and baby son, Arturus, were now prisoners, along with my half sister, Eurwen. We would not return without them.

I knew that Tadgh and his pirates had a good start on us; it had taken some time to gather the men and the ships together. My twenty eight men were the smallest crew while Prince Butar's drekar had over fifty warriors. Jarl Erik, my brother in law, commanded the third boat. A hundred and odd warriors sound like a large warband but we knew that we were entering an environment where everyone would be an enemy. The Hibernians were a treacherous people who would happily slit a neighbour's throat for a cow or two. We were under no illusions, we would have to fight for our families.

We were still wary of our sneaky neighbours and our oldest and best warrior, Olaf had remained behind to defend Duboglassio. With Jarl Erik with us, his settlement was undefended. There were many Hibernians and we had made our island prosperous. Olaf would defend it along with Jarl Harald and his men. We had temporarily abandoned Hrams-a for it had been devastated by the raiders. It was a brutal and stark reminder of the perils of a surprise attack. We would, once again, rebuild it but we needed to wait until we had recovered our families and our slaves.

My ship was the fastest of the three; she was slim and had the shallowest draft. We were leading the others and heading west. Our ship acted as the scout for the other two. We had no idea where the raiders had gone. We had discussed where Tadgh might go. We could not imagine him sailing too far with overloaded boats. We would make the earliest landfall we could. We would land as soon as we could and search for them.

The night before we had sailed we held a council of war. We were under no illusions, this was war. They had come in the night and killed the old and taken the young and the women. If we did not fight for our families then there would be no one left on Man. We selected the men who would sail and those who would remain. Every warrior wanted to go.

My step-father, Prince Butar, had become old almost overnight. My mother had been the love of his life and Eurwen the sun in his sky. Without my mother, he was half a man and without his child, he was little more than a dead man walking. It was as though the heart had been ripped from him. He cared for his people and it showed. Jarls Erik and Harald had both brought their families and oathsworn to serve under

Prince Butar on our newly conquered island. The settlements and their families were safe. They had no need to follow us. Jarl Erik would not be left behind; his sister was my wife.

"Tomorrow Dragon Heart and I will take our drekar and we will sail to Hibernia to bring back our families." He had looked at Olaf, his oldest friend, "I leave Olaf the Toothless in command until I return. Jarl Erik is oath bound to rescue his sister and Olaf will protect all our people at Jarl Erik's home." He had stopped as though he couldn't find the words but I knew it was my mother's death which preyed on his mind. "I ask no man to follow me. All those who wish to sail with us do so of their own volition." There had been a clamour of men shouting to become part of this attack to wreak revenge on the renegades. Prince Butar had held up his hands. "Some must stay to defend our home. If we succeed and lose the island then we have lost all."

Jarl Harald stood, "I would follow you across the oceans to the edge of the world and back Prince Butar but what you say makes sense." He had spread his arm in the direction of his men. "We lost many men in the raid on the Dee and others protecting our home. We would not be able to add great numbers to those sailing. I will stay and I swear that I will defend the island against all who try to wrest it from us." I did not know how he could be willing to stay when there was a chance for revenge but he had suffered no losses as yet.

And so we had our warbands. Prince Butar had the largest number of men although in truth many of them were barely boys. Erik had some doughty warriors but he was forced to leave some to protect his wife and family and there was my band of Ulfheonar. We were the fewest in number but I knew our enemies would fear us. We were well trained in fighting at night. We were adept at infiltrating enemy camps and there was no one who could face us man to man. Although I was younger than some of those who followed me, they had all fought alongside me since we had come to the island. We had fought Saxons, Hibernians and now Norse; we had never been beaten.

It had been hard to leave Scanlan, my slave, for his wife and family, had been kidnapped but I needed him at home. I needed him to keep what little we had for our return. He had begged permission to follow me but I had had to be ruthless. He was a slave and could not fight with my warriors. If he fought alone he would die. I cared too much for him and his family to risk that and so it was just the handful of us who pulled across that cold Hibernian Sea to the unknown land to the west.

I had two of the boys who would be warriors with me as crew. They acted as lookouts and brought the rowers sustenance. They would also guard the boat when we went raiding. It was a way of blooding young warriors. We had the sail raised to make the fastest crossing we could and their young eyes were invaluable. Snorri perched precariously at the top of the mainmast; his legs astride it and dangling over the red and white sail. It was he who first sighted land.

"Land to the north west!"

His small voiced carried aft on the wind and I waved to acknowledge it. I turned the tiller slightly and we headed in the direction of the distant land. We had all seen Hibernia when we sailed south but we knew better than to land on this island of half naked madmen. It was an unknown quantity. We sought somewhere without people but yet close enough for us to explore. Bjorn the blacksmith's son and the only survivor of the raid had told us that there was at least one drekar. The Hibernians did not use our ships and so if we found the drekar we would have found our families.

"It is an island! There are houses!"

That meant we could not land there. "Is there land beyond it?"

"Yes, my lord, to the west."

I leaned on the tiller. The people on the island would see us and know us for what we were, they would call us Lochlannach or Gaill. They would hide their animals and bar their gates. The word would spread and it would reach Tadgh. It was now a race against time. Would we reach my wife before Tadgh heard that we were hunting him and were close?

I did not have to worry about the other two ships. They would follow me. We had been lucky that the sea was so calm and we had not had to bail. The wind, too, had helped us. Perhaps the gods were being kind to us now having been so cruel to us before.

I could now see the land spied by Snorri. There were low hills which reminded me of our island home and, to the south, I saw the smoke of a settlement. "Snorri, is there anything ahead of us? Any settlements?"

"Just the one to the south, my lord."

I decided to head into the lee of the hills that we could see. Hopefully, there would be a beach for us to run our boats upon. "Haaken and Egill, get the sail down."

Olaf had taught me to sail and he had drilled into me the importance of a safe beaching. If I hit the beach too hard I could rip the bottom out of my boat. As he said to me once, "There is always time to go in slowly. It is getting out that sometimes has to be quick!"

I was also thinking about the two bigger ships. They would see my sail being lowered and know that we were landing. As Ulfheonar we were the scouts and the first to land. It was a great responsibility but you learned to make decisions beyond your years.

I saw the beach ahead and there was no sign of rocks. The white caps just reflected the tide and not savage underwater obstructions ready to rip out your keel. I judged the moment was right and I shouted, "Up oars!" With only twenty odd men it was a slick operation. Prince Butar would struggle to achieve the same quick and efficient movement. My warriors began to ship the oars and store them out of the way. They donned helmets and grabbed their shields from the side where they had added protection from the elements. There might not be any hostile force waiting to greet us but we would take no chances. We would be ready to fight the moment we stepped ashore.

I felt relieved as the keel gently slid along the sand. I left it to my men to secure the boat to the shore and I donned my helmet, shield and cloak. My sword, *Ragnar's Spirit*, hung from my side. It was a deadly and powerful weapon having been made from the finest Frankish iron and forged by lightning. None of us used axes; that was the way of the Dane. Swords had a heart of their own and lived in a way that an axe could not. We were true warriors.

By the time I reached the prow most of the men were on the shore in a defensive half circle. *'Wolf'* was tied to two trees which had somehow managed to grow on a grassy knoll above the beach. I looked behind me and saw the other ships coming into shore.

"Snorri, watch the ship. We will scout." I did not issue any more orders; it was unnecessary as the men of the Ulfheonar knew exactly what to do. I began to climb the hill. There was no settlement to the north of us; we had seen that as we had entered the small bay. The hill proved to be higher than we had anticipated. It seemed to climb up into the sky. There were no rocky gullies and precipices but each time we thought we had reached the top we had not. Eventually, I could see no more hills before us. Just below the ridge, we dropped to our hands and knees. It was undignified but, with our wolf cloaks, we appeared like animals from a distance.

Cnut reached the top first and he waved his hand to signal that he could see something. I took off my helmet and slithered towards the bracken crowned crest. There was a village on the other side of the inlet. It looked to be about the same distance as that which we had climbed. It was a good, safe bay and would make a perfect anchorage. The people had built a wooden palisade around their huts. I looked at Haaken, who had just joined me. "This is not Tadgh's settlement." There was disappointment in my voice. I had hoped for a little luck.

"No, he would have his ships there if that was the case."

"You and the others stay here and keep a watch. I will go and report to Prince Butar. Egill, come with me."

When we reached the bottom the other warbands waited expectantly. There was no criticism from my father in law, just a question. "Did you have a problem?"

"No, Prince Butar. The hill was higher than we thought. It looked to be the same as the one at home but it is bigger. Beyond the mountains there is an inlet and, on the other side, a settlement with a wall around it. The anchorage is a good one but it is empty. It would be safer to anchor there than here."

Butar stroked his beard as he weighed up his options. Erik looked up at the mountain. "Then Tadgh is not there?"

"If he is then he has no ships and that seems unlikely."

Prince Butar nodded as though reaching a decision. "We will visit this settlement."

"With our ships?"

"No, Jarl Erik, for that would alarm the people. I will go with the Ulfheonar. We will walk there. Keep a watch from the hill tops and when I signal then bring in the ships."

I could see doubt on my brother in law's face. "Suppose they attack you?"

He laughed, "With Dragon Heart and the Ulfheonar? I think I will be safe enough." He looked at me, "How many huts are there?"

"No more than fifteen."

"Then we will be safe. That would only mean ten or twelve men who could be warriors. I do not wish to harm these people. I just want our women and children returned. Spread the crews out in the three ships to bring them around."

"Egill, go and tell the men to join us. It will be easier to walk around the mountain than go over it."

We walked slowly; this was partly to allow our men to catch up with us and partly to avoid walking into an enemy. I glanced at Prince Butar who looked distracted. We had not been alone since my mother's death. We had both grieved as she had been buried but our thoughts remained our own. I knew that she would not be shedding tears in the Otherworld. She was too strong for that. She would, I knew, want her child and my wife and son bringing safely home. She had been enslaved twice and it was only the second enslavement which had been a happy time for her. The first, with my father, had been a living hell. Happiness came with Prince Butar.

Perhaps Butar sensed my thoughts for he said, quietly, "We will find them. Of that I am certain."

I nodded, "I know. We will find them but I wonder in what condition? Tadgh is cruel and he hates us both. I dread to think what he might do to her." I had sent those dark thoughts far away. Therein lay madness.

"Do not let anger cloud your judgment. Do not become a berserker."

His father had been Ragnar a crippled and half blind warrior but he had made me into a warrior. "Your father trained me too well for that. I will kill Tadgh. I should have killed him when I had my chance but pity stayed my hand; pity and the remembrance that we were children together once."

"Good." He peered around the land. "There seem to be few people around here."

I too had noticed the lack of farms. The soil looked good enough and I knew they had the same weather we did. There had to be a reason. It was soon after Egill and the Ulfheonar caught up with us that we discovered a possible reason for the lack of people. We found a burnt-out village. From the chewed and discarded bones, this had been destroyed some years earlier. We halted to examine the remains. We could see that the bones had savage cut marks on them, as well as the marks of the teeth of animals. These people had been butchered. We had heard of the internecine warfare of these people and now we had evidence of it.

"Who rules here, Prince Butar?"

He shrugged. "They have a High King but his power depends upon his popularity. Otherwise, they have smaller kings and warlords. It is easy to see why they would hire someone like Tadgh and the others. We are better prepared for war than these people."

When we reached the bay, we sheltered behind the trees and bushes so that we could spy out the settlement. They had no guards on the gates and we could see no armed men. We had to approach quietly without frightening them and making them retreat behind their walls.

Haaken shook his head, "They will see us long before we reach them." He pointed, "Look it is open land right up to the walls."

I scanned the opposite side of the bay. "But if you notice the bay shelves and anyone approaching along the water would be hidden."

Prince Butar said, "You are right. I will walk slowly, with Haaken here while the rest of you make your way to the point over there where the shelf hides you. Keep yourselves close to the bank and to the walls and then hide." He smiled, "It is one of the things Ulfheonar are good at is it not?" We grinned and nodded. We prided ourselves on our ability to hide in plain sight. "Haaken and I will walk up to them. They will not fear two men and when we are close you can reveal yourselves."

It was decided and we quickly ran through the woods towards the head of the bay. When we reached the edge of the woods we crouched in the undergrowth. Although there were people a mile or so away I thought we could make the water without being seen.

"Egill, you bring them through and I will go first." I crouched down and crawled towards the water. I reached down to the river mud and smeared some on my face and hands. I then pulled my wolf cloak over my helmet. My shield was already hidden and I was as dark as I was going to get. All that anyone would see would be a shadow and not a man. I waited until I judged that I could not be seen and then I plunged into the water. It seemed icily cold but I knew that was an illusion. It came up to my waist but, more importantly, I was well below the bank of the river which led to the bay. I could not be seen. I waded east, towards the sea.

The sound of the sea masked all other noises. I would have to rely on my sense of smell to tell me when I was near to the village. I had marked a spot on the opposite bank which was approximately level with the village but I didn't know for certain. It was hard pushing through the water and trying to stay upright in the current. By this, I knew that I was nearer to the village. The sudden splash of me hitting the water would be sure to alert the villagers. I halted. I glanced over my shoulders and saw that the rest of the Ulfheonar were also in the water. I could see that the bank was much higher than their heads.

When I judged that I had reached the right point I stopped and turned to the bank. It was hard to get purchase on the slippery, muddy earthen wall which rose above me. I had to grip with my hands and haul myself up. When my blackened muddy hand clutched air I paused and slowly raised my head above the bank. Had anyone been looking in my direction all that they would have seen would have been an animal, nothing more. I could see the village; I was about sixty paces too far away. We had not travelled far enough. I slithered down just as Cnut appeared next to me. I pointed towards the sea and he nodded.

I counted out sixty paces and then repeated my climb. It was the perfect position. I could see the gate and I was between the settlement and the sea. I waved for Cnut to climb and he did so.

The settlement was just forty yards away. My original plan had been to crawl towards it and hide even closer. That plan would have to change for the villagers were returning to their huts and we would have been seen had we attempted to move. I looked down the line and waved at the others. I used my flattened palms to make them lower themselves. They all knew what we had to do. It might be wet and uncomfortable but we were Ulfheonar.

I slid my sword from my scabbard and laid it on the bank next to me. We now had to wait until Prince Butar appeared; hopefully, it would not be long. I peered through the marram grass at the settlement. It looked to be self contained. There were small coracles for fishing drying against the palisade. Through the gate I could see women weaving baskets from reeds and others, churning butter. I wondered why I could see no larger fishing boats; perhaps they were still at sea or they just used the one man coracles like the people of Cymru.

I could see men returning with animals they had hunted and I saw animals being herded into the enclosure. That told me a great deal. There were raiders in this land who would steal their beasts. They had to keep them protected at night. It made it a little more likely that Tadgh or other predators were in the vicinity.

It was the movement and reaction of the villagers which heralded the approach of Prince Butar and Haaken. The women and children quickly rushed inside driving the animals before them and some of the men picked up their weapons to form a defensive barrier in front of the gate. I signalled to the rest to be ready. The eight men approached our two comrades and they had their swords and spears aimed at both of them. It was foolish. The two of them could have slaughtered the eight easily had they chosen to do so. Prince Butar had chosen Haaken as he was one of the other men who owned a mail shirt. I was another. Their crude weapons would have been useless against armour.

As they moved forward to meet them I raised my sword and we silently slid from the bank and ran across to the gate. Everyone's attention was on our two warriors who were striding boldly towards the waiting villagers and no one seemed to see us. Moving silently, we had almost reached the gate when there was a scream as a woman, standing inside the village, saw us. By then it was too late. We stood, back to back, with weapons drawn in the gateway. The settlement was ours.

Chapter 2

Prince Butar and Haaken held their hands palm uppermost; a sign for peace. I lowered my sword too and the rest of the Ulfheonar followed suit. Prince Butar was a fierce warrior but he was also a friendly and affable man, some even called him kind. He smiled at them and it was not the wolf's smile of Harold One Eye, our former jarl; it was a smile which invited conversation and not war. They were too far for me to hear the words but when I saw the ten of them approach us then I knew we would not be fighting.

"Let us move inside the walls. The gate is secure."

As we did so the people fled inside their huts. I almost laughed. We could have taken anything we wished to and their huts would not have stopped us. This was a land ripe for raiding. When they had entered the settlement, I waved at two of the men to stand guard at the gate. "Cnut, take Egill and light the signal fire although it is light enough for the men on the hill to have seen us. They should know that we have succeeded."

Even with four men otherwise occupied there were still plenty of us to prevent any trouble. Prince Butar came over to me. "I do not understand them and they do not understand me. We have a problem."

"Have you tried Saxon?"

He shook his head, "I will try." He turned to the eight men, for they were the only ones he could see; the rest were hidden. He spoke in Saxon, "I am Prince Butar of Man and I come here in peace."

Two of the men looked at each other and one of them shouted something. After a short while, a woman with the yoke of a thrall around her neck was led over to us from the largest hut. The two men spoke harshly to her. She looked terrified and shook her head. The oldest man slapped her across the face. Still, she shook her head when he raised his arm for another smack I grabbed it and said, in Saxon, "No! We just need someone who can speak Saxon!"

The woman gave me a half smile. "I am Seara and I can speak Saxon."

Prince Butar nodded, "Tell them we come in peace, Seara."

She told them and they began to speak. She translated, "The headman is called Padraigh and he asks why you sneak up and come armed if you come in peace."

The conversation took some time because of the translation. "If we had come unarmed wouldn't they have hidden behind their walls?"

His cunning smile was answer enough. "Then what do you seek here? We are a poor people and we have nothing worth taking."

I suddenly said, in our language, "Excuse me, Prince Butar may I speak?"

"Of course. You have something in mind?"

"It seems to me that she might know as much as they do. If we ask them then when we leave they may reveal what they have learned of us." I turned to the woman and spoke Saxon again, "Where were you captured?"

"In the land to the west, the land of Northumbria."

"How long have you been here?"

"Five summers."

"Are you alone?"

Her eyes filled with tears and she nodded. "My husband was killed and my son and daughter died when the coughing sickness came."

"We are looking for our families who were taken as slaves. I know that they are not here for the ships which took them are not close by. Were you brought here first?"

She shook her head, "There is a bigger place with a market and many ships. It is half a day south of here."

"There is nothing north of here?"

"Not that I know. They take me to the market when they go and I carry back the heavy goods."

The woman was little more than a two-legged horse. "You see our armour and our weapons?" Again, she nodded, "Have you ever seen warriors with these kinds of weapons before? Perhaps in the place with the market and the ships?"

She was now eager to please; I was speaking quietly and smiling at her. There were no blows and no harsh words. "There were. They came towards the end of the last year and they serve the king there, Colm the Mighty."

I saw Prince Butar's eyes widen as he took in the import of the message. I took her hands in mine; they were red and thin, much as she was. The men frowned as I did so. "Two last questions. Did they have a ship there? It may have had a dragon at the front."

She shook her head, "The dragon was not at the front." I felt disappointed. It was not Norse. "The dragon's head was laid next to the boat." I almost cheered out loud when she said that. Some warriors believed it was unlucky to have the dragon prow on a boat in port and removed it. "My second question, would you like to be free?"

She nodded, tears filling her eyes. "More than anything."

I looked the village elder in the eyes as I said to her, "Tell them we would like to buy you. When they ask why say that we are men and wish to use you." I smiled, "We do not but it will make them believe the reason for us taking you."

For the first time, she smiled and said, "I do believe you but that would not be as bad as living here with these…"

"Just ask them."

She did so and they looked curiously at me. After a brief discussion, they spoke to Seara and she said, "What have you to trade for me. You do not look as if you have any wealth. They say you do not even have a ship."

I laughed. "Then they know little." I reached into my pouch and withdrew some small black stones. I counted out five. "Ask them if five pieces of jet are worth the price."

Their eyes widened as they looked at the jet and saw how many pieces there were. I had offered far more than they thought she was worth. They spoke to her and she said. "They ask for ten."

I drew *Ragnar's Spirit* and it made a savage rasping sound as I did so. I put the point at the elder's throat. "Tell him I could take you for nothing and slaughter his entire village. Ask him to reconsider."

He was frightened enough with the blade but when she translated he nodded and held up five fingers. I threw the stones at the feet and he scrabbled after them. "Stand behind me. We will take your yoke off later on."

Cnut's voice sounded, "The ships, they are here, as are the village boats."

The demeanour of the men changed instantly, their shoulders slumped. I think they had counted on delaying us here until their fishing boats arrived with the rest of their men. No wonder he had acceded to my request so easily. They had thought to surprise us with their extra men.

Prince Butar's eyes narrowed. He now saw their treachery. He turned to Seara. "Did you know the fishing boats would return now?"

She shook her head and pointed inside the settlement. "They do not let me near the sea in case I try to escape. Another slave did just that last year and so I am kept within the walls of the village." Her eyes pleaded with Butar, "I knew they fished but I swear, my lord, that I knew not when they returned."

His face softened into a smile. "I believe you. Stay with us a while longer while you translate for us and then, as my son promised, you shall be free and the yoke will be removed." He turned to the rest of us. "Disarm them! We cannot trust them."

They were not expecting that and within a moment or two, they were all disarmed. I pointed into the village, "Haaken, take a couple of men and search the village. They may have arms hidden."

The sound, as the men went through the village, was like that when a fox moves through a hen coop. There were squeals of indignation as Haaken and his men searched for weapons. They had a good haul and returned with five axes and three swords. His one eye twinkled, "I wonder how many of us would have woken up to Hibernian steel up our backsides?"

When Sweyn and Erik brought the rest of the men from the ships they also brought the fishermen. Unable to speak their language Sweyn had used the universal language of the tip of a sword to make his point.

"Dragon Heart, see if there is another entrance to this village."

I sheathed my sword and strode around the outside of the palisade. The ditch, I noticed, was a pitiful affair which would not have stopped a ten-year-old. It led me to believe that this village was protected by some warlord or king. I was even more hopeful about finding Tadgh. As a warrior, I always examined defences when I saw them. People had learned to hide behind walls when we came and I needed to know how to destroy those defences. These were only as high as I was. I could see beyond them into the village. It helped that I was bigger than most of the Hibernians but, even so, I would have had a higher wall and fighting platform if this had been mine to protect. I saw that, at the far side of the village, they had dumped their waste there. It stank like a midden!

By the time I had returned to the only gate the settlement had, Prince Butar had the men kneeling in a circle. He was addressing them through Seara. "You have tried to deceive me and for that alone, I could raze your wooden walls to the ground." The women nearby, who heard that began to whimper. "But I will not do that. Instead, we will allow you to feed us and then, tomorrow we will be gone from here so long as I have your assurance that you will not tell anyone of our presence." Seara paused as Butar held up his hand.

The village elder smiled and said something. Seara said, "He so swears."

Sweyn laughed, "I would not take his word that day followed night without the evidence of my own eyes."

"And neither would I. Seara, which is the headman's son. Do not point, just tell me where he is. Dragon Heart when he is identified, grab him and bind him."

"He is the small boy hiding behind his mother; she is the one with the raven hair and the eyes like daggers."

It was a good description. The woman oozed hatred while the boy's eyes were wide with wonder. In four strides, I was next to them and I reached down to grab the boy. The woman squealed and, pulling a knife, tried to stab me with it. The blow would have pierced my flesh had it not struck, first my cloak and then my byrnie. I reached out with my left hand and twisted her arm sharply. There was a crack and she dropped the weapon. I leaned down and picked up the dagger. "Seara, tell her I could kill her for that but I know she was protecting her son. If her husband keeps his word then the child will be returned unharmed."

Seara translated and the woman began to wail. I do not think the news that her son was to be a hostage caused the wail but her broken wrist and my treatment of her. She barely looked at the boy and the headman also appeared unconcerned.

"Dragon Heart, take Seara and the boy on to my boat."

The boy did not seem to struggle as I led him. Perhaps the treatment of his mother has made him wary of perhaps she was indifferent about him. Seara followed me gratefully. The boys who were guarding the boat were eager for news.

"My lord, what has happened?"

"This boy is to be our hostage." I looked at Seara, "What is his name?"

"Aiden."

"His name is Aiden and he does not speak our language." Snorri from my boat was the eldest of the ship's boys. "Snorri, he is your responsibility. Arrange watches and keep him tethered." Snorri nodded and grinned. I pointed my newly acquired dagger at him, "He is not to be hurt. I will inflict any pain he receives on you. Understand?"

He nodded fearfully; they all knew I was a man of my word. I casually threw the dagger so that it landed in the sand between his legs and grinned, "There is payment for you."

"Thank you, my lord."

"Come with me Seara, and I will remove your yoke." I had suffered a yoke and knew how painful it could be. "Kneel down." Once she had knelt down I used the pommel of my own dagger to knock out the wooden pin securing it and the two halves fell to the floor. Her neck was red and angry. It would take her some time to fully recover. I held my hand to allow her to rise. "That is my ship, *'Wolf'*. You can sleep on there." I pointed to the spare sail which was rolled up close to the bow. I saw the unspoken question in her eyes. "You will be safe. My men are Ulfheonar and they are honourable. Your time of suffering is at an end."

"You are Saxon too."

"I was and I was a slave like you. Now I am a Norse and I have put my former life behind me. You would be advised to do the same. You can never recover what you have lost. It is better to start anew."

"And yet you seek your family which is lost to you."

"You are wise, Seara. True but they are not yet lost and we will find them. Come let us see what food they have to serve to us."

The next day, before we left, we towed the fishing boats out into the bay and, filling them with stones, we sank them. We did not destroy them. They would be able to recover them but it would take them some time. We had Aiden but I still not trust the headman. He did not seem bothered that we had taken the silent Aiden. He just watched all that was going on. He did not appear to be afraid. We sailed south. Aiden and Seara were on my ship and the boy seemed remarkably calm. He reminded me of me when I had been captured by Harald One-Eye. The difference was that he was alone and I had had my mother.

Seara's description of somewhere half a day's journey south was not as helpful as it might have been. We sailed slowly down the coast and kept well out to sea. Our sails were furled and we would be hard to identify as Norse from the land. We needed to find somewhere to land close to this unknown slave market. We eventually spied the town. The smoke spiralling from their fires marked it clearly. It looked to be a much bigger version of the one from which we had rescued Seara. More importantly, we saw the masts of ships. It was impossible to see if one was a drekar but it was worth investigating.

We passed the inlet and sailed until it disappeared from sight and then I headed due west. We saw no other signs of habitation and I beached my ship in the shelter of some sand dunes. This time we had to set up a camp proper. We did not know how long we would be here. Sweyn organised sentries while the ships were turned around ready for a speedy launch should that prove necessary. Erik, Butar and I met while the rest of the men busied themselves.

"It looks like the place but we need more information before we try to rescue them."

Both Erik and Butar looked at me and I nodded, "The Ulfheonar."

"You are perfect for this role. How long will you need?"

"Although it is not far we will have to be careful. I would not expect us to be back before morning at the earliest."

"Good. Then gather your men." He clasped my arm, "Take care, my son, I would not wish to lose someone else as precious as your mother."

I smiled, "Remember Prince Butar, Ragnar still watches over me."

Chapter 3

I led the way. In the Ulfheonar we had no leaders; we were all young men who had grown up as warriors together. Sweyn had been our leader but he was much older and now led Prince Butar's oathsworn. The rest were of an age with me. We did not move in a single file but walked in an arrow formation. We moved like a wolf pack. Each person protected someone else. I had good reflexes and was able to react quickly which was why I was at the front. Unlike the rest of the warriors, we went to war quietly. There was neither banter nor bravado. Our shields were slung behind our backs and our swords remained sheathed. I ran without a helmet; it hung from my shield. I needed my eyes and ears as well as my sense of smell.

We had never crossed this land before but we knew in which direction the settlement lay. We kept heading in the right direction. We would smell it before we saw it. The smells told me that it was not far away. It was the smell of smoke mixed with animal and human dung. By an hour after noon, we were within sight of it. There was precious little cover close to the water but I spied a wood not far inland and we trotted there. There were no farms on this southern side of the palisade. It made it less likely that we would stumble over anyone when we approached for a closer inspection. Once inside the cover of the wood we halted and took a drink from our water skins. It would be a long day.

"How do we get in? If we try now we will be stopped and if we wait until after dark then the gates will be barred."

Cnut was right and I had no immediate answer. Haaken came up with the only solution which we thought might stand a chance of working, "If we all crawl closer to the walls and watch then we may gain more information that way. We only need to find out if there are Norsemen within those walls and, if they are, then is it Tadgh's band."

Harold Blue Eye was not certain, "It is a long time to wait. We would have to be very still and very lucky."

"I have done this before Harold. I have hidden in plain view. Choose your watching place wisely and blend into your background."

There were no more questions. We slipped to the ground and began to crawl towards the distant walls. I had learned to move sinuously like a blind worm. It made fewer disturbances and looked more natural. When moving through grass it simulated the action of the wind. The trick was to get as close as possible and wait without being seen. I had taken the position at the end of the line of warriors and I was the closest to the sea. Its sound made listening more difficult but I knew that it

Viking Warrior

would be my eyes which would tell me more. I moved so slowly that sometimes I stiffened as I spied out the land ahead and sought out the hollows and the limited cover available. I found a small depression which gave me the opportunity to creep faster towards the wooden walls. I could not see the others but I knew that they were doing as I was. After what seemed an age I saw some gorse bushes forty paces or so from the walls. They masked my approach and, when I was safely ensconced beneath their prickly protection, I was hidden and I was safe.

Sometimes you wait for hours and see nothing. We all knew we would have to lie there until dark and then make our way back. That day however I struck gold within the first hour. Not only did I see warriors armed and dressed as we were; I saw Tadgh himself. He was dressed in fine clothes; he had neither armour nor helmet. That made it easier to identify him. He now braided his hair and his moustache. The sword which hung from his baldric was a long one of Frankish origin. He was with two other mailed warriors. From their deference, I deduced that he was some kind of leader. The next question was if he was here where were the captives?

My view was limited to the side of the settlement close to the boats. As such I could see that they were preparing the nearest ship for a voyage. She was a drekar. I assumed that she was Tadgh's ship. Now that I had the information that this was the correct village I set to counting the warriors and the men. If this had been one of our villages then every man would have been a potential warrior but the Hibernians were like the Saxons and had elite warriors. They were easy to identify as they all wore a sword. I counted thirty such warriors. At least half of them were warriors such as we had while the rest were Hibernians. It looked like they had farms from the carts which came in filled with produce. This was an important town.

Dusk seemed to take forever to arrive. I was in such a prominent position that any movement would give me away. As soon as the gate was shut and barred then I knew that it was safe to leave. I still had to be careful for the drekar was crewed and ready to sail. I backed out and kept going that way until I reached the depression. Once there I rolled down and moved a little quicker to the woods where I hoped my brothers would await me.

"At last! We thought you had decided to stay the night!"

"No Haaken, but I had the furthest to go did I not?"

"Enough! We have some way to go before we are safe and we have talked too much already." Egill hated wasting time and we left duly chastised. Egill loped along at the head of us. We hoped not to meet anyone on the way back. The Hibernians were a superstitious people and the dark places were avoided at night.

We reached our boats faster than we had taken to reach the walls. Prince Butar, Erik and Sweyn were eager for news. As we had not shared our information with each other all of the Ulfheonar were present. We each had some information and none knew which was valuable and which was not.

I began because I could give them the vital information they needed. "Tadgh is there and the drekar too. They are preparing her for sea."

A murmur ran around all the men. Prince Butar held up his hand. "Let us hear from all of the scouts."

From the rest, we learned that there were, at least, some of the captives there. They had been seen. We calculated that there were at least thirty warriors such as us and another forty or more Hibernians. The numbers did not worry us. We knew there would be more inside that we had not counted. It was how many there were like Tadgh.

"You have done well, Ulfheonar. Go and take food and drink while we ponder what to do."

Haaken could not resist having the last word. "If the drekar leaves tomorrow then we should go back now. Strike while they sleep."

Prince Butar sent him away with an irritated wave of his hand. "We will travel when I say, Haaken One Eye!"

Jarl Erik smiled, "He may have spoken out of turn but he is right."

"I agree," said my stepfather, "but there are two considerations. One, if we went back and attacked at night then we do not know who we might harm by accident and two, the Ulfheonar will be tired and need a couple of hours sleep at least."

I stood defiantly, "I could go now!"

Smiling, Prince Butar said, "I know but if Tadgh sails it is unlikely that he will take the captives with them. It is probable that he raids somewhere else."

"I want to kill Tadgh!" I was aware that I sounded like a petulant child but I was angry.

"Yes, Dragon Heart. As do Erik and myself but first let us get the captives. If not then we might be dooming our families to a life of servitude and slavery."

I knew that he was right but it sat hard with me. I nodded and Erik put his arm around my shoulders. "Get some food and some rest. We will be leaving before dawn."

I knew that the two of them would have planned the rescue while we were scouting it out and assumed this was the place. It was a little annoying to be left out of the planning but I was still younger than any of those who made the decisions. I would have to bide my time. One day it would be me who would plan how to use our men. I would give the orders and not just take them.

It was decided that the Ulfheonar would attack the drekar when we reached the town. That suited me. I wanted to deal with Tadgh sooner rather than later. The rest of the warriors would slip over the palisade and use surprise. We had noticed that it was just like the one we had seen when we landed; just the height of a man. They were easy to scale. Two men held a shield and a third vaulted over. A good palisade was twice the height of a man.

We moved quickly over ground that we had travelled twice the previous day. Although not familiar with it we knew where the cover was and used it to our advantage. It was still dark when we saw the settlement. We did not know how many guards they had but we were confident that we could overcome them. They would not have expected us to find them so soon. Meeting Seara had been an unexpected event which had brought us good fortune. The Ulfheonar left the main band and headed towards the sea, which we could smell, and the jetty. The sky was pitch-black and we could see nothing. I drew *Ragnar's Spirit* and hefted my shield before me in preparation. With our black mail and wolf skins, we were invisible in the night. Suddenly I realised that we had reached the sea and the drekar had sailed. I had been within touching distance of Tadgh and missed him. There was no point in berating myself we could now join the attack proper.

"To the gates."

Prince Butar had decided that we would leave the gate alone; it would be too well defended. I was angry that Tadgh had fled and I decided that the Ulfheonar would destroy the gate. We moved like wraiths as we left the harbour and ran towards the gate. The sentries were either asleep or absent for they did not see us. Suddenly I heard the clamour of battle as the rest of the warband attacked the walls. It may have been that the sentries at the front gate were distracted. Whatever the reason, we reached the gate without hurt. "Hit the bar!"

We saw that there was a gap between the gates and Haaken and Cnut took it in turns to hack at the bar which held the gate in place. Within a few moments, it was destroyed. We put our shoulders to the gate and burst in. Immediately we entered we had our shields and swords ready to defend ourselves. We were all alert to danger and to the captives. Our priority was to kill warriors and then rescue our families.

A half naked Hibernian warrior launched himself at me wielding a double handed Danish axe. It looked a fearsome weapon but it was easily avoided. I angled my shield and dipped below the blow. The edge of the wicked looking weapon caught my boss but by then I had ripped open his bare midriff with my blade. I pushed him out of the way and leapt forwards. Two men had spears and were charging towards me. I just tucked my shield tighter to my body and ran towards them. Perhaps they had thought I would retreat. They did not know who they fought. Their spears hit my shield and splintered against the nail studded oak. I slashed at one and stamped on the head of the other as he slipped beneath my feet. One of my comrades would despatch him. I raced on as I was anxious to find my wife.

A warrior leapt at me from the side. He swung a skeggox with his two hands. It was a powerful blow and had it connected it would have ripped through my mail. I dropped to a knee and braced myself behind my shield. The blow shook both my arm and my shield. The tip stuck in the shield and, as he struggled to remove it I stabbed him in the chest. After I had removed the axe I looked around and saw that the gate behind me was secure. Two Ulfheonar guarded it. No one would escape that way. Cnut and Haaken were by my side, the blood on their weapons testament to their endeavours.

"Let us find the captives."

We ran through the village like a small wedge. No one could withstand us. The weight of our arms and armour were too much. Clutches of warriors ran at us but they fell to our blades. As we passed each hut we peered inside looking for our kin; they were not in the first ones. Then we began to shout, "Erika! Eurwen!"

We were halfway through the huts when we heard a cry in our own language. "In here!"

We darted through a door and found some of our women folk and children tethered to the walls with ropes and with hands tied. We quickly freed them. "Thank you, lord,"

"Where are my wife and my child?"

In answer, they pointed towards the large hut which looked like a warrior hall at the far end of the village. "They were taken there, along with your slaves."

"Make your way back to the gate. You are safe now."

Even though we had seen Tadgh, until that moment I did not know, for certain, that this was where my family was held. Although the wily and lucky Tadgh had flown I could still recover my family. By now Erik and Prince Butar's men were flooding over the wall and the Hibernians were retreating towards the large hut. They were herding their women and children inside in a forlorn attempt to protect them. It would serve them no good at all. Once they had captured our people they had lost any chance of mercy. They would either die or become our slaves.

As we made our way steadily towards them, despatching the wounded we found, their warriors began hurling insults at us in their unintelligible language. The fact that we remained silent must have given them confidence, suggesting we were afraid. It was a mistaken assumption. We did not need words to make us fight; we were warriors and fought because we could.

One enormous Hibernian, a hand span taller than me swung his two-handed sword above his head. He was clearing a space in front of him. One of Erik's men rushed towards him and mistimed his attack. His severed head rolled towards us. The Hibernians took heart and cheered. I could not wait for someone else to break through and I raced forward. I relied on my speed and the strength of my weapons. He grinned as he shouted at me. He raised his lethal weapon once more as he prepared to decapitate another Norseman foolish enough to come close. He could keep anyone almost three paces away from him.

I held my shield up higher than I normally did. He took the bait and swung at my shield. I dropped my shoulder and leapt towards him. The blow would not strike my head. I knew that I would have to take a savage hit on my shield but I counted on the strength of my well-made shield. It was a race against time; I saw the arc of the mighty weapon as it closed with me and I struggled to reach him to strike a killing hit. I saw him grin in the anticipation of another victory and then he saw *Ragnar's Spirit* as it sprang at him like the tongue of a dragon. His sword struck my shield but, by then, I had lunged forward and my own weapon found his unprotected middle. The blow to my shield had unbalanced me and I fell sideways with my sword embedded deep within him. Its edge sliced him open and his entrails and guts flopped out like bloody eels as my blade emerged, having eviscerated him.

One of the warriors next to the mighty Hibernian took the opportunity to stab down at me with his spear as I lay like a stranded fish. Haaken's sword was quicker and it flicked death. The death of the warrior was like the flood when the dam is breached. We fell into and upon them slaughtering all before us.

When none remained alive I followed Prince Butar into the large hut. It was filled with women. Half of them were keening and wailing while the others had smiles upon their faces. The ones who smiled were our people.

I saw Scanlan's wife, Maewe, and she fell at my feet weeping. "My lord you are here; thank the Allfather."

I lifted her up. "My son, Eurwen, my wife?"

She turned and lifted a blanket beneath which were my son, my half sister and Scanlan's children. I looked around the room where other warriors were greeting their wives and sisters. Maewe shook her head. "Tadgh came in the night and took your wife. She fought him but they tied her. I promised to watch over the children."

Blackness came over me. I wanted to slaughter every man woman and child in that Hibernian town. I think Haaken recognised the signs for he came and took my sword from me. "This is no time for revenge."

I turned to him and spat out, "But Erika!"

"I heard and we will follow him. What you need, my brother is to use your mind as Ragnar taught you. We need to discover where they have gone."

I suddenly wished that we had not killed all the men. Would the women know where he had gone? There was one woman with a torc around her neck in clothes which were better than the others. I turned to Maewe, "Watch my children and go with the other captives. Haaken, come with me."

Two of the ships would still be where we left them but mine would be approaching the village with a smaller crew and, more importantly, Seara who could question this woman for us. I grabbed the woman with the torc. Her eyes flashed angrily and she tried to rake my face with her nails. I still had my helmet on and she merely hurt herself.

"Now then, none of that!" Haaken grabbed her hands and her shoulders slumped in resignation.

I took off my helmet. I saw Prince Butar approaching. Lifting her chin so that she had to look at me, I asked, "Where is Tadgh? Where has he gone?"

She looked at me dumbly; she had not understood a word.

Prince Butar asked, "Where is Erika? I have seen Maewe with the children."

"Tadgh took her. We came too late." I could not keep the bitterness out of my voice. He had been close enough for me to kill and now he and my wife were lost to me.

"We will find her. Who is this?"

I roughly ripped the torc from her neck the edge drew blood. "By this token, I take her to be the wife of the chief. I will ask Seara to find out where they have gone." I saw a piece of rope on the floor. It had been used to tie the slaves to the walls. I tied it around her hands and then put a loop around her neck. "I will see if the ship is here yet."

I yanked on the rope and she fell to her knees. Haaken helped her to rise, "Dragon Heart, calm your anger. You need this woman to answer your questions. She is not Tadgh."

"No, but she and her people sheltered him. That makes them all guilty." Then I realised he was right. I took a deep breath, "But you are right to chastise me. I will be calmer. Come, woman."

I gave a half smile and she began to walk. Haaken was always the voice of reason. The captives were all at the side of the shore with six or seven of Prince Butar's warriors. When they saw the chief's wife they began to spit at her and throw stones. I let them do it for a few moments, it would not hurt to let her know how perilous her position was and then I shouted, "Enough!" and they all stopped. She gratefully sidled closer to me. I did not think I would have any trouble from her.

I went over to Maewe. She had rocked my son to sleep. I nodded my thanks. Eurwen clung to Maewe's dress. I knelt down and picked her up. "Do not worry little sister. Your father will be here soon and you will be safe again."

"Where is mama?"

I hugged her tighter. She did not know our mother was dead and I could not tell her. I was a coward; I would let Butar tell her. "Stay close to Maewe and we will sail back to our home."

Haaken had brought the double handed sword with him. It was almost as tall as a normal warrior. He handed it to me, "Here, you earned it, you mad berserker!"

I shook my head, "I was no berserker I knew precisely what I was doing."

"You could have fooled me. Have you seen your shield?"

I hadn't. I swung it around from my back and saw that the sword had gouged through the leather, ripped out many of the nails and had scored the wood beneath, Haaken was right. I had come closer to death than I had thought. I would have to repair my shield before I could use it in combat again. The trouble was I needed to pursue Tadgh as soon as possible. I looked at the sword which lay embedded in the sand, "What will I do with such a weapon?"

"Sell it? Trade it?"

"Who would want such an unwieldy weapon?"

He nodded at the chief's wife, "The Hibernians. It would make a good bargaining tool."

Haaken was correct and I was glad that I listened to him. It proved crucial in the next weeks.

It seemed to take an age for *'Wolf'* to reach us. I felt guilty when the exhausted crew stepped ashore but I quickly forgot that as I grabbed Seara and led her to my captive. "Ask her where Tadgh has gone."

She nodded and then began to speak. The chief's wife shook her head. I had had enough of this and I drew my seax. I held it to her eye.

She screamed and then fell to her knees and began to jabber. After she had finished I said to Seara, "Well?"

"They have sailed to Tara and the court of Áed Oirdnide; he is the high king."

My heart sank. That would be the most defended place in the whole of Hibernia. My wife was lost.

Chapter 4

By the time Prince Butar had returned I had my men aboard my ship along with Maewe, Seara and a few more captives. I had the men preparing the ship for sea. I would catch them. *'Wolf'* was the fastest ship afloat; she would catch them. My step father looked at me curiously, "Where are you going, my son?"

"We have to get to Tara; Tadgh has gone there."

"And you would risk my daughter and your son by taking them there?"

I had not thought this through. "But they are escaping. Each moment takes them further away from us."

"And where is Tara?"

I looked around as though I might find the answer on someone's face. I looked in desperation at Seara. "Ask her where is Tara?"

Seara asked and the chief's wife shook her head. I drew my seax again but Seara held her hand out. "She does not know my lord! Her husband visited but not her. Please believe me!"

I knew how much Seara hated her former oppressor. The woman was telling the truth. Prince Butar put his arm around me. "Take some men back to our ships so that they can row around the headland and bring our ships here. Then we will sail back to our island. We will get your wife back but it may take longer than you think. She is alive and Tadgh will not hurt her." I was not convinced. He added, heavily, "You have your son. Would you throw away his life too?" I shook my head and resigned myself to a further delay before I could sail after Erika.

It seemed to take forever to reach the other ships and land enough men to sail them back to the Hibernian's home. As we sailed back I saw the flames licking the huts and the palisade of the Hibernian settlement. It was a warning to others that we were not to be crossed. We left the warriors lying where they fell. They had no honour and they deserved no respect. The crows and the foxes would destroy them.

We left for Duboglassio while the other two ships were loading the plunder, both human and animal. I let Haaken steer while I spoke with Maewe. "How is Erika?"

"She is strong my lord. She knows that you will come for her."

There was an unspoken question in my mouth but I could not bring myself to ask it. Instead, I asked how Eurwen and my son had coped with captivity. She spoke slowly and patiently. I could see she was afraid of upsetting me. All the time Seara was rocking my son who had fallen asleep. Eventually, I was satisfied. I had all my questions

26

answered but one. My son and my step sister had not been harmed and Erika believed in me still. I turned to Aiden. He had not said a word which was not surprising as we were all speaking a foreign language.

"Seara, ask Aiden about his father. Is he an honourable man?"

She asked the question and Aiden just shrugged. The concept was not one with which he was familiar. "Then ask him if he is a warrior. Has he a sword like mine?"

This time Aiden smiled and began to gabble. Seara nodded, "His father has a sword, a shield and helmet but none are as fine as yours." She hesitated, "He would like to touch the hilt and see the blade."

I saw no harm in that. The boy had not shown any attempt at escape and he had been docile and cooperative throughout. His interest was understandable. I drew the sword and held the hilt towards him. He touched it and shivered. He stared in wonder at the shining blade. I took it and sheathed it.

"Can I ask you, my lord, why did you ask the boy those questions?"

"I need to find Tara and the only way for me to do so is to get his father or someone from the village to show me. He may want that." I pointed to the two-handed sword lying on the deck.

She still rocked the boy in her arms. "Then you will still need me to speak your words for you."

I had not thought that far ahead but she was correct. "I would. Are you willing to return to the village with me?"

"Aye my lord but I would beg a boon from you."

I wondered what she meant and I was wary of a trick. "If I can then I will."

She sighed, "The Hibernians hurt me when I was with them. I cannot have children. I would if you would allow me, nurse your son. Perhaps when you have his mother returned to you I could work in your hall."

Her eyes pleaded with me and I could see how tenderly she held young Arturus. I could see no harm in it and if it brought Erika to me a little quicker then perhaps it was ordained. Certainly, I could see the weird sisters' hands in this.

"I think that would be a good idea. You must learn to speak our language though. My wife does not speak Saxon" I nodded to Maewe. "Maewe can teach you." Maewe had been listening and she nodded. Her smile showed me that they would get on. Now I just needed to prepare to find my wife.

Olaf had had men watching from the hill top and he was waiting for me when we reached Duboglassio. He smiled when he saw the two children. Scanlan, too, was waiting and Maewe and his children rushed to his arms. He frowned when he saw there were no others.

"Where are Butar and Erik?" Olaf came directly to the point. He was a blunt man.

"They are following with the other captives."

He smiled, "And Erika is with them?"

"No, old friend, Tadgh has taken her to Tara. She has been taken to the High King. My search for my wife must continue."

He put an arm around my shoulder. I noticed then how stooped and old he was. His voice was sad as he said, "Ragnar will watch over her and you will find her."

"I hope so. I think that Prince Butar will want to begin rebuilding Hrams-a soon."

"I am not so sure, Dragon Heart. This is an easier place to defend and a better harbour." He pointed to the small hill above the beach. "We could build a good warrior hall there with a stout wooden palisade."

"I cannot think of such things as yet. Is there somewhere for my family?"

He pointed to a hut. "Scanlan has made that for you. It is sturdy and will suffice until we know the Butar's mind."

When we reached the hut, I had Scanlan help me off with my byrnie. "I am going down to the sea to bathe. This Hibernian blood is beginning to clog my nostrils. I need to cleanse myself."

Just as I was leaving, Haaken arrived with the Hibernian sword. "If you are going to use this then it had better be cleaned."

I took it from him and handed it to Scanlan. "Seara will come with us when we return the boy. I will see if it buys us favour." He nodded, "Scanlan, clean the sword and watch the captive. He has behaved so far but we will need to watch him. Seara can speak his language."

I reached the sea and took off my tunic. I waded out. The water chilled me and I lay down so that I was completely immersed. It was true; I needed to wash away the blood and the smell of death but I also found the sea water and the waves soothing. I had grown up next to an estuary and each morning I had had to wade out to remove fish from the nets. This was something similar. The water chilled you and then made you sleepy. I closed my eyes and saw, once more, my mother. This time she was on the river beach when I was a child and she was calling me. When I heard her voice in my head then I knew that I was not alone. Ragnar was there, as he always was, but now he had been joined by my mother.

Then the voice changed and this time it was Haaken. I opened my eyes and saw him on the sand shaking his head and laughing. "What in the name of the Allfather are you doing?"

"I find it soothes me."

"Well get out and get dried. The other two ships are approaching."

I needed no further urging and I dried myself on my tunic and hurried back to the harbour. I saw the two drekar as they edged their way to their moorings. The whole of Duboglassio had turned out to greet the returned captives. As was his custom, Prince Butar stepped ashore first to be greeted by cheers. This time there was no speech for we were not yet successful. When Erik landed, the three of us headed, with Sweyn and Olaf, for Erik's Hall.

We sat around the table and a slave brought us ale. It was for refreshment and not for toasting. I was keen and eager to begin the plans for Erika's rescue but it was not my place to initiate the discussion. Prince Butar still ruled.

"It is good that we have recovered most of the captives but it grieves me that Erika is still a prisoner and Tadgh remains at large. How do you propose that we secure her release?"

Although the question was asked of the whole table it was aimed at me. I took a deep breath. "I would take Seara and the hostage back to their village. I will ask the headman for a guide to take me to Tara."

Erik laughed, "And you think he will?"

"He might for the chief's sword I captured. His son says that his sword is a plain one. Now that we have destroyed that village it struck me that his village might be the next most important." I shrugged, "If that fails then I will think of something else."

They all nodded. Prince Butar said, "That is a sound strategy." He looked around the table again. "And who shall go with Dragon Heart?"

I saw that Erik looked uncomfortable and shuffled in his seat. There was silence around the table. I would not make anyone join me unwillingly. "It is my wife and I will take the Ulfheonar for they are sworn to rescue her."

Erik looked embarrassed, "I would go but I am afraid to leave my family unprotected again."

Olaf snorted, "I thought that she was your sister; is she, not family?"

Erik coloured and his hand went to his sword. Prince Butar's voice roared, "No one touches a sword in my presence." Erik nodded and put his hands on the table again, "And, Olaf, you are an old comrade but do not presume too much." He looked at me. "I, too, think that I should stay here. We need to make this stronghold even stronger."

"I understand, Prince Butar, and I do not blame anyone who does not wish to journey with me. We will be going into the unknown and we do not know what kind of reception we will get."

Olaf drank his ale and said, "I will be your steersman Dragon Heart. I have one more adventure left in me." He flashed an angry look in the direction of Prince Butar and Erik. "And I still believe in honour."

Prince Butar's voice growled, "Olaf!"

"So, a man may not speak his mind here? I thought that was why we left Harald One-Eye's town? Or was I wrong?"

I had to smile, Olaf was the only one who could stand up to Prince Butar and get away with it. Butar smiled, "You are right, old friend. Put it down to the fact that I feel guilty about this. Perhaps a smaller band might succeed. I promise you this, Dragon Heart, I will watch over your family until you return."

"I know. We sail on the morning tide!"

I had little to do as we set sail from Duboglassio. Olaf steered and I stood with Seara and Aiden watching the land recede. He was a strange child. He had never cried or shown any distress since being held hostage by us. He seemed curious and interested in all that surrounded him. Strange as it might seem I would be sad to be returning him to his family. My son, Arturus, was little more than a baby compared with Aiden.

We sailed directly to the village. I knew that they would be wary. '*Wolf's*' sails would be seen from some distance. As I had expected the gates were barred and the palisade had armed men on its fighting platform. I took only Seara, Aiden and Haaken who carried, hidden by a sheepskin, the two-handed sword. We stood beyond bow range and waited. Eventually, Aiden's father and five other warriors emerged. I almost laughed when I saw the poor quality of their arms. The way that they strode towards us you would have thought that they were encased in mail with mighty weapons.

I had told Seara what to say and she began without preamble. "As the lord promised you your son is returned to you unharmed." She looked down at Aiden, "You can return to your father now." He reluctantly let go of Seara's hand and then smiled at me and gave a slight bow before he trudged towards his father. They were about to turn and re-enter their village when Seara continued. "The lord would like one of your men to come with us and show us where Tara is. We would speak with the High King."

He turned, laughed and then said something. Seara nodded and translated, "He says it might be worth taking you there to watch you die but neither he nor his warriors have the time to spare."

As they turned again I said to Haaken, "The sword."

As soon as Haaken unwrapped the sword from its protective sheepskin the warriors crowded round and excitement filled their faces.

They began to jabber amongst themselves. Seara smiled and translated, "It is the high sword of the tribe. It is only wielded by the chief." She paused and listened, "They are saying that Murchad should take it and then he will be chief of the tribe."

"Who is Murchad?"

"He is Aiden's father."

Murchad went to touch the sword and I put my foot on it. "When I have a guide and I have reached Tara then the sword will be his."

She translated. Once again, they spoke amongst themselves. They seem oblivious to the fact that Seara was translating all of their words. "They say that Murchad should go to Tara and show the High King that he is now the chief."

Finally, Murchad came up to me and spoke directly to me. "He says he and two of his warriors will come with you." I nodded and then Aiden began to talk. His father shouted at him but he stood defiantly. Seara smiled, "Aiden wishes to come."

"Tell Murchad that his son is welcome. Haaken, take the sword back on board the ship and tell Olaf we will be sailing soon."

Murchad nodded his agreement and the warriors returned to the village. "Where are they going?"

"They wish to make a good impression on the High King. They are going to change."

I noticed that Aiden had not left Seara's side and we went back on board '*Wolf*' with Aiden gripping her hand. When Murchad and his men returned we set sail. Murchad pointed to the south. Olaf put the rudder over and we headed back towards the destroyed village. It was still a smouldering ruin and Murchad and his two companions cast black looks in our direction. They had obviously been kin to those we had killed. As we sailed I could not help but notice that Murchad seemed indifferent to his son. How different was my reunion with Arturus? No wonder the boy had wanted to stay with us. He had, at least, had some affection from Seara and Maewe.

We continued to head south. There were few inhabited places which were close to the coast. The land seemed empty. Perhaps they all lived inland. We passed one estuary where we saw the masts of ships. "Olaf, sail a little closer to them." Murchad became agitated. I turned to Seara, "Tell him we are not landing but I am curious."

He jabbered back at Seara. "He says that the people here are warlike and may try to take your ship."

I wondered at that. I could not see Murchad being that concerned for our welfare and perhaps it was his own life he feared losing. And then

Murchad was put from my thoughts as I saw Tadgh's drekar. "Ask him if we are close to Tara."

He spoke at length and Seara nodded. "He says it is many miles inland and we can land further south. It will make the journey shorter than from here but you will have to leave your ship on the beach. There is no port."

"Ask him if there is a landing site closer to the north."

I could see that Murchad and his companions were concerned about that. I drew my sword and put the point to Murchad's throat. "The truth or he dies along with his companions."

The threat in my words and face were enough and Murchad nodded. He spoke to Seara. "There is a place we passed some miles back."

"Olaf, turn her around we are going north."

"Make up your mind!"

I laughed, "Why have you something better to do?"

He grumbled, "I might have."

The small bay was totally deserted when we reached it. Before we landed I questioned our captives. "How far is it to Tara?"

Murchad looked shifty eyed again but he could see the determination on my face. "Half a day."

"And from the place, we just left?"

"A little longer."

I knew then that Murchad had had something planned. There must have been somewhere along the route which would have been suitable for an ambush. He could still do that. "Seara, get a description of Tara and the route we take to get there."

She did so. It seemed to me that we would be unlikely to run into trouble before we reached this Tara. From what I could gather it was a place with religious significance. It was a place where violence was forbidden. For the first time, I felt a little hopeful.

I turned to Olaf. "I am only going to take half the men. I think this may be a trap. You can take Seara with you and return to Man. Try to persuade Prince Butar to raid the port we just passed. I would like Tadgh's ship destroying."

Seara protested, "I will come with you."

"No, I need you to look after Aiden. As he is with us I will retain him as a hostage."

"How will you understand their words?"

"I will get by. You have done more than enough."

The hard part was choosing the warriors who would accompany me. All of them wanted to go; they were oathsworn. In the end, I took

Haaken, Cnut, Egill, Harald, Bjorn, Oleg, Sigismund and Stig. Olaf looked at me with a sceptical eye. "And will that be enough?"

"I am not here to fight the whole Hibernian tribe. I am here to kill Tadgh and rescue my wife. If it is not enough then we will have a glorious death."

He nodded his understanding. He pointed at Murchad. "I would not trust that rat. He will slit your throat as soon as look at you."

"And I know that already."

Murchad frowned when he saw that his son and Seara were not joining us. He jabbered at me. I pointed west and just said, "You, Tara!" He tried to push past me to get to the ship and his son. I hit him with my mailed fist and he fell in an unconscious heap.

My Ulfheonar laughed and Olaf shouted, "I see you have learned the art of negotiation. We will be here tomorrow."

Then my ship's sails filled and she turned to sail to my home. I was resolved that I would be able to accomplish what I needed to without risking losing all of the finest warriors my people had. I nodded to Haaken, "Keep that sword safe. It is our insurance."

"I will."

Murchad came to. His nose was a bloody mess. I pointed west and snapped, "Tara!"

Casting me murderous looks he turned and began to walk west with his two comrades behind him. "Egill, keep way behind us in case we are being followed."

As we trudged west I wondered about this new High King. From what I had gathered he had ruled for only a few years. As such he would be wary of both friend and foes. He would not be secure in his position. Perhaps that was why Tadgh had sought him out. It would be a way to ingratiate himself into the king's favour by offering him, such renowned warriors.

Chapter 5

The land, we passed through, was green and dotted with isolated farms. There appeared to be no danger for we saw no-one. I was not worried about ambush for the country was too open and we were too well armed. When we closed with the hill fort that was Tara, then that would change. I had learned that this hill had religious significance and was the main reason I had chosen so few warriors to accompany me. The High King would not risk any bloodshed on such a religious site. We were too few for our deaths to bring any honour and I counted on the fact that he would want to talk first. He might still wish us dead later on but I just needed time to speak with him.

Surprisingly our three guides did not appear to want to leave us. From what I knew of this land it was full of clans with blood feuds and memories as old as the mountains. We were their protection. Seara had told me that Murchad needed the High King to confirm him as chief. The warrior I had killed must have been the last holder of that office. Perhaps they had been related in some way. The bones from the nearby village were testament to the brutal nature of life in Hibernia.

We saw the hill fort some time before we reached it. It dominated the land around it. The hill was the highest point for miles around and the wooden walls looked formidable. We had the advantage that we were travelling from the east which would keep us hidden for longer. The sun was low in the western sky now and I judged that we would just reach it before sunset. The Ulfheonar were calm as we marched west. We had yet to taste defeat. From what we had seen of the Irish they were not as skilled in arms as we were. It remained to be seen if the High King had gathered better warriors around him. I hoped we would not have to fight but if we had to then my warriors could match any that we might meet.

We were spotted some half a mile from the gate. Four warriors on small ponies galloped out to meet us. We waited as they rode up. In the time it took for them to reach us Egill arrived. He shook his head, "No one followed."

The four warriors who reached us were lightly armed. They looked at us as though we were a strange new phenomenon. They spoke to us. I smiled and pointed to Murchad. I hoped he would say what we wanted him to. Haaken still had his sword and I had seen the greed and the desire in his eyes. Until he got his hands on that weapon he would be more compliant. Murchad spoke with the riders who looked at each other and then pointed us in the direction of the main gate. The sun was now setting. Had we arrived an hour later then it might have been seen as a threat. As it was the four men on ponies rode behind us to ensure that we had no tricks.

Cnut laughed, "As if those four little boys could stop us if we chose to go back from whence we came." I was just glad that they could not understand our language. It would not do to upset them. We needed to see how the land lay. We were the strangers in this land.

There were many warriors on the ramparts as we rode up. It was an old hill fort with concentric circles of ditches and mounds. I could see why it had been chosen; it was the only high spot for miles around. The wooden walls were sturdy too and the gateway was a real obstacle. It would take a mighty army to assault it. Half naked warriors with tattoos and limed hair lined the entrance. Their wild rolling eyes showed that they were trying to intimidate us. It would take more than spiky hair to do that. Once inside I saw that there were hundreds of warriors gathered. I was desperately looking for a sign of Tadgh and my wife but I could not see either of them. Nor could I see any warriors such as us. Had I been misled?

The lines of warriors led to a raised dais and a throne. On it sat a man, younger than I had expected. He had red hair and blue eyes. They were both striking and handsome features. He was dressed in a mail byrnie and from his side hung a long sword. Behind him and to the right was a white-haired man dressed in white robes. He had the longest hair and beard I had ever seen. He stared at me and my men as though he knew us.

Murchad approached him and dropped to his knee. The king, for I assumed it was he, spoke to Murchad. The man spoke quickly with many gestures towards us. When he had finished the king looked at us and then beckoned us forward. We all kept our hands before us, palms up. We wanted them to know that we came in peace.

The king spoke to the white-haired man who nodded. He walked forwards and began to speak with us in our own language. "I am the high priest here, Myrddyn is my name. King Áed Oirdnide wishes to know why men from the north have brought this man here to this most holy of places." He smiled, "The punishment for coming uninvited is normally death."

"Our village was raided by some Hibernians and renegades. They took my wife. We destroyed the village of the Hibernians who raided us and we were told that Tadgh and his renegades were here."

He translated for the king whose face remained impassive. "So, you killed Colm the Mighty and I believe you promised his sword to this man?"

"Haaken."

Haaken took out the sword and laid it at the king's feet. The king picked up the sword and balanced it in his hands. He spoke to the priest who smiled. "You are lucky young warrior for the king did not like Colm. It seems he had desires on the throne. For that, you shall live. He wishes to know your name."

"I am Garth also known as Dragon Heart."

The priest's eyes widened. "Are you the one with the sword touched by the gods?"

I nodded and tapped the pommel, "Aye, *Ragnar's Spirit.*"

He translated. This time even the king's impassive features cracked and he spoke to Myrddyn. "The king would like to see the sword."

I nodded and, very carefully, took the sword out. I held it by the blade and offered the hilt to the king. He took it and balanced it as he had done with the other one. He smiled and he gave it back to me with the hilt towards me. It was a sign that he trusted me; a little anyway.

"You are brave men to come here into this stronghold. King Áed Oirdnide appreciates bravery and you may stay the night." He gave an apologetic shrug. "You will, of course, be guarded."

"Of course."

"Now this man you are seeking. Why did you think he was coming here?"

"Colm's wife told us that Tadgh and his Norse renegades had set off for here."

This time the priest and the king frowned as this information was digested. "It seems, Garth of the Dragon Heart, that your coming here was not an accident. The king would hear more but you must be tired. Come, I will take you to the warrior hall where you can rest before we feast."

As he led us I asked, "And what of Murchad?"

The priest gave me a baleful stare. "Murchad is tainted too much with his cousin's greed. The king will make a judgement tomorrow."

When we were in the hall the Hibernian warriors who were there afforded us some privacy and we found a corner, close to the fire, where we could talk. I was not certain how many others could speak our language and we kept our voices low.

"So where do you think Tadgh is?"

"He could be on his way here. We saw his ship in that port. He may have been delayed there. We had a shorter route and we did not tarry."

I nodded, Haaken was right. "The question is what is he doing here? Things have changed since we arrived. I assumed that this Colm, whom I slew, was an ally of the king. That is obviously not true. I had thought that Tadgh's journey was to be to consolidate that friendship."

"Why did Murchad come here then?"

"You are right Egill; it does not look good for him. Hibernian politics look complicated and deadly. There is treachery on all sides and we know that Tadgh is the most treacherous and untrustworthy of all. I think we should not drink too much tonight and keep one of us awake at all times. I am not certain we are safe here."

All of us were in agreement and we kept a close watch on each other when we were summoned to the feast. The king had given us one long table and the priest sat at the end so that he could translate for us if we needed it. Haaken nudged me and pointed, surreptitiously to the wall above the king's head. There hung the two-handed sword we had brought. He shrugged, "And no sign of Murchad or his companions."

"It seems our Hibernian friend miscalculated." I did not think that Murchad had much of a future as a chief.

The room was filled with warriors. Most of them had the same arms and clothes as Murchad had had but the bodyguards of the king looked as though they knew their business. They had the warrior bands and the scars which bespoke of combat. Yet there were only twenty of them. If Prince Butar had brought all of our warriors then we could have easily overcome them. This was a backward country in terms of weapons. The king was the only one who was well armed.

The priest saw me appraising the warriors. "Tell me, Norseman, what you think of our warriors." He saw me hesitate. "I am the only one who speaks your language. You can speak the truth." He smiled, "There are those who say I can read minds anyway."

I laughed, "If that were the case then you would not have needed to ask me the question."

"You are wise beyond your years. But come, indulge an old man."

"Your warriors look brave but apart from the twenty bodyguards they are ill armed."

"And if the rest of your warriors came then we would be defeated." I let the words hang in the air and he nodded his understanding. "This is why the alliance of Tadgh and Colm was a worry to the king." He waved a hand at our table. "Had you come with more men then we might have thought that you, too, have desires on the High King's throne."

"I told you, priest, I came here for my wife. I have no desire to conquer Hibernia."

"And yet you have taken Manau from the Saxons."

"I believe the Saxons took it from the Cymri first."

"True. And that little rock is enough for you and your people?"

"Probably but if not then the lands to the east are a more attractive prospect. No offence but I have not seen many riches here."

"You are shrewd and you are correct. We have little; the Allfather just gives us a home which is bound to the land."

"You still follow the old ways then?"

"The followers of the White Christ are growing, especially in the north and the west but this is the heart of the old ways." He looked wistfully towards the south east, "Much as Wyddfa is the heart of the old ways on the mainland."

The food and the drink we consumed was simple enough fare but tasty. My companions heeded my words and we were sparing in our drinking. The Hibernians were not and fights broke out. Some of them were bloody with daggers and swords being used. Myrddyn shook his head, "I had heard that your people were fierce drinkers too."

I smiled, "We can be but I deemed it imprudent to be so here, so far from home."

"You show great self control. I can see that your coming here was not an accident."

"I came for my wife."

"Yet had you followed the ship which took her you might have met this Tadgh on the road and not reached us here. Murchad would not be talking and the sword would not hang upon the wall."

"Murchad is talking?"

"Let us say he knew of Colm's plans." He shook his head, "He is a simple man who has ambitions. Had he been less ambitious and a cleverer man then things might be different."

When the feast was over we returned to the side of the hall where our sleeping robes lay. We had decided who would stay awake and the men rolled themselves in their furs and fell asleep. Cnut nudged me awake when it was my turn to watch. "It is quiet and no one stirs. The only sounds you will hear will be the snores and the farts of the drunk."

I sat with my back to the wall listening to the noises but inside my head, I was seeking my wife and wondering what Tadgh's plans were. I could see him offering his sword to the High King but why bring Erika? He could have left her with Colm. I knew that he hated me and his need to defeat me was driving him but there was something else which I could not, as yet, see. Why was he coming to Tara? Was he still coming to Tara? Perhaps he had deliberately misled Colm's wife and was going elsewhere. When I judged that enough time had passed I woke Egill and tried to sleep. I might as well have stayed awake for sleep eluded me. I tossed and I turned, worrying about my wife and her fate.

When we awoke the next day, we saw that there were two more adornments on the walls. Murchad and one of his companion's heads were impaled upon two spears. The warriors were all standing and watching. We looked and wondered where the third warrior was. Our question was answered when he was led out by the king's bodyguards. King Áed Oirdnide followed holding the sword we had brought. He spoke some words and everyone cheered. The warriors banged their shields and the third warrior trudged out of the gates.

The priest came for me. "The king would speak with you."

"What will happen to that warrior?" I pointed towards the departing figure.

"He is the new chief of Murchad's settlement. He will return to warn them of the dangers of fermenting rebellion." He smiled, "These are dangerous times and King Áed Oirdnide has much to think on."

My companions were kept back while the priest took me close to the king.

"The king is pleased that you appear to be honourable men and he understands your need to find your wife. This renegade who has taken your wife has not yet appeared and the king wishes you to stay here until he does."

I saw the warning in the priest's eyes. The king did not yet trust us. He thought that we were working with Tadgh. It was ironic that I needed my enemy to arrive so that we could leave. He smiled, "The king suggests that you enjoy his hospitality for a few more days."

I returned to Haaken and the others. "It seems that we are prisoners, albeit temporarily."

Oleg growled, "We could soon escape if we wanted to."

Haaken shook his head, "We could get beyond the gate if that is what you mean but could we reach the safety of the coast and '*Wolf*'? I think not. We will stay here I think and use the time well."

"What do you mean?"

"Let us learn some of the language. I do not like others forming our words for us. I don't trust the old wizard."

I found myself in agreement with Haaken. "And we might as well investigate this fort, just in case we ever have to capture it! Divide yourselves up try to pick up some of the words and knowledge of their defences."

I went alone to the gatehouse. The sentries there looked at me warily when I approached. I smiled and looked out of the gate. It was obvious to me that any sudden move out of the gate would have resulted in them trying to stop me. They would have both died, of course. They had no mail and their spears were not the best. I was not trying to escape- not yet anyway. The gate was solidly made and the wooden bar would have withstood an initial attack. However, there was nothing to stop a determined group of axe men from hacking it to pieces. The gate itself was not studded with iron and an axe can cut through any wooden door. The ditches were more of a problem. They looked to be ancient. The entrances were offset which would make any attacker have to suffer a barrage of missiles from the side. Once again it showed me that they had not fought warriors like us who had good shields, sound helmets and mail byrnies.

I waved to the sentries as I returned to the interior. I had only seen the warrior hall up until now. I found that they had stables and they contained a number of small horses and ponies. If we had to escape then that would be the best way. They had a small blacksmith hut but all I saw was the smith working horseshoes and spear heads. Their skills were not as advanced as ours. I wandered in and gestured at the wheel with the grindstone. He nodded and said something to the boy who began to turn it for me. I took out *Ragnar's Spirit* and sparks flew as I made it sharp enough to shave with. The boy's eyes were wide with wonder.

By now I had explored the whole of the fortress and picked up a few simple Hibernian words. I would not be able to hold a conversation but I would understand some of what they said. The others joined me and we shared our information and words. I was wondering how best to employ our time when there was a sudden shout from the gate and the sentries barred the gate. The king himself and the priest raced out and stood on top of the ramparts.

Haaken said, "I just heard the word Lochlannach!" We knew that was their name for us.

Tadgh! It had to be. The priest waved me up to the ramparts. The guard at the bottom allowed me up but not the others. I heard Oleg begin to complain, "It is fine, Oleg. I do not need a minder, not yet anyway."

When I reached the top I saw, in the distance a large warband of Norsemen. They were too far away to make them out but I saw that half of them were mounted on the Irish ponies. I frowned. There were more men than I had thought. It looked to me as though there were at least fifty warriors. Where had Tadgh, if this was Tadgh, acquired so many men?

Myrddyn looked at me, "Do you know them?"

"They are too far away to make out."

"But this could be the man, you say, is your enemy."

I stared at him with hard cold eyes. "Priest, do not question my word. I have spoken the truth and no man calls me a liar. I do not care if he is a king or priest."

The man did not seem at all put out by this. "I am just saying that these men are of your people." He shrugged, "They could be working with you. With you inside then they could be here to join you."

"Then if that is the case let us leave now. You are the ones holding us."

Myrddyn translated for the king who gave me a mirthless smile and spoke.

"The king says he will see what these new visitors have to say first."

I saw that the bodyguards were all ready to fight and the rest of the garrison was massing behind them. If these warriors did wish to take Tara then the men I had seen would not be able to withstand them. I peered east to try to discern their identity. It was Erika who told me who they were. She was being led by a halter behind a warrior on a pony. She was the only one not wearing a helmet and as soon as I recognised her I saw Tadgh next to the man with the halter.

"It is the man I seek and that is my wife."

Myrddyn smiled, "I hoped that you would be speaking the truth. Now what does he want I wonder?" he turned to the king who nodded and then shouted orders.

Within a few moments, two warriors were astride ponies and were galloping through the maze of ditches towards them. The warband halted. They did not display their arms and appeared to have peaceful intentions. I saw the riders halt before them and then a discussion ensued. I was desperate just to run down and fight Tadgh there and then but I knew it would not be so simple. It seemed an age before the two riders returned and reported to the king. He looked at me and then spoke to Myrddyn.

"It seems, Dragon Heart, that you were correct. The warrior is called Tadgh and that is your wife with him." he paused, "He is offering her to the king as a concubine as a sign of his honourable intentions."

I saw the two of them watching my reaction. I forced myself to remain impassive although inside I was screaming. I said, as calmly as I could, "And what are his intentions?"

"He is here offering his services as a leader of what he describes as the finest warriors on this island."

I remained silent. I was in a helpless position. If the king took up Tadgh's offer then my men and I would die. Even the Ulfheonar could not fight fifty men armed in the same manner as us. They both watched me and then the king said something to Myrddyn who nodded. "We will allow this Tadgh and your wife within the walls so that the king can make a judgement."

I saw Tadgh and two warriors detach themselves from the warband who began to make a camp beyond the last ditch. Leaving the ponies with his men, Tadgh walked towards the gate. I noticed that his helmet and his byrnie gleamed. They were expensively made. They disappeared around a ditch and Myrddyn said, "If you and your men would wait inside the warrior hall…" I hesitated. He shrugged almost apologetically. "It is forbidden to shed blood within these walls." I glanced up at Murchad's head. "He and his fellow were executed beyond the walls."

I shouted down to the others. "We have to go to the warrior hall." They gave me questioning looks. I nodded, "Yes, it is Tadgh."

They all looked happy at that prospect. I would have to tell when we entered the warrior hall of the sanctity of this site. At last, I had my enemy and soon he would be within a sword length of me.

Chapter 6

As we made our way to the hall I explained what was happening. Oleg snorted, "They do not worry me Dragon Heart. We can fight our way out." Oleg was always one to act first and think later.

Haaken gave a derisory laugh, "With Erika fighting too I suppose?"

Abashed, Oleg shook his head, "Sorry. I was not thinking." Oleg was the most loyal of warriors but he was never the one to send out as a scout. He tended to rush into things too quickly but as a warrior to back you unto death, there was none better.

When we reached the warrior hall, two of the king's bodyguards awaited us. They took us to an area behind the throne. I had only seen what I took to be a hessian sack but it turned out to be an old curtain or tapestry. They had probably raided it from the mainland. It looked to be the sort of thing the Romans would have owned. The images on it were so faded that they looked like stains. The guards stood on either side of us. We were being kept hidden for a reason. This King Áed Oirdnide was a careful man. It would not do to underestimate him. I could see why he had attained the throne at a young age. He was clever.

We heard the people as they came in and we knew when the king had sat down. There was silence. I could picture the other side of the curtain. The king would be seated and the priest would be standing alongside him. I wondered if Tadgh would recognise Colm's sword hanging above the throne on the beam. Surprisingly Tadgh spoke Hibernian. It sounded halting but they could obviously understand him. That was annoying for it kept us in the dark. I only caught one or two of the words and, out of context, they made no sense. Then I heard the priest say. "And who are you?"

Tadgh's voice sounded only to be silenced by a roar from the king. There was a brief silence and then I heard Erika speak. "I am Erika, wife of the Dragon Heart and this man has abducted me."

"You are still my slave and my property!" Tadgh had spoken our language and he sounded petulant. He had not had the reception from the king that he had anticipated.

"Not while my husband lives. He will come for you, you treacherous snake."

The king shouted again and then the priest spoke, "I will speak for the king, Tadgh, in your own language so that you may know his questions and there will be no misunderstanding. Why have you come here?"

"To serve the king."

"And be paid for doing so?"

"Of course."

"Did you also serve Colm the Mighty?"

There was a slight hesitation. "I knew him."

"We have heard that he planned to take over this fort and, it is said, that you were part of the plan. Your warriors were to attack us."

I could now see the king's dilemma. He could not afford a battle with Tadgh's men. Even if he won his forces would be so weakened that another could wrest the crown from him. I wondered how he would extricate himself from this parlous position.

"That is a lie! Show me who says this and I will separate his head from his body!"

"You passed his head when you came through the gate. That was Murchad his brother and, as you can see, Colm's sword is here with the king for he is dead." There was another maddening silence and I could picture Tadgh seeing the sword for the first time. Had he been expecting Colm to bring more forces along? He had his own dilemma. Was he arrogant enough to think that he could capture the hill fort with his warband? "I will ask you again, did you plan to kill the king and take over this fort?"

I heard swords being drawn and then Myrddyn shouted, "It is forbidden to spill blood in this sanctified place." The silence which ensued seemed to last forever. Then Myrddyn said, "You are not the first of your people to come here. We have had others like you who arrived earlier." He said something in Hibernian and the guards gestured for us to move from behind the curtain.

As we stepped out I heard Erika give a cry of joy. She was no longer tethered. She stood protected by two of the king's oathsworn. Tadgh had his helmet in his hand and I could see his face which was black with fury.

The king pointed at Tadgh and spoke. Myrddyn translated for us. "The king says that he has learned that you speak the truth, Dragon Heart, and this man lies for Murchad told him that this warrior was an ally of Colm."

I pointed my finger at Tadgh. I could see him working out if he could escape from this obvious trap. "And I claim the right of combat. I will kill this thing of evil, this nithing!"

"Gladly!" Tadgh seemed almost relieved that I had given him a way out. It suited me. The last thing I needed was Tadgh and his men waylaying my tiny band as we headed for our ships.

The priest had a strangely satisfied smile upon his lips and he pointed to the gateway. "Go beyond the walls, Tadgh. Do not try to escape with your men or you will be hunted like dogs. The combat will take place before the walls of Tara."

He and his warriors stormed out, followed by some of the bodyguards of the king. Erika rushed into my arms. "I knew you would come." She kissed me, hard. "And Arturus?"

"Safe at home with the rest of the captives. I am sorry we did not arrive in time to stop you being taken." I held her at arm's length. "Did he...?" I could not bring myself to say the words in case she answered in the affirmative.

She shook her head. "I would have died first."

I turned to the Ulfheonar. "Guard her with your lives."

Erika gripped my arm, "Beware of him. He is cunning and does not fight fair."

"I grew up with him. I remember what he was like."

As we emerged from the gate I saw that Tadgh's warband had been surrounded by a ring of the king's warriors. It looked as though they were enclosed but the reality was that warriors like us could break through the flimsy circle as easily as cracking spring ice in the river. This was an illusion. The only way out of this would be if I killed Tadgh. His men would then be leaderless. The king and the priest walked just behind us and the other half of the bodyguards flanked them. The king was being careful still and they were taking no chances.

I turned to the priest, "What happens to Tadgh's warriors when I kill him?"

"You are confident. That is good. When he is dead the king will see if they will serve him."

"You would have them even though they fought for Colm?"

"You have to be practical. With an army of such warriors, the king would be safe, even from Lochlannach." This Hibernia was a different place to my own world. Here you bought your swords and had others die for you.

Tadgh's warriors formed a double line and behind them stood the king's spearmen. There was a large area between the warriors and us. Tadgh stood there with his helmet on, his shield ready and his sword already unsheathed. I took in the fact that my sword was longer, not by much but enough. His blade was Frankish too- it would not break. I also saw that he had a small axe and a second sword on his belt. He was ready to use any means possible to defeat me. I just had my sword and a seax which was tucked into my boot.

This was a blood feud and there was no need for any announcement. There would be no rules. One of us would live and the other would die. It was not a first blood fight. This would be a fight to the death.

As I had expected Tadgh could not resist insulting me. "The little boy thinks he can defeat me now that he has a shiny sword. You were pathetic as a child and you are still pathetic." He pointed his sword at the Ulfheonar. "And you can only manage a handful of men in silly wolf cloaks to follow you! I have a warband and when you are dead I will take this kingdom and your woman."

"And that is the only way you could get a woman. None would choose you of their own volition. And as for taking this kingdom? That does not surprise me for you have no honour. You are a killer in the night. You face me now but you would prefer to stab me in the back! You are a nithing!"

He suddenly roared at me and smashed his sword overhand at my head. I took the blow on my shield. His arm was powerful and his sword heavier than mine. I felt my whole side judder with the blow. My blade had just been sharpened and I had no intention of blunting it on his shield. I feinted at his left and he brought up his shield; I turned the sword and slashed at his thigh. The blade severed some of the mail links. He swung again at my head. I stepped forwards to close with him and held my shield up. He only struck my shield with his hilt. As I moved forward I sliced and stabbed at him and felt more of the mail links rip. As we stepped away I could see what he could not; his byrnie was now holed.

"You are afraid of my shield. Well, you should be for it is protected by a charm from a witch." Tadgh took the fact that I was not striking his shield as fear.

"I thought your mother was dead!"

That enraged him and he swung at me wildly. I stepped back and his blade struck nothing but air. I did not strike but I waited. His sword was heavy and soon his arm would tire. He thought that I was weakening and came at me, furiously again. This time I turned my shield as he struck it and felt his sword rasp down the metal studs and nails. It would not be as sharp as it had been. I saw that it was a Frankish blade but it had not been finished as well as mine. He was not a true warrior; had he been then he would have chosen a better sword.

I could see that he was now becoming weaker; he was out of breath. He swung again and the blow was weaker when it struck my shield. It bounced off and still, I waited. I could see links dropping from his armour with every movement he made. His eyes began to show fear for the first time. He would be wondering why I was not attacking him.

"So, Ragnar's bum boy, you just learned to take punishment. You do not know how to fight."

"I know how to fight but this is the first time I have ever fought a snake and I am learning."

Suddenly I lunged at him with my sword. He brought his shield down too slowly and merely succeeded in forcing my sword lower. It slid through the last few links of the weakened lower section of his byrnie and sliced a long cut across his leg. He screamed and the Ulfheonar cheered as they saw the blood.

He tried a different tactic and this time tried to emulate me and hack across at my neck. My shield came up and this time his sword struck the boss. When he stepped back I could see that a piece of metal had been chipped from his sword. I brought my sword over my head and downwards. He put his own blade up and it shivered as *Ragnar's Spirit* caught it near the chip. The sword shattered in two. He stepped backwards, panicking and glanced over his shoulder to his men.

"They cannot help you now."

He took out his second sword. I could see that the wound in his leg was making him limp. I feinted with my sword again and, when he brought the shield down to protect his wound I punched him hard in the face with my shield. The boss caught him squarely in the face. He fell backwards and then leapt to his feet. I could see that I had bent the nasal on his helmet and blood was pouring from his nose.

"I will take you a piece at a time if I have to but you will die." This was no idle boast or taunt. I was deadly serious and the look on his face showed me that he knew it.

We had moved further away from the warriors and my men now and were much closer to his warband. His next attack showed how much he had tired and it barely registered that he had hit my shield. I dropped my shoulder as I swung and twisted my sword to the side. It penetrated the mail links and cut him along his side. He screamed again and, as he dropped to his knee, turned and yelled, "Tostig!"

Suddenly a war axe flew at my head. I barely had time to bring my shield up. It hit my shield and the force threw me to the ground. As I lay there I saw two of his men rush at me while the others dragged him to his feet and towards the waiting ponies. I was now tired too and I struggled to rise and defend myself against this treacherous attack. I swung my sword more in hope than expectation and felt it slice into the leg of the one who had thrown the axe. He fell screaming as his leg was sliced in two. The second warrior swung his two-handed axe and it cracked my shield rendering it useless. Before he could withdraw it, I kicked his legs from under him and he fell down next to me. I rolled on top of him and put the whole weight of my body and armour onto the edge of my sword which lay across his neck. His head rolled away.

I could hear the clamour of battle as the Hibernians fell upon the warband. They had dishonoured the combat. They would not be joining the king's army. As I reached my feet the Ulfheonar had surrounded me. I looked at Haaken, "Erika?"

"The king and the priest are guarding her with his bodyguards."

As I looked east I saw the Hibernians being slaughtered by the mailed warriors. "Let us end this!"

I had no shield and so I picked up Tadgh's discarded sword. Tadgh's warriors were no match for my Ulfheonar who had had to watch in frustration at the treachery of our enemies. We ran at them in a wedge. My two blades came down together and severed the first warrior's head. On either side of me, my companions punched a hole in their line. Without a solid line, they were no match for even the poorly armed Hibernians. Some fell while the rest ran, pursued by the angry Irish. I could see that Tadgh and those with horses were too far away for us to catch and we halted.

The Ulfheonar cheered me. I shook my head. "I do not deserve your cheers for I failed; I did not kill him."

Cnut shook his head, "You defeated him and now every warrior will know that he is a coward. Tadgh's days as a leader are numbered."

I was not so sure. I noticed the remnants of his warband still followed him and they were still a potent force. Tadgh had always had a glib tongue. He would turn this defeat to his advantage.

We made our way back to the king. Those warriors who had been wounded were now being despatched by the Irish. They were not doing it mercifully. The Norse warriors screamed as their manhoods were hacked from their bodies before they were finally killed. Erika threw her arms around me. "I told you he was not to be trusted."

"So you did."

The king walked over to me with a smile on his face. He put his arms around me and slapped me on my back. Myrddyn translated his words. "The king says that you truly are a man of honour and a great warrior. He would have you and your men fight for him. He will pay you whatever you wish."

I shook my head, "Tell the king I thank him for his offer but I have a family on Man." I did not add that I did not trust him either. "You might suggest using the armour and weapons you salvage to arm your warriors better. They are brave but they will die unless they are better protected."

The priest nodded. "Is there anything we can do for you?"

"Loan us some ponies and a guide to get to the coast. We have a ship waiting."

The king acceded to our request and we left as soon as we were mounted. I wished to be away from this place as soon as possible. The king sent ten men with us as our guards. I think he wanted to make sure that we actually left his land. The fact that we had destroyed Tadgh's band and his own army had been outclassed themselves showed him that we were a danger to him

As we rode east I knew that if we wanted to we could easily conquer this land. The warriors were brave but they were not well led.

When we reached the beach, it was deserted and it was night time. Our guards and guides looked perplexed. Haaken used the few words he had acquired and told them to go. They looked reluctant to do so but we insisted. When they had gone we lit a bonfire on the beach and prepared for a foodless night.

Erika and I snuggled in each other's arms and shared our experiences. If anything, the nightmare strengthened our love for I saw that I had married a strong woman, I had married a woman who was just like my own mother. Arturus was lucky to have her as his protector.

We had just set the sentries when the ship came. It ghosted from the south. It was a drekar but was it Tadgh and his men? We took no chances; we moved away from the fire and formed a protective circle around Erika. I gave her my seax. There was nowhere we could run to; if this was Tadgh then the best that we could hope for was to kill as many of them before we succumbed.

The dragon's head loomed up through the surf and a figure in a helmet leapt ashore. It was Erik! "Is that you hiding in the dark Dragon Heart?"

We stepped back into the light. "We thought you must have thought we were dead."

Erik threw his arms around his sister. "We decided to keep coming back as often as was necessary." He looked at me, "Tadgh?"

"The slippery eel wriggled away."

Erik laughed, "It he returns to his ship he will have a shock."

"And why is that?"

"Jarl Harald destroyed it yesterday along with the other Hibernian ships."

Chapter 7

The winds were with us and we reached Duboglassio before dawn. The keen-eyed sentries recognised my ship when we were some way out to sea and Prince Butar was waiting for us as we landed. He embraced Erika and I saw the relief on his face. He clasped my arm, "It is good that we have the whole family together again. Come let us get you something to eat and drink."

Erika shook her head, "I must go to Arturus."

Butar nodded, "He is with Maewe and Seara."

"Seara?"

"She is the Saxon slave we rescued. It was she who led us to Colm's home and to our son."

"Then I have much to thank her for."

They were all asleep inside the hut. We stood in the doorway with the early light of dawn casting golden shards of light on their faces and Erika began to weep. I put my arm around her and led her from the hut. My stepfather stepped away from us and we walked to his hall. There was nothing I could say to Erika; she needed to get the tears out and to release the emotion which she had contained during her captivity. My thoughts were murderous ones; Tadgh had not yet begun to pay for his evil act. It was not our way to rant and rave. We cried a little and kept it all within us.

The slaves brought us food and drink. Erika was silent as she nibbled at the cold meats and biscuits. I told the others who were present, between mouthfuls, of our journey and of the fight.

"This High King then, he is a plotter?" I could see that Prince Butar was interested in the character of this near neighbour.

I nodded vigorously. "He is and it seems to me that his land is ripe for plucking. The warriors are brave but both reckless and poorly armed. They could not stand up to us. Had the seven of us not intervened then I think that Tadgh and his small warband would have prevailed."

"And you think we should do so?" There was a wry smile on his face.

I shook my head, "No, definitely not. There would be little to be gained. We need to put warriors on the island to control it. We are not numerous enough as yet. Besides, Tadgh is still on the island and, if he were to gather others of a similar mind, they could control the whole land easily. That would bring us into a conflict which would only result in deaths we could ill afford. For me this small island suits."

"Good for I have no wish to go to war again. Jarl Harald and Jarl Erik may think differently. They both have ambitions for more land and riches." He nodded towards Erika who had fallen asleep on the table. "Your wife has survived this well my son but she will need love and care."

"I know." I looked at him, "Will you stay here or return to Hrams-a?"

"I have come to love this place and, if I am, to be honest with you, Hrams-a has too many painful memories. I returned there and found myself crying like a baby. I just see your mother's burned remains. I shall stay here." He scrutinised my face. "But not you?"

"No. I wish to return there and make it strong enough to withstand another raid. We were happy there and we will be again. Besides we need it occupying. It gives us warning of any raider from the north."

"And who do you think will raid from the north?"

"Tadgh came that way and I cannot believe that Harald One-Eye will have forgotten us. He has an evil heart."

"The last news we had from home was that he was raiding the east coast of the land of the Angles."

"All the more reason for vigilance."

"Then I will ask you to rule Hrams-a for me. Will your Ulfheonar go with you?"

"They are not mine to command but I will ask them and, hopefully, they will. They have fulfilled their oath to return my family to me. Their other oath was the one I also swore and that was to you."

"Then perhaps we will make you Jarl and you start your own warband."

I laughed, "Me? I am too young. The men would laugh at me. No, I will just continue to be a warrior and watch over my family. That is enough responsibility for me."

He looked at me with sad old eyes, "I will do as you wish but know that you are highly respected even amongst the older warriors such as Olaf. They see in you, a leader. Your age does not matter. And remember that one day you will lead all of our people."

"Hopefully that day will be many years hence."

I left Erika sleeping and went outside. I was not ready for sleep. My mind was filled with too many thoughts. I watched the sun fully rise from the east. I had a task to do which I was dreading. I would have to tell Aiden that his father was dead. We would have to take him home to his village. I felt sorry for the boy. He had been another of the victims like my family and Scanlan's. Tadgh had set a series of events in motion and he could not have known the consequences would be so far reaching. It was like throwing a stone into a pond and watching the ripples become progressively smaller but stretching further. There were people who were affected who had no idea what had caused the disaster in their lives. Aiden was the smallest of ripples. Of course, Tadgh would not care about that. He only cared for himself. I knew then why I could not sleep; I had unfinished business. Until Tadgh was dead I would have more sleepless nights.

I heard the noise of Arturus from the hut behind me. He could not yet make words but his sounds were purposeful. The one he was making now was the one for food. I smiled. Arturus just needed company and food; anything else was a bonus.

I headed towards the hut. I saw Erika emerge from Prince Butar's hall and rush towards our hut. She would have heard his noise and panicked. "I think he just needs food."

As soon as I spoke she understood and nodded. "You let me sleep."

I shrugged, "I could not sleep and I knew that you needed it."

She kissed me, gently, "You cannot always be the tough warrior, my husband. You must promise me that you will let others do some of the things you seem to take on yourself."

I did not answer for I would not lie to her. "I need to give Aiden, the hostage some bad news before I do anything else. I will wait until you have met them first."

She knew of Aiden's plight; we had spoken on the journey home. The mother in her felt for the boy, now fatherless and in a strange land.

When we entered, Arturus squealed and threw himself at Erika. She hugged him tightly. Scanlan bowed. "I am pleased to see you safe my lord and thank you for saving my family. I will be forever in your debt."

In answer, I just smiled and said, "We will be leaving for Hrams-a this afternoon. I would build my home again."

He nodded, "That is good. This is a fine town but it is too crowded for me."

I saw Aiden clinging to Seara who looked nervously at my wife. I knew how women were about their domains. "Seara, Aiden, this is my wife, the Lady Erika."

When she saw Aiden, her face beamed. She could only speak a little Saxon and poor Aiden could understand nothing. She did the best thing she could. She picked him up and she hugged him. She turned to the former slave and said, "Thank you Seara."

Seara did not need to know our language to understand the sentiment and she blushed. Erika laid Aiden down who looked bemused by it all.

I reached out for Aiden. "I am ready to eat, Maewe, but first I need to speak with Seara and Aiden."

We went outside. It would be a glorious day. Aiden skipped happily with Seara but she, I think, knew that bad news was coming and she had a sad expression upon her face. We walked to the beach and felt the morning breeze fly from the mainland and into our faces. How did one tell a child that his father was a traitor and had been executed? I picked up a pebble and threw it to skim across the waves. I counted the bounces. I did it again and then watched as Aiden picked one up and tried to copy me. It flopped into the surf after one desultory bounce. I chose a flat stone and threw it. I managed to achieve seven bounces. When I had been a child seven bounces meant that I would have good luck for the day. Aiden reached down to pick up a stone. It was round and I knew that it would not work. I took it from him and discarded it. I chose a flat one and then placed it so that it rested on his second finger while being held by his thumb and first finger. I then mimed pulling back my arm and spinning the stone. He nodded, seriously, and I stepped away. Concentrating hard he threw it and he managed four bounces. He squealed with delight and then threw his arms around my legs and hugged me.

Seara put her hand on his head and said, "Now would be a good time, my lord. What is this bad news I need to give to him?"

I took a deep breath, "His father died. He was executed as a traitor by the king but he does not need to know that. He just needs to know that his father died and I will take him home."

She shook her head. "You are wrong, my lord. He does need to know that. Some time, probably soon, someone will tell him the truth and that will hurt far more. Let him have the hurt now whilst he is young and he will be able to live it."

I could see the sense in what she said, "You are wise Seara. Go ahead."

She turned him to face her and then she spoke slowly. He nodded a few times and then she hugged him. He spoke to her and then picked up a stone and threw it into the sea. He didn't say a word. He merely smiled when he managed to bounce one a few times. I looked at Seara, she explained. "He understands. He says his father never liked him. Murchad thought he was not strong enough to be a warrior." She smiled, "Apparently they were happy to let him be the hostage."

I found myself struggling to believe that a family would not miss any of their members. Perhaps I had been lucky. I had been loved and cared for by my mother and Arturus had the same love from two of us.

"Tell him we will take him home to his mother."

She told him and, for the first time, he became upset. He shook his head and he shouted at Seara who, like me, was taken aback. She spoke to him and he turned away again to throw stones angrily at the sea. I noticed this time that there was more aggression in the throws. I had rid myself of anger in the same way when I had been a child. When Tadgh and the others had bullied me, I had set my lip and thrown stones into the Dunum. I had imagined that I was throwing them at my tormentors.

"Well, what did he say?"

"He says he has no home now save this one." She shook her head, "He says I am a better mother than his own. I do not think he means it. He is just angry for some reason." She looked at me carefully, "I told him I would ask you."

I picked up my own stone and threw it. I did not mind having Aiden in my family. He seemed a good boy. Was it the right thing to do? I closed my eyes and listened to the sea. I heard my mother's voice and, perhaps it was the surf, I don't know, but it sounded like 'yes'. Then I thought of Ragnar. I was no kin of his and yet he had been a better father than my own had ever been.

"I will speak with Erika."

She nodded, "He is happy playing here, my lord."

When I told Erika, she smiled as though I had given her the greatest jewel in the world. "Of course. This is the work of the sisters. You know that don't you?" I was confused both by her reaction and her answer. "Tadgh stole us from you. You have regained a second son. This cannot be ill my husband. This is the work of higher beings than us."

I turned to Scanlan, "Go and tell Seara that we say yes and then start to gather your belongings together. I would like my new family to get to our home sooner rather than later."

Erika said, "And that means we have much to do, Maewe, as well as our men."

I left them to get their belongings organised and then I headed for my ship. Snorri and Erik Short Toe, my two ship's boys were asleep on the boat. I knew that I would not need to ask them if they wished to settle with me in Hrams-a. They jumped to their feet. "Sorry Dragon Heart, we were tired."

"Do not worry Snorri, I am not here to chastise you. I am leaving here to return to Hrams-a. We will have cargo to carry. Prepare *'Wolf'*."

They happily set to, "Aye my lord."

They quickly began to lift the benches and then the deck upon which the rowers sat. *'Wolf'* might be the smallest ship we had but there was enough cargo space to carry all our belongings. "When Scanlan comes show him how to load the cargo." I pointed a finger at them. "If we capsize I will know who to blame!"

"We will not let you down."

I knew that they wouldn't. The heavier items would be loaded down the centre of the ship under the planks which were removed to allow us to do this. The lighter goods were stacked towards the stern, bows and the sides. I was not that worried, we did not have a long journey ahead of us. I headed back to Prince Butar's hall. He was playing a game with Eurwen and she squealed when I entered. "My brother, the warrior!" She hurled herself at me.

"And what of you, my little princess? You are now safely returned from your adventure."

She affected a cross look, "I did not like those people, they smelled!" My stepfather could see that I wished to speak with him and he waved over the slave who looked after Eurwen. "Go with Hilda and play outside. You can see Dragon Heart later."

She skipped off and waved as she left. She would not have the tormented childhood I had suffered. She would be happy and for that I was glad.

"I am going to return to Hrams-a."

"You have decided then?"

"I think it was meant to be. The hostage, Aiden, wishes to be part of my family. I can see the hands of my mother and your father in this."

"I think you are right." He frowned, "Perhaps if you waited then more people might like to return with you."

"They might but they can always walk there. It is not far. And I would like them to reflect and choose rather than rushing into it. I will gladly care for all who come."

"And you will rebuild Hrams-a?"

"No, I will build it anew. I have ideas. I have seen other places now and know what it is that I want. I will ask the Ulfheonar to row back with me and then give them the choice." I took a deep breath, "I will need a crew when I begin to trade."

For the first time, I think I truly surprised Butar. "I had thought that you would go a-raiding?"

"There may be a time when I return to that way of life but Tadgh and his actions have made me yearn for a more peaceful time; just until Arturus is older." I enjoyed travelling to Frankia and I seemed to be quite lucky in the trades we made. "If we are richer then we can arm our men better. I have seen now, the advantage of good weapons and armour."

Butar relaxed a little, "I see and so you are not becoming too peaceful then?"

I laughed, "I do not think I will have a choice in the matter. War and fighting will come here no matter what I do. At least, for the time being, we have time to build. The Ulfheonar are young. They will become better warriors in time."

"You are wise beyond your years. Even if you do not accept it you will be a good Jarl."

"Perhaps… when the time is right."

I went to find the Ulfheonar. I knew that they would be in the warrior hall and that some would be awake. When I entered, I saw that most of them were already up and drinking the first ale of the day. They looked at me expectantly as I walked through the doors. This would be harder than the last two speeches I had made.

There was no other way than to launch into it. "I am returning to Hrams-a to build a better town and fort. Then I will go to Frankia to trade. I would ask you to row my ship back to Hrams-a and then I release you from your oath."

There was a strange silence and they looked at each other. Haaken stood, "I don't know about the rest of you but I do not want to be released from my oath." He grinned, "Life would be too boring with another leader."

"But I am not your leader! I am just one of the Ulfheonar."

Cnut almost choked on his beer, "You were the first of the Ulfheonar. It was you who had the first wolf cloak. We follow Dragon Heart and *Ragnar's Spirit* and there is an end to it."

Chapter 8

We had not been away from the burnt-out settlement of Hrams-a for long, less than three weeks and yet it had the look and feel of something long abandoned. We had been given much timber by the people of Duboglassio which we had towed behind us. The fort on the hill still stood and we put our families inside the walls while we set too to build the warrior hall. The town would be built next to the sea. I would use the sea to protect two sides and the other two would have ditches. Our previous mistake had been to rely on the fort on the hill. I could see now that that had been our undoing. It relied on the people knowing when an enemy might come. As Colm had found you needed to protect against enemies all of the time. The walls could come later. First, we needed shelter.

We laboured all day. Some of the men cut turf from the hills while the rest cut timber and laid out the bones of their new home. My hall could wait. We had canvas and the weather still held. Erika had not only Seara and Maewe to help her but our slaves. None of the Ulfheonar had women but that would come. Until then my wife would have to be mother to them all.

Our first recruit was, perhaps, not surprising. It was Bjorn Bagsecgson the son of the dead blacksmith and the only survivor of the massacre.

"If you will have me, lord, I will be the blacksmith here as my father was."

I clasped his hand. "And you will be more than welcome."

Over the next few days, as the buildings grew from the debris and the shambles that had been our home, more and more warriors and their families arrived. For some, it was because they had settled there when we had first come and for others, it was the allure of Dragon Heart. I was touched that they wished to live under my protection.

Once the warrior hall was built half of the men built the walls while the rest built my home. That was not my choice and was the scene of my first argument with my men. All of them were unanimous that our home had to be built first. By late autumn Hrams-a was largely finished. Where my mother had died we built a rock cairn. It lay just at the rear of my hall and was a place of comfort and reflection for me. When I found myself troubled I would go there and find that her spirit and presence calmed me. We made sure that we had enough space so that it was quiet. We built the other halls and huts of the settlement so that the rest of the homes radiated out from mine.

Our livestock had thrived over the summer and we made sure that we
protected it over the winter. Enclosures were built and more lookout
towers erected. We had plenty of grain which we had liberated from the
Saxons and it allowed us to build a better harbour for our handful of
fishing boats and *'Wolf'*. And over the winter we waited and we
watched for any unknown sail. We worked and we trained; we all
needed to be better warriors. We wrote sagas about our deeds and we
made children. That year saw more babies conceived than anyone, even
Olaf could ever remember. Half of the Ulfheonar married and chose the
winter solstice to do so. The long nights of winter were fruitful.

When the nights began to shorten, imperceptibly at first, we gathered
our trade goods to take to Frankia. The seal oil we traded from our
brothers to the north was sought after further south as were the
sheepskins we produced ourselves. We sought weapons and fine armour
in return. Bjorn was a good blacksmith but the blank blades produced in
Frankia were superior in every way to the ones we were able to
produce. Bjorn could turn them into the best of weapons. When he had
to use metal produced closer to home then he was only able to make
adequate weapons. It might have been that we could have traded closer
to home but that meant the Saxons and we did not trust them.

I chose the men I would take, carefully, for we did not want to leave
our newly made home undefended. The winter had been benign enough
to allow us to make it even stronger and more comfortable. I left Egill
in command of those at home. I knew that I would want Haaken and
Cnut by my side. They were my oldest and most reliable friends. We
took only twenty warriors. We were not going for war and that allowed
us to take a little more cargo than we might otherwise have done. My
drekar was not a trader, it was neither tubby nor slow but it was not
capacious. Our advantage lay in a swift passage and the dragon's teeth
of our swords to fight off pirates.

Aiden, of course, wished to come. He had learned our language well
and he knew Snorri and Erik Short Toe travelled with me and wondered
why he could not.

"When you are a little older and those two have taught you some of
what they know then you can come with me. Until then I need you to
stay here and protect my son."

The last argument convinced him. He already saw himself as the
guard of Arturus as well as his playmate. Erika, like many of the other
women, was also with child again and that meant a unique shopping list
for her. She thought that there were places on the lower parts of the
Rinaz which made something called lace. It seems it was pretty and it
was expensive. Where my wife had seen it, I had no idea but I was

instructed to get some if I could. She had convinced herself that the next child would be a girl and she wanted pretty things for her.

"I know you will be buying the metal for the weapons which will be made for Arturus, indulge me and our daughter."

There seemed little point in telling her that we did not know what the new child would be. She had, however, the other women of the house and the village on her side. They kept going on about one life departing and another one arriving. Maewe and Erika were convinced that the new child would be my mother reincarnated. Life was simpler when I didn't argue.

Each family in the settlement brought things for me to trade. We kept a record of what they were. The warriors who went with us would have their own goods too. The exception was Bjorn. He had gold and silver to trade. Warriors who wanted a fine blade happily paid Bjorn in valuable metals or jewels if they had them. The dead warriors we had fought at Tara had yielded much in the way of booty. We had done the fighting and the killing; the reward was ours. It meant that Bjorn could afford to buy the valuable and expensive Frankish blades to turn them into swords.

We left one cold morning with a driving rain which seemed to penetrate beneath our very skin; the rain and wind, however, came from the north and would speed us on our way. We had no need to row as we flew south along the coast of Cymru. The wind took us faster than any boat propelled by men. I wanted a swift passage as I did not like to leave my family alone for too long. Jarl Erik and Jarl Harald planned to raid the Saxons and Hibernia in the spring but, until then, they would watch over our island. We had sailed this route before and we knew where the dangerous parts were. The rocky toe of the mainland was one such place. The rocks had hidden teeth to rip out the bottom of an unwary ship. We were lucky that ours had such a shallow draught. We kept well out to sea. The wind made us move even faster once we turned east as it was on our beam.

Oleg grumbled that this would mean we would have to row all the way back with a hull filled with iron. Cnut laughed at him, "If you found a half-filled beaker of ale you would complain. Take what the gods give us and be grateful."

Cnut had been with me that night when the gods had struck my sword. Of all the warriors with whom I fought, Cnut had the greatest respect for the gods.

Once we had cleared the rocks we sailed closer to the coast rather than risking the dangers of the open sea. I knew that the Saxons who saw us would fear even a single drekar. They had come to this island some years earlier as we did. They were now the sheep to be fleeced and we were the wolves. There would come a time when we would begin to take what they had. They were a rich people with many golden objects and fine jewels. The time was not ripe as yet but one day it would be.

We took turns at sleeping while the wind was with us. Anchoring was a dangerous thing to do and both Haaken and Cnut could steer. We would not stop until we made landfall again. Snorri and Erik Short Toe kept us supplied with ale and food. As Harold Blue Eye pointed out, at least we didn't need to season our food; the sea did that for us.

When we saw the northern coast of Frankia we all felt a sense of relief. We had done the hard part. Now came the dangerous part. This land was not peaceful. When we reached Cologne then we would be safe. Until then there would be danger from river pirates and other warriors keen to take what we had.

Once we reached the river then the backbreaking job of rowing began. We lowered the sail and stepped the mast. We wanted to attract little attention as we passed through the dangerous lower reaches of the Rinaz. The rowers rowed without armour but our weapons were close to hand and Snorri watched from the bows to see both obstacles and dangers to our passage. We had removed our shields from the side of the ship for we wished to advertise our peaceful intentions. It could be dangerous if a larger ship tried to attack us. That was where Snorri and his sharp eyes came into their own.

It was a hard pull to Cologne but we made it safely and without incident. We left most of the crew on board while Haaken, Cnut and I left the ship to visit Sigismund. When we reached his home, I thought that it was deserted. We knocked on the door and called his name. There was neither answer nor sign that the house was inhabited. We were about to leave when the door was opened. A man peered warily through a crack. He took in our weapons and our attire and his eyes widened. I spoke in Saxon which Sigismund had understood. "We are traders. Sigismund knows us. We once brought him some amber he liked."

There was a slight relaxation and the man said, "If you wait here. I will not be long."

"I have had better welcomes."

"Haaken be patient, you know not what might have happened since we last saw him. Have faith."

Eventually, the door opened and the man bowed apologetically. "I am sorry for the rudeness but my uncle is not well. I am Sigurd, the nephew of Sigismund. Come, he is in the back room."

Sigismund looked older and he was wrapped in blankets and lying on a bed. I was shocked for he looked to be at death's door. He laughed, "Do not worry my friend. I am not about to die. At least not yet."

I could see soiled and bloodstained bandages by the side of his bed and a slave was removing them. "What happened?"

"There are more thieves and robbers in Cologne than there used to be. I made the mistake of stepping out of doors with just a single slave as an escort. I was robbed."

"But you have men who work for you at your warehouse?"

He nodded, "They are not armed warriors. The ones who robbed me were dressed and armed as you are. Luckily my nephew was visiting otherwise I might have died of my wounds. He paid for a doctor and I am on the mend." He spread his arms, "The problem is that my business is suffering. I do not want to risk Sigurd by sending him alone on the streets. These are dangerous times." He shook his head, "However this is rude of me. You did not come here to listen to the troubles of an old merchant. How can I be of service?" His eyes glinted, "Have you any more amber?"

I laughed, "I am sorry but that pot has been emptied. However, we do have some gold and silver to trade as well as seal oil and sheepskins."

He looked disappointed. "I would dearly love to trade with you but, as I said, my hands are tied."

An idea struck me. "Perhaps we can be of service to you. We three could escort your nephew to the warehouse and then my crew will bring the trade goods. After the trade then we can escort your nephew back here."

Sigismund nodded, "That would keep me solvent at least. I can find buyers for those goods. Sigurd can arrange the trades for the sheepskin and the oil but bring the precious metals to me. I have scales here." He saw a dubious look pass over Haaken's face. "Oh, do not worry, I trust my nephew but where metal is concerned then the scales are essential."

I looked at the nephew. He was older than I was and he had the haggard look of a man with worries. "And does that arrangement suit you?"

His face showed the relief he obviously felt. "It does but I would ask you to accompany me to the Jewish quarter too for we are short of funds."

"You are short of money?"

"Oh no! We have money but the Jews hold it for us. They keep it safe and we make a little money on it while they hold it. The problem is getting there and back without being robbed."

"If I might suggest you hire a couple of men such as us. We will be gone soon but I would expect there to be warriors looking for employment."

The uncle and nephew looked at each other. Sigismund said, "We are no judges of such things. I would not know a good warrior from a bad one or," he added ominously, an honourable man from a cut purse."

I could see his dilemma. It was in my interest and that of my people to keep this honest trader in business. "Tonight, we will try to find such men as you need and if we find some we will bring them tomorrow."

That satisfied both men and we left the house. I walked with Sigurd while Haaken and Cnut trailed us by four or five paces. We were not trying to trap anyone but the distance would allow them to draw their swords if they needed to. I sensed the danger as we made our way through the narrow streets. This was not Hrams-a where everyone knew each other. This was a disparate mass of humanity who had nothing in common save that they lived on the same street. I saw dark looks as we walked. My martial appearance deterred any action but I was aware that we would have to go back and that might be dangerous. We travelled through parts of the town I did not recognise. When we reached the Jewish quarter then every door and window was shut to us. We looked a little too dangerous to allow us close. Sigurd was allowed into the house of the Jew who held their money and we waited outside. We did not feel welcome.

We finally reached the warehouse and the relief on Sigurd's face was obvious. "Thank you. I feel safer now that I am here."

"I will return with more of my men and trade goods." I paused, "We will need Frankish sword blanks. You have them?" He nodded and I gave him a list of other items. He smiled and nodded. I hesitated and then took a deep breath. "My wife wishes something called lace. Is that easy to come by?"

He shook his head, "No, and it is expensive. I know of no one here in Cologne. Any that we do get is bought by the priests of the White Christ who adorn their vestments with it. I am sorry. I will keep watch for any which comes in the future but it will be a high price."

"Do not worry about that. I will have to pay whatever the going rate is. I will have to explain to my wife that I tried."

Haaken and Cnut had similar problems. Their wives had asked for combs for their hair and brooches. We were good traders when it came to useful things but not these knick knacks which they seemed to adore.

Back at the ship the rest of the men were pleased to see us. Harald Olafson pointed to the men lurking by the harbour walls. "This is a lot rougher than it used to be. There look to be armed gangs all around."

"I know Harald. We will leave half of the men on board when we take the trade goods. Arm yourselves and let no-one close to the boat."

I collected the precious metals and put them in a leather bag which I slung around my neck and shoulder so that it could not be torn from me easily. The rest unpacked our trade goods. I had more than enough men to carry and to protect our precious cargo. The only heavy items were the barrels of seal oil and they rolled. Haaken and I acted as guards and led the way back. I could see men eyeing up our barrels and sheepskins. They were wondering when to strike; on our way or on our way back. They had to be desperate men for few thieves would chance his arm with a Norseman.

Rather like Sigurd earlier, I was relieved when we reached the warehouse. He looked at the oil and the sheepskins and gave me a value. It seemed reasonable and we used that to purchase those items which the other villagers had requested. He handed us coins as well. "The sword blanks?"

He took me to a pile of Frankish blanks. They looked like iron bars with a tapered handle but they could, when Bjorn had worked his magic with them, become the deadliest of weapons. I distributed the coins between the men and then haggled a price for the blanks.

"You still have the precious metal?" I nodded and showed it to him. "I can give a rough price and then you can take the blanks. You will have coin left over."

"Good."

He counted out fifteen sword blanks. Bjorn's share would be ten of them. They were distributed between my warriors to carry back to the boat. "Are you ready to come back to Sigismund's yet or shall we return for you?"

"Return when you have delivered your goods. I will take this opportunity of conducting a little more business." He smiled. "It was good fortune which brought you today. We have done more trade than in the past month. My uncle will be pleased."

As we made our way back I reflected that carrying the blanks was like carrying gold in plain view. Everyone could see the valuable cargo. In the right hands, they could make ten times what we had paid. Had we used our trade for Frankish swords then I would be carrying just one. A Frankish sword was the most valuable weapon you could possess and men would kill for one.

We were half way back to the ship and close to the river when the robbers struck. I had noted where all of the gangs had congregated on our way to the warehouse. We had tried to vary our route but the river drew all roads. The closer to the river then the more predators lurked there. They were still in the shadows when we returned; all apart from one gang. There had been one crew who were now absent. Where had they gone?

"Be ready for an ambush. The ones who had the blanks had a readymade weapon in their hand and the rest had their trade goods on their backs. I loosened *Ragnar's Spirit*. Suddenly wooden logs were dropped from the buildings above us. I was lucky; I was just struck a glancing blow. Jorgen was knocked cold by the one which struck him and some of the others fell to the ground caught by the heavy pieces of timber.

The thieves came at us like rats swarming over spilled corn. I did not hesitate but swung my sword in an arc. All those before me were enemies and I had to protect the warriors of mine who had fallen beneath my feet. Two robbers fell, gushing blood. I swung the blade above my head and brought it down on to the skull of the thief who had his dagger out to slit Jorgen's throat. The head opened like a ripe plum. Cnut and Haaken had killed their enemies just as quickly and the rest fled as they realised that we were not easy prey. We had been saved only by our armour and our helmets. It had been a well conceived trap.

"Haaken, see to Jorgen. Cnut, search the bodies. The rest of you keep your eyes peeled."

It was as though the street and alleys which led off had emptied. There was no one in sight and the only sound was the screeching of the gulls. Jorgen slowly came to and Haaken helped him to his feet.

"Can you walk Jorgen?" He nodded and picked up the fallen blade. "Back to the boat as quickly as we can."

The dead and bleeding bodies just lay where they had fallen. Soon we reached the safety of the boat. Once on board, we secured the blanks below the decks. "Harold, take charge here. Move the ship a little further away from the bank. You can always pull it closer when we return." Cnut deposited the swords, daggers and coins he had taken from the dead robbers. If you were a thief then you assumed that everyone else was one too and you kept your treasure about yourself.

Oleg shook his head, "We have the swords let us leave."

"It is not honourable."

He shrugged, "Who cares?"

"Me for one but realistically we need Sigismund to continue our trades. We still owe him for the blades and he trusted us. I gave my word. Would you have me break it?" His silence was eloquent. "As soon as we are ashore, begin to let out the lines. It will keep you safer."

The three of us were more alert as we headed along the river bank to get to Sigurd at the warehouse. I dared not risk the street with the dead robbers. This route might be as dangerous. We had no choice. We moved with drawn blades. I had been surprised once; the second time I would be ready.

Thankfully we reached the warehouse without incident. Sigurd looked up, he was unconcerned. He had no idea of our ordeal. "I just have to..."

He got no further, "We go now or you go alone! We were attacked on the way back to our ship and I fear for the safety of my men."

He nodded, "I understand." Panic filled his face. "What about the men you said you would find?"

"I gave my word. I will try to find you, men." Haaken rolled his eyes in exasperation.

On the way to the house of Sigismund, I kept watch for suitable places to find men. This time we kept to the main thoroughfares. It was safer that way. We passed two or three drinking houses; I saw the sheaf of barley hung from the door which marked them as alehouses. We would try those three. I had made a promise but I would not risk my men and my ship to keep it. If there were none within them then Sigismund would have to find his own protectors.

Sigismund was relieved to see us. When I told him of the attack he frowned. "The city will have to take action. We survive because of trade. If traders cannot conduct their business then the town will die."

"It was not like this last time. What happened?"

"Count Conrad is off in the east fighting a war and the men he has left are not the best." He shook his head, "War is the enemy of trade."

"And yet if we did not need the weapons of war then we would have no need to trade here. We could trade our oil and our sheepskins closer to home."

"Perhaps." He rubbed his hands together and then winced with the pain. "Show me what you have for me."

I emptied the metal out and he carefully divided into the different qualities. He weighed each one and made a mark on a wax tablet. "These would pay for fifteen blanks."

"We bought fifteen."

Although he said, "Good," Sigismund flashed a look of annoyance at his nephew and then handed me some coins. I think he wanted his nephew to have sold more. It irked him that we were taking coins away from a trade. "Hopefully I will be well the next time you come and the city will be safer."

I nodded, "We will go and see if we can find some men for you. There are three places we can try. We will return here either with them or without them." I shrugged, "We cannot make such warriors."

"I know and I thank you."

The first alehouse we entered was almost deserted and the men who were within looked more like the kind of criminals who might wish to bring harm to Sigurd. None had the look of warriors and that was what we sought; warriors such as us. We did not bother drinking there but entered the second one. This one looked to have more potential. There were warriors within. We sat at a table. There was no choice over our fare. We were brought three horns of beer. I put some coins on the table and the man took two of them.

The ale was drinkable. We looked around at the other drinkers. One table looked to have warriors dressed much like we were and they were having a drinking contest. They would not be suitable candidates. The table next to us, however, had three warriors. They were nursing their beer and taking sips. I noticed that the only things which looked as though they were cared for were their weapons. They looked unwashed and their clothes were torn. These were warriors who had fallen on hard times. It happened to the best of warriors. Olaf had told me. Men followed a leader because of an oath and when that leader died they often found themselves many miles from home or friends.

I waved to the man with the beer and held three fingers up. He brought three more over. I pointed to the men at the next table. He shrugged, took the money, and put the beer before them. They looked surprised and asked him a question which I could not hear. One of them, obviously the leader, stood and came over to us.

He spoke our language. "Before I drink the beer you have paid for, can I ask, do I know you?"

I smiled, "I have never seen you before in my life."

"Are you one of those who prefers men to women? If so I have to disappoint you. None of us are like that."

Cnut began to rise and I restrained him, "Peace, Cnut. There was no offence meant. I bought you the beer for we have money and, I think, you have not. You are warriors like we are but appear to have had less luck."

"That is true. Our ship was sunk off the coast and we made our way here. They have no need for warriors here." He suddenly leaned forward, "Do you have a ship? Are you raiding?"

"Yes, I have a ship but we are not raiding. We are here for trade and we will return to our home soon."

"You look a little young to have a ship. Who are you?"

"I am Garth."

The man looked as though the name meant nothing. Cnut said irritably, "You may have heard of him. He is called Dragon Heart and he has the sword touched by the gods."

The man looked at me in amazement. "I have heard the name and the stories. I thought they had been made by drink."

Cnut said proudly, "No, they are true. I was there when the gods touched the blade."

"We will serve with you."

"At the moment, I have neither need nor room for more crew but I will be returning soon and then I will offer you places. However, until then, I can offer you employment, shelter and money. If you are interested then bring your friends over and I will explain."

He brought them over and introduced them, "I am Rolf, this is Erik Redhead and the other is Ham the Silent. We thank you for the ale."

"You are welcome. There is a trader who lives not far from here and he was recently attacked. He needs men to protect him and his nephew. I said I would get him some men he could trust."

"And you trust us? You barely know us."

"I am a good judge of men. You are warriors; I can see that. You have little money yet your weapons are in perfect condition. You ask sensible questions and you wish to be warriors still. However, if I am wrong and you let me down then I will hunt you down and kill you."

I said those words without anger and without any animosity. The aptly named Erik the Redhead began to rise but Rolf pushed him easily down. "Calm down my excitable friend. This is Dragon Heart and I can see that, despite his years, he is a warrior and I would do the same. I say this to you, Garth the Dragon Heart, I will serve this man, if he will have us, for half a year and then I would serve you."

I gave him my arm. "And I will offer the three of you a place on my ship and we will raid Saxons together."

Chapter 9

I felt good as we boarded my ship. Rolf and Sigismund had liked each other as soon as they saw each other. Sigismund was happy to have warriors in his home although he did ask them to bathe. Rolf and his men were just pleased to have a roof over their heads. Events had turned out well and we were able to leave the city in the middle of the night. I was anxious to depart as soon as possible. We also had a bonus. Sigismund had heard of Erika's desire for lace and he gave me a piece of white lace. At least he said it was lace. It seemed small and flimsy to me. It was only as wide as my hand and as long as my arm. It appeared to have more holes than material. If it were not for the fact that the holes were regular I would have said it was the work of mice. He told me that it had been ordered by a bishop of the White Christ who had decided to rebel against the king and he had paid the price with his life. I was satisfied and happy for Erika for she would be pleased.

Oleg smelled the ale on our breath when we returned. "You could have brought some for us."

Haaken loved to tease Oleg. "You wouldn't have liked it. It was sour."

"Better sour ale than no ale."

We hoisted the sail and let the current leisurely take us west towards the sea. I felt relief when we hit the sea. It was daylight and there was not a sail in sight. I knew how lucky we had been to avoid serious trouble. Perhaps the next time I would bring a bigger crew or a bigger ship. Even as those thoughts tiptoed into my head I knew that '*Wolf*' was the only ship for me. I ran my hand down the oak rail. This was a sturdy and swift ship. Her small size merely made the boat livelier and more responsive to the helm. I knew that I could turn inside any ship which was bigger and, with the right wind, out run anything that sailed. Her only weakness was when there was no wind. The small number of rowers meant that, in a sea chase, we would be caught.

The men cheered as we left the estuary for the wind was from the south; it meant no rowing for them. We fairly leapt across the water as the water on our quarter made '*Wolf*' run as though alive. I needed Cnut's help to fight the sea. It took two of us to keep the ship heading north west.

A day and a half later we had just passed the island they called Wight. It was a fearful place for it was believed to be inhabited by spirits. Of course, no one had ever met anyone who had seen one of these unearthly creatures but that did not stop the legends and stories spreading. I knew the crew would want us to give it a wide berth but the wind seemed determined to make us strike the shore. I managed to miss the jagged rocks but we passed close enough to see the cliffs and rocks; they were far too close for comfort.

"Well Dragon Heart, if we can avoid the evils spirits on Wight then we may escape with our lives on this journey."

Haaken's words proved hollow for as we cleared the island we spied three Saxon ships laying in wait for us. They began rowing after us. The wind was still in our favour and took us further from them but I knew that once they cleared the island then their sails and their superior numbers would begin to tell. "Out oars. Cnut, you had better row. Snorri, come and help me. Erik, go to the bows and watch for rocks."

The warriors had been rested but, if the Saxons had been waiting then they too would be rested. This would be a test of ships and of men. I prayed that my faith in *'Wolf'* would be justified. I risked a glance astern. They were about half a mile back. So long as the wind and my men's backs held then we might hold them but if the wind failed us then they would draw us in like a fisherman landing a catch. They were tubbier than we were and there was no dragon at the prow. That might mean little to them but to us, it meant that we had the gods of war on our side. I knew that the men rowing on *'Wolf'* regarded it as a good omen that they had a dragon at the prow and a Dragon Heart steering. To the Saxons, it would mean nothing except a fear of the warriors within.

Snorri was rapidly growing and would be joining the warriors soon. He put his weight on the tiller. He snorted his derision, "It takes three Saxons to try to fight one drekar."

I laughed. He was right. "Never forget, Snorri, that a wolf can bite and this wolf is full of wolves with sharp teeth. They may yet regret their action."

As the wind caught their sails I could see that they began to close the gap. They were slowly and inexorably gaining on us. The worst action I could have taken was to panic. We were sailing with the wind on our quarter which was the most efficient. The rollers coming in from the west negated some of the advantage their extra oars gave them. This would not end quickly. Cnut was keeping the beat by singing our rowing song which Haaken had composed.

Push your arms
Row the boat
Use your back
The Wolf will fly

Ulfheonar
Are real men
Teeth like iron
Arms like trees

Push your arms
Row the boat
Use your back
The Wolf will fly

Ragnar's Spirit
Guides us still
Dragon Heart
Wields it well

Push your arms
Row the boat
Use your back
The Wolf will fly

And so it went on. The rhythm could be changed by the addition or subtraction of a word. The men rowed better when we sang.

I looked astern and saw a glimmer of hope. The first ship was moving away from the other two which were less well sailed. If this continued then I would get Cnut to increase the speed of our rowing and try to lose them. It was easier to lose one ship than three. The jagged rocks of the land to the west would need care and caution; not speed. I had been pleased to see the daylight all those hours ago but now I prayed for the dark to consume us.

"Rocks ahead!" Erik's shrill voice carried aft as he pointed to the south, the left of the boat. The land was to the right. I had a dilemma. I did not know if the rocks extended all the way to the land. The Saxons behind me might know that. I glanced astern and saw that they had not deviated from their course. They followed our wake still. I closed my eyes and listened for the voices. I heard the sound of the sea. It seemed to say 'yes.'

I grinned at Snorri. "Let us see if Ran is with us. We will sail between the rocks and the land."

The gap we were aiming for was about four hundred paces wide. I put the ship so that we would be the same distance from both dangers; the rocks and the shore. When I looked behind me I saw that the lead ship had followed us but the other two had headed out to sea to avoid the rocks. They would catch us on the other side of the danger. If I was wrong then the bottom would be ripped out of my ship and we would all drown.

Erik's voice sent a chill down my spine, "Breakers ahead!" That could mean rocks or shallows. Both spelled danger to us. I saw Tostig suddenly pitch from his bench as his oar caught something and shattered. I felt a shudder under the keel and we began to move off course. I made a small correction on the tiller and waited from the grinding noise which would signify our end. There was nothing. Tostig quickly withdrew the broken oar and grabbed one of the three spares we carried. It seemed an age before he got the oar back into the sea. The delay allowed the Saxon to close with us and I could now see that there were twenty oars on each side. They would outnumber us if it came to a fight.

Snorri pointed down and said, "Look Dragon Heart."

I peered over the side and saw the rocks below the surface. Our keel had barely passed over the tops of them safely. It was with some relief that I felt the extra surge as Tostig rowed once again and we moved away a little from the Saxon astern of us.

"Cnut, up the rate." His face showed that he doubted my sanity but he did so. He dropped a word a line. Within a few strokes, we had leapt forwards. I looked at the Saxon ship. It too tried to keep up. In his hurry to catch us the captain had not kept a good watch and it was though someone had grabbed hold of his stern. The ship stopped and then suddenly began to lean to one side. He had struck the rocks as we had. The difference was he was a deeper, larger ship. The mast leaned alarmingly and then, with a crack, it snapped into the sea. The boat began to sink and the men leapt from her decks to the water below. Some would make it ashore but many would drown. We had been fortunate.

"You can slow the rate again Cnut we have lost one of them."

The crew cheered and Haaken said, wryly, "Try not to use up all your luck all at once, Dragon Heart. I would like to see my unborn children, however briefly."

I glanced to the left where the two other ships now had a dilemma. They could either try to catch us or sail to the rescue of their comrades. I think that it was the distance we had put between us which decided them to help their friends and give up the chase.

"Well done Ulfheonar! We showed them."

As we began rowing again Tostig shouted, "We are leaking. There is a hole!"

I could see that he was right. Water was sloshing around the rower's feet. We had no choice in the matter. We had to head into shore. Luckily for us, the sky was darkening and we would be hidden from the Saxons who were already disappearing east to help their comrades.

"Snorri, Erik, lower the sail."

With the sail lowered we would slow down and that would minimise the amount of water we would ship. This coast was a mystery to me. I knew that Saxons lived here but also that, further west, were people who had lived in this land since before the Romans had come. We would need to tread very carefully.

I grabbed my shield and my sword. As *'Wolf'* gently slid on to the sand I ran forwards and leapt ashore. "Snorri and Erik secure the boat."

I left my crew to the ship while I raced along the beach. We had had little opportunity to select our landing site but we had done well. There was a low cliff which hid us from view and I could see a path leading inland. I made sure that there was no one around and then returned to the men.

Cnut was lying half in the water and half out. He spluttered as he lifted his head from the water. "We have sprung a couple of planks. What we could do with is some of that seal oil we just traded."

Haaken shook his head, "Which we haven't got. Wish for a workshop while you are at it!"

I could sense the tension. "Be silent! Bickering will get us nowhere. Do not bring me problems. How can we solve this dilemma?"

Oleg was a miserable warrior and one of the older Ulfheonar but he had sailed before. "If we had a spare sail then we could wrap it around the hull and tie it tightly. It would hold the water out. We wouldn't be able to sail as fast but it might work."

"That's better. So, we need another sail. We haven't got one I suppose?"

Haaken laughed, "That would be real luck, Dragon Heart."

"Then I will take some men to get a sail while the rest of you guard the boat and try to repair the sprung planks."

"How?"

"We have candles. Melt the candles and used them. Even with Oleg's sail, we will still need all the help we can get." They all nodded. "Haaken, Cnut, Snorri, come with me."

Oleg said, "Snorri? Why not take a warrior?"

"Because we may need someone who can appear harmless yet who can sneak into places. We are in Saxon land. Every hand will be turned against us."

Rollo gave his cloak to Snorri, "You damage that and you have to kill me a wolf to replace it."

From the look on Snorri's face, he relished the prospect of killing a wolf so that he could join the Ulfheonar.

"Take the chests with the cargo out. It will help you to empty the water and stop the leaks."

We headed up the path. I saw once we crested the cliff, lights in the distance and the smell of wood smoke. There was life close by. I led the way with Snorri and his sharp ears bringing up the rear. I soon saw that it was a collection of small buildings with a low palisade around it. I was disappointed. I had hoped for fishermen but this was too far from the sea. A fisherman might have a sail. I was about to avoid it when a voice inside my head told me to investigate. The one thing we didn't have was time. If we were not afloat by dawn then our bones would whiten on the sand. If I could not find a sail then I would have to find something else.

I waved my arm to spread the other three out on either side of me and I crouched as I ran. It was dark and our cloaks hid us from any prying eyes but it paid to be careful. I saw that there was a cross on the top of one of the small buildings. This was a church of the White Christ. I felt even more disappointed. There would be no sail here. Yet the voice still told me to advance. I heard voices from one of the huts and I halted to listen. It was the sound of a man and woman coupling. I saw Snorri begin to giggle and I flashed him a warning look. He ceased.

We moved towards the building which was the church. It was a wooden building but more substantial than the huts which surrounded it. I gestured for Cnut and Snorri to stand guard while we went inside. It was dark and I tripped on something as I entered. It did not seem to make much of a sound but we paused anyway. We needed light. I knew that the priests of the White Christ had a table at the end furthest from the door and they used candles to light it. We made our way cautiously through the church. As I had expected I felt candles and tapers lying on a table at the side. I took out my flint and eventually sparked a flame on the taper. I lit the candle and the church was suddenly bathed in a soft yellow light. There was the usual cross but, behind the table, was a large curtain depicting some scene to do with the White Christ. It provided an area of privacy behind the table but, more importantly, it was like a small sail.

Haaken realised its importance and we began to take it down, quietly. Once down, we folded it to make it easier to carry. It was when we had folded it that we saw the candlesticks and the platter which had been behind the curtain. They were metal; we could not tell the type but the jewels on them suggested they had value. We stuffed them in our belts and cloaks. The curtain was heavy and took two of us to carry it. I think that was the reason why we did not see the priest emerge from the cell to the side. He held, in his hand, a staff with a metal cross upon it. He swung it hard and shouted something. The end struck Haaken on the side of the head and he fell to the floor. I just reacted. Dropping the curtain, I whipped out my sword and stabbed him before he could strike again.

Cnut came in. "Quickly, get Snorri to help Haaken and then grab this sheet."

He ducked his head outside as Haaken rose, groggily. He saw the dead priest. "I thought they were supposed to dislike killing!"

I shrugged, "Perhaps that does not apply when we are stealing from them. Grab that staff, it might come in handy."

Cnut and Snorri appeared and we picked up the curtain and moved outside. The noise had alerted the others in the settlement. Even though we were struggling to carry the curtain we held our swords in our hands, Haaken handed the staff to Snorri and then drew his sword.

As we passed the hut where the couple had lain they both ran out. The man had a sword and he swung ineffectually at Cnut who skewered him. I pointed my sword at the woman and said, in Saxon, "Go back inside and you live!"

She nodded and acquiesced. Two other men ran out of their huts but when they saw, in the moonlight, our weapons they fled. "That's it then, the locals will be after us soon."

"Back to the ship."

Our journey back was, perforce, slower and I was acutely aware that the survivors would have raced to get help. As we descended the cliff path I tried to remember if we had passed any coastal settlements when we had sailed west and I could not recall seeing any. Those three Saxon ships had to have a port somewhere. *'Wolf'* was half out of the water when we reached the beach.

I shouted to alert the men. "There could be trouble. The Saxons know we are here. We have to work quickly. Have you managed to do anything with the keel?"

Harold nodded, "We have used the oil and the wax. I am glad you have," he looked at the curtain as Cnut and Oleg unfolded it, "whatever that is."

"Get it secured around the keel and tightened." I turned and pointed at the nearest ten warriors. "Come, we need to strip and pull *'Wolf'* from the beach. Saxons will be here soon. Snorri, help me off with my byrnie."

Snorri pulled the mail shirt from me and I handed him my wolf cloak and helmet. "Put these and the objects we gathered in the hold. Haaken and Cnut, keep your eyes peeled for any Saxons." I saw that my warriors had stripped to the waist as I had and I waved them forwards. "Grab a rope and throw it to Erik." Erik stood at the stern and waited for each warrior to throw his rope. I was the last one. "Harold, let me know when the seal is secured."

I saw that they had succeeded in drawing the curtain beneath the bows. They had used the waves to do so. As each wave had lifted the bows a little they had pulled the curtain a little further towards the middle. I saw that Harold was tying the material as tightly as he could through the holes for the oars.

Suddenly Haaken shouted, "Saxons!" I could just make out a dark line of warriors descending the slope. Those warriors not with me and not tying the ropes ran to join Cnut and Haaken. There were just four of them.

"Harold, we are going to have to launch the ship or we will die." He waved and I shouted. "Ulfheonar, pull!" We heaved with all of our might and nothing seemed to happen. I waited until another wave struck us and then I shouted, "Pull!" At first, I thought we had not moved it but then it felt easier. We pulled again and again. *'Wolf'* was almost afloat. "Pull!"

I heard Harold shout, "Secured!"

"Get the sail hoisted and the others on board. Right boys, one more pull and then we go back aboard." We pulled so hard that some of us fell into the sea. I sprang up, spluttering salty water but *'Wolf'* was, at last, moving without our help. We began to wade back through the sea. To my horror, I saw that there were warriors lying on the beach and they were Ulfheonar.

"Harold, take command. The rest of you get aboard." I drew the seax from my leggings and forced my tired legs against the current. I could see that Haaken and Cnut were fighting seven Saxons. They were defending the bodies of two Ulfheonar who had fallen. As the pressure of the water lessened I raised my seax and screamed, "Ulfheonar!" I saw the sword of one of my dead men lying on the sand and I picked it up.

The Saxons I struck had their right sides to me and there were no shields. My blade sliced through the first one and severed his body in two. I reversed the swing and sliced down to decapitate the second warrior. The other Saxons turned to face me. I yelled to Haaken. "Get them on board!" I did not wait for a reply but hacked aside the blade that sliced towards me with my seax and stabbed its owner in the throat. A spear came at me and raked across my middle. I grabbed the ash shaft and pulled the warrior onto my sword. I reversed the spear and threw it towards another warrior who ducked out of the way.

"Dragon Heart, down!"

I trusted my companions and I dropped to my knees. The air filled with arrows and the remaining warriors cowered behind shields. "Run!"

I turned and ran towards *'Wolf'*. It was thirty paces from the beach. I sheathed the borrowed sword and dived into the water. I began to swim. The weight of the sword threatened to drag me down. I was relieved when the rope snaked towards me and I was dragged to safety.

Cnut and Haaken threw my wolf cloak about my shivering shoulders. "That was foolish, brave and honourable, but foolish."

I pointed at the bodies of the two men they had fought to save. "And this was intelligent?"

"We could not let their bodies and weapons be despoiled. And the Ulfheonar leave no man behind. It is not our way, is it Dragon Heart?"

I nodded. I could understand that. We had lost two Ulfheonar and two others were wounded but we had defied the Weird Sisters and survived. "Let us go home." They nodded their agreement and, as they took their places at the benches I walked to the stern. "How is your repair holding?"

Harold handed the steering board to me, "We will only know that once we turn north. If we manage to do that then the repair has worked and if not then we will all be joining Sweyn Three Fingers and Gotfried."

Snorri and Erik brought around some ale and dried meat. I was not hungry but knew that I needed to eat. We still had a long way to go. We had been lucky I knew that. The voices in my head had made me go into the church and we had been rewarded. I determined to listen to the voices more closely the next time they spoke with me. Perhaps the spirits of the dead were watching over me. My mother's people were mystical. They had powerful wizards. Who knew?

The rocks around the savage tip of land we had to pass before turning north were wild and stormy. Had our ship been whole we would have sailed further out to sea but we did not have that luxury; we needed to get home as fast as possible. Even Snorri and Erik grabbed one of the spare oars as we fought the sea and the wind. At times, we appeared so close to the rocks I thought that we would rip the bottom out of her again. Either Ran was with us or I was a more skilful steersman. We survived. As dawn broke I saw that we were finally heading north; we had completed the worst part of the journey. We just needed Harold's repair to hold for another day or two. The waves were now smaller but, more importantly, were not striking us in the bows where the hole was. We were shipping less water.

Harold grinned up at me, his beard rimed with salt. "I think the White Christ might like us. His shroud appears to keep out the water!"

That made all the men laugh. We knew that the Saxons were largely followers of the White Christ. We felt that weakened a warrior but we knew that their priests feared and hated us as the wolves of the sea. They might show charity to many but any Norse or Dane suffered a cruel and painful death. We had heard of one who was thrown into a wolf pit and another who suffered a snake pit. That was not the way for a warrior to die. It was ironic to think that a relic from a church of theirs had saved us.

Chapter 10

All of us thanked the gods for our safe return as we edged the wounded and sluggish *'Wolf'* into the harbour. The last half a day had seen us become slower and slower as water gradually entered the hull. The curtain had done its job but we had barely made it safely home. The ports for the oars were only just above the water. I could see the concern of those on the harbour as we threw them the mooring ropes.

Egill and the others we had left guarding our families trooped down to inspect the ship. He looked at the water sloshing around the ankles of the rowers. "It looks like there is a tale to tell here."

"We were pursued by three Saxon ships and Dragon Heart thought that we could fly across rocks." Cnut laughed at his own joke, "He nearly succeeded."

We quickly removed the benches and then the deck so that we could reach the cargo. Luckily, we had chests in the bottom of the hull otherwise much of our trade goods would have been ruined. Once the chests came ashore the boat rose a little in the water. Harold stroked his beard. "We will have to put her on the beach to work on her. I will get some men to take down the mast and we will drag her yonder."

"When I have seen my wife, I will go and see Olaf and Prince Butar. Olaf knows more about ships than anyone. I would like his advice on how to make *'Wolf'* better."

Most of the chests had been taken ashore already and there only remained the chest with my byrnie and trade goods. Snorri and Erik carried it for me. "You did well, both of you." I looked at Snorri and saw that he was now up to my shoulder. "Snorri, would you like to begin your training as a warrior?" His smile and nod were only matched by the disappointment and the slumping of Erik's shoulders. "And Erik, with Snorri not on the boat you would become assistant steersman and you would have to train another boy. How does that sound?"

"I am honoured, my lord. Which boy?"

"The one we brought back last time, Aiden." I did not like the look on Erik's face. Images of Tadgh and the others bullying me came to mind. "You will treat him well, Erik, or you will not work on *'Wolf'*. Is that clear?"

His face showed the fear he felt at being threatened with such a sanction. "I swear I will treat him fairly, Dragon Heart."

"Good. This is the first time that you have given your word. You know what that means?"

"I do."

"Good."

We had reached my hall and Erika and Arturus were there to greet me. It had only been a matter of ten days or so since I had last seen him but I could see changes already. He looked to be taking more notice and recognising not just me but the others too. Of course, he still gurgled and made noises which made no sense to me but I knew that would change.

Erika threw her arms around me and noticed, for the first time, that I wore no mail. "What happened to your war shirt?"

"I had to drag the ship from the beach and I did not relish the prospect of drowning 'neath that mail. We stored it in the ship with the trade goods."

Her eyes were bright with expectation. "Did your trades go well?"

I smiled, "They did but no one had any lace to sell. It seems the priests of the White Christ like it more than any others and they are rich enough to be able to buy it."

I felt guilty when I saw her face fall. I went to the chest and opened it. "However, because I did Sigismund a favour I have some for you." As I handed it to her I wondered if she would be disappointed. When she looked at me with her eyes wide and aglow I knew that she was not.

"Thank you!" She kissed and embraced me. "I will be the envy of all the other wives. Our daughter, when she is born, will be the only one with a lace collar on her dress."

She was happy and I knew I had much to do. "I must visit with Olaf. I need words with him."

"But you will be back to sup here this night?"

"Of course. I will not be long. I will take a pony."

Scanlan had been training some hill ponies. They were tough little beasts and they would easily carry me across the hills and back before dark. Aiden was with Scanlan when I found my slave. "Come, Scanlan, we must visit Duboglassio."

He nodded and then saw that Aiden looked disappointed. Scanlan was kind and he had children of his own. "Could the boy not come with us? We have three ponies."

I looked at him dubiously, "Can he ride?"

Suddenly he said, "Yes master."

I laughed with surprise. "He has learned our language then?"

Scanlan nodded, "Some words he has. He is a quick learner."

"Then he can come with us and impress me with his words."

I enjoyed the journey over the hill. Aiden was desperate to please and did not shut up all the way across. He talked of throwing stones across the water, apparently, he had become quite competent. He told me of the words Arturus tried to say. He told me of all that he had done with Scanlan. In short, I knew every event which had happened to Aiden since I had left.

As we neared the larger town I said to Scanlan. "Is my wife coping well with the new child?"

"She seems to be. You know women, my lord. All three of them are nest building and that makes them happy." He hesitated, "My lord you once said that I would be able to bear arms. When will that be?"

I remembered that conversation. I could see no reason not to give him the chance save that no one else had armed a slave. Then I thought, '*He is mine. It is my decision.*"

"As soon as we get back. Then you can help me to train Snorri."

"But I am not a warrior."

"No, but you will be able to train him to become stronger, and the two of you will both become better warriors as a result. Being a warrior means having strength to bear arms. It is not just about waving a sword and wearing armour."

We were warmly greeted by the guards at the gate and ushered into Prince Butar's Hall. Scanlan and Aiden went to find Olaf while I drank with my stepfather and told him of our journey.

"So, the Rinaz is not as safe as it was?"

"No, and the Saxons are becoming more aggressive too. We barely escaped with our lives."

He laughed, "And yet you still made a profit from the church?"

I nodded sad with the memory of my dead men, "It cost me two Ulfheonar."

"I would not worry about that. They died with their swords in their hands and will be in Valhalla awaiting you. More and more warriors are seeking employment here. The word of our success is spreading and the fact that we appear to welcome warriors also helps. I will find some suitable volunteers."

I shook my head, "A Ulfheonar is chosen. They do not volunteer. Send those warriors to me who are young enough not to have attachments and we will let them serve in the town for a while. It will give us the chance to see if they have what it takes."

He gave me a curious look; it was a mixture of appraisal and question. "Are you happy to become a jarl yet?"

"I am not ready, father. I will tell you when I feel I have earned the right. Besides we are still a small community. How are Erik and Harald doing?"

"They are both planning a raid on the Hibernians in the summer. Jarl Harald was emboldened by his raid to destroy Tadgh's ship and your comments about their poor quality of warriors means he can take warriors who have yet to be blooded and know they have a good chance of returning safely with booty."

"It will be hardly worth the effort."

"Jarl Harald has many young men and he must train them to be warriors. He needs to earn the respect of the others. You have garnered all the glory up until now. Do not begrudge Jarl Harald the same opportunity. This will suffice and Jarl Erik still smarts over the kidnap of his sister. He wishes to punish them."

"And you, Prince Butar, do you have plans to raid?"

He gave me a smile which made him look years younger. "I think we will pay the Saxons another visit. Their land is rich and I have heard that they all worship the White Christ now. It makes them weaker warriors. This time we will raid the land a little further north. Will you come?"

"If my ship is repaired and if there are enough men left to protect my family then you shall have my sword."

There was a noise at the door and Olaf stood there, "What's this I hear about you trying to rip out the keel of your ship? Did I teach you nothing about sailing?" He came over and gave me a bear hug. "I am pleased that you are safe."

"'*Wolf*' did well. There were three Saxon ships trying to take us and we flew like the wind. The waters around the southern coast are treacherous."

Both older warriors nodded. "Aye, they are. I will come in the morning and look at your boat. She will be out of the water by then?"

"She should be out by the time I get home tonight."

Both men looked disappointed. "You do not stay then?"

"I can see that neither of you have a wife who is with child and without husband! I dare not tarry."

Olaf laughed, "I am glad that I have chosen the life of a bachelor. I answer only to Prince Butar and myself. That is how I like it."

My stepfather looked sad. "I would trade all this for my wife returned to me."

I suddenly felt guilty, "I am sorry Prince Butar I …"

He held up his hand, "Do not walk around me as though I am an invalid. Your words were true. Return to your wife and I will visit and bring Eurwen with me too. She would like to see her brother again."

The next day was a joyous one. I suddenly felt important. Olaf and Prince Butar did not come alone. They brought eight young warriors who wished to serve on board '*Wolf*'. Two of them were older than me but they still wished to learn to be warriors like me. None had mail but all had a good helmet, a shield and a sword. Their eyes danced enviously between my wolf cloak and my sword. I wondered if, some day, my fame would be my undoing. It seems the whole world had heard of the sword touched by the gods. We left Eurwen with Erika while we went to inspect the damaged drekar. A boat out of the water can be an ugly thing but not *'Wolf'*. I still thought that the drekar looked ready to leap into the air and fly.

I could see that the rocks had not punctured the hull they had struck it so hard that the nails had popped out. Olaf nodded when he saw it. "You were unlucky that is all. I can repair it." He stroked his beard. "When I was raiding down close to Africa I spoke with a warrior who told me of a wood they have down there that can soak up water and yet float. It is a soft wood called cork. I think if we got some and packed it close to the hull it would mean you could still sail even if you had a hole."

I liked that idea and I also wish to travel further south and investigate the warmer regions. I had heard that the land around Africa had gold tumbling from its rivers as well as valuable spices. A drekar like *'Wolf'* could make a fortune carrying the spices which weighed little but cost the earth.

I left Olaf and Harold to repair the ship. Snorri and Scanlan were waiting patiently for me. I had searched through my chests earlier to find the wooden sword which Ragnar had made me make. I threw it to the ground. "Here is your first piece of training. I want you to make a sword like this which you feel you can handle."

Seara was standing nearby. Snorri looked confused "You will find an axe and a knife over there. Use them. I will see you tomorrow when you have made a weapon such as this."

Scanlan looked at me. "Lord, who made this?"

I smiled, "I did when I was just a little older than Aiden."

The rest of the day I spent with my family and Eurwen who loved playing with Arturus and being fussed by Erika. I knew that Erika was not seeing my little sister, but her unborn child. It was good to watch Prince Butar as a doting father. Since my mother had been taken from us he had had slaves to look after his daughter. Maewe and Seara were more than slaves; they were like family. Seara had fitted seamlessly into our lives. She was older than Erika and had become the big sister my wife had never had. Having spoken to Seara I knew that she gained more than they did for she could not have children and suddenly she had this extended family. I would trust Seara with not only my life but that of my children. She had had her future ripped from her and she would defend my family with her life.

By the time my stepfather and Olaf left, many days after they arrived, I felt I had recovered from the trauma of our journey and the closeness of death. *'Wolf'* was healed and would sail again. Scanlan and Aiden had not found the process of making a sword easy but I knew they had learned from it. I saw the discarded early versions. The ones they practised with were well balanced and finely finished. They were learning that a sword was more than a piece of metal. You put part of yourself into it; even a wooden one. I wondered if I should ask them to make a shield but decided that that task would be one for a later time.

The next month was a pleasant time of my life. My wife became larger as did the number of my warriors. I found more men wishing to serve with me. Scanlan and Snorri came on in leaps and bounds. Snorri grew almost daily and soon he and Scanlan were having bouts which tested them both as well as leaving them both black and blue.

Haaken and Cnut took it upon themselves to train the new men and they had high standards. One of them, Dargh, came to me after three weeks. "Lord, I wish to serve you but I cannot be the warrior that Cnut wishes me to be." I knew that Cnut could be short with the men and would not allow any deviation from his standards. He looked distraught.

"They mean well but they are looking for warriors who can be Ulfheonar."

"I can be a warrior my lord but not an Ulfheonar." He looked unhappy. "I have not the skills."

I nodded. Scanlan and Snorri were nearby. "You two, bring me your swords." They handed over their weapons and I gave one to Dargh. "Have a go at me."

He looked hesitant and I swung the wooden sword hard at his knee. It cracked and made Scanlan wince. It stiffened Dargh and he swung his sword at my head. It was not a clumsy blow but I saw it coming and I countered it easily. I made a move to his head and he smacked the wooden sword away. We sparred for some time and I saw him sweating. He would never be an Ulfheonar but he would make a warrior who could defend my settlement.

"You will never be Ulfheonar." His shoulders sagged, "But you could be the warrior who protects the hill and my town."

He suddenly brightened. "You are not just being kind my lord?"

"No. You have skills. I need warriors who can stay here while my men and I are raiding and watch our families. It is a great responsibility. Will you accept it?"

He knelt, "I will my lord."

"There is a warrior hall in the castle on the hill. At the moment you will be the only occupant. Until we get others you will guard that alone but I will send more men to aid you as they are sent to me. When there are enough you will organise them so that they can watch the port and the hill."

I thought that he would burst into tears. He gave a bow and then raced up the hill. He was the first of my town guards. I told Haaken and Cnut to send me all the men who were not good enough to be Ulfheonar. Soon Dargh had ten men under his command and he made sure that they were the best trained men in Hrams-a. He took his new post and responsibility very seriously. For myself, I now had the satisfaction of knowing that my family would be safe when I sailed across the seas.

As the days grew longer so did the desire of my warriors to go raiding. I had given my word to Prince Butar that I would go with him but I was tempted to take my little ship and try somewhere alone. Fortunately, a message came to prepare to sail to Duboglassio in two day's time. Erika was a little unhappy as she was in that stage of pregnancy when tears are frequent. Seara and Maewe came into their own and they chivvied and joked Erika into becoming happy about it. We had so many Ulfheonar that I was able to leave six men to help Dargh and his warriors protect our families. Hrams-a would be safe. Scanlan and Snorri persuaded me to take them. They both accepted that they would be useless but both wished to learn how to serve with warriors. I made sure they both had a helmet and they both had their first shield. I hoped that they would both return but I was not sure.

This was the first time we had sailed *'Wolf'* since her repair and I was pleased with the way she handled. The short crossing helped me to trim her rowers and make her fly. Aiden and Erik appeared to get on well. I saw Snorri casting a critical eye over their performance but he could not find fault with either of them.

This would be Prince Butar's cruise and we followed. I was happy to do so. Whatever we found would help my people at home and I would find out the mettle of my new warriors. The new Ulfheonar, who had no wolf cloaks, were excited to be travelling to the mainland where they might be able to kill their own wolf. I did not think they would be returning with such cloaks but they could dream.

We headed north east towards the land we had travelled to years earlier. Prince Butar knew that the Saxon hold on this land was tenuous at best and it was a rich land. We were not seeking glory, we were seeking riches. Saxons were known to love gold and to be richer than almost any other people. Now that they had become followers of the White Christ their churches, too were filled with gold and precious metals. We could make our people richer at little cost to ourselves.

It had been some time since we had sailed together and we had many new men on board. The rowing helped to bond them into a well trained and drilled band. Cnut and Haaken sang and soon they were all in the rhythm. Every bench was filled and we had four spare warriors, as well as Snorri and Scanlan so that we could relieve benches if we needed. It was not a long crossing making it unlikely that we would need to do so. Soon we were rowing up a wide estuary which promised much. It also meant that we could sail out boats up the river and find targets who felt themselves safe from raiders. We had seen the mountains to the north and knew that was where we had found wolves all those years ago.

Prince Butar was looking for slaves and animals. The slaves we could either use or sell on. There was always a ready market for slaves. This land did not produce grain but the sheep and cattle were renowned for their meat. We would take back a bull and a cow while slaughtering the rest. The sheep we would capture. We were all confident. No one had raided this land before and it promised to be fruit ripe for the plucking. The Saxons who lived there were protected by the mountains in the middle of the country and ranges to the north and the south. The king of this land lived far to the east and the north. There would be no warriors to come hunting us.

I left Scanlan and Snorri with Aiden and Erik to guard the boat. They were not happy about the task but none of them were warriors. They had to learn the discipline of obeying orders. The estuary meant that they could fish and they did not have to worry overmuch about tides. Prince Butar left eight men with his ship. This was my stepfather's raid and we followed him and his men inland.

This was verdant country. It was green, rolling and full of growth. We sought a settlement. Prince Butar halted the column of men and waved me forward.

"I think it is time to find some Saxons to rob." I grinned. This was where the Ulfheonar came into their own. My men eagerly followed me in a double file. We ranged ahead of the main warrior band. We knew how to find where people lived. People need a hill for security and water. They sought a site with both for obvious reasons. We just followed the water courses. One line of warriors followed the water and the second line was a mile or so uphill of them. We had found this to be an effective way of discovering villages and farms. Half a day inland and we found our first one.

Haaken waved the signal to halt us. We lay down like a flock of sheep in a field and we were as still as rocks. Haaken and Egill, who were closest, edged their way forwards and disappeared from view. We waited patiently. Eventually, they returned and made their way down to the rest of us.

Haaken grinned, "They have an old hill fort." I wondered why he looked so happy. We knew from the Hibernian experience that hill forts came with their own problems. "They have not occupied it but built their settlement lower down the hill, closer to the river. There is a palisade. It is as high as young Snorri."

That told us all we needed to know. "Egill, return to Prince Butar and tell him what you have found. Cnut, stay here with half of the men. Haaken, bring the rest with me. We will go around the other side of the village." This was a tactic we had developed. When we attacked then the tendency would be to flee. We prevented too many escaping.

We dropped down the valley and made our way through the undergrowth to remain out of sight. We used the cover of the many trees and bushes which littered the valley side. We had learned that having a small group such as ours beyond the walls captured those who fled. Usually, they were fleeing with the most valuable objects that they possessed. I only had ten warriors with me but we would be more than a match for any fleeing Saxons.

Haaken moved his arm left signifying that we had travelled far enough east and we began to climb the hill. Without being told, we all swung our shields around and unsheathed our swords. We had all experienced surprise before and we wished to avoid having to react quickly. That was how good warriors suffered avoidable wounds. We had lost fewer men than might have been expected because we always prepared for the worst.

The wind was blowing from the west and we could smell the wood smoke from the village. We moved slowly through the undergrowth trying to avoid making a disturbance. We could hear the bleating of the goats and the sounds of chickens and ducks noisily scratching food. The sound that was absent was the sound of children and that was worrying.

When we were level with the village I left most of the men there and took Haaken higher up so that we could peer down into the settlement. I could see now that the people were all gathered around the centre of the enclosed village. The huts radiated out from a central cross. This was a village of the White Christ.

Haaken looked puzzled, "Why are they gathered?"

"I think this is their holy day; this is the day of the White Christ. See how they are all kneeling and facing the man with the brown tunic and hood. See how he has a golden cross of their god."

Haaken shook his head. "These truly are sheep to be fleeced. Where are their warriors? Where are their sentries?"

I pointed to the open gate where two armed men faced, not outwards as they should, but inwards, watching the ceremony. "The gods smile on us today. Let us rejoin the others. We can close with the walls. There is no one watching."

As we moved our warriors closer, we explained what lay ahead. The wind would take our voices away from the people listening to the priest. Our task was now to wait until we heard the shouts of panic as Prince Butar fell amongst the helpless Saxons. We reached the wooden wall. As Haaken had said it was little bigger than Snorri and would only serve to keep the sheep in at night. As a defence, it was useless. I risked a glance over the top and saw that the backs of the people were still to me. I could see the priest's head was bowed. As he raised it I could see his eyes open as he spied us but before he could say anything a spear suddenly erupted from his chest and he fell dead with a surprised look on his face.

"Over the wall!"

We scaled the wall easily and then raced towards the people, many of whom were still kneeling. They were mainly facing the warriors who followed my stepfather. Prince Butar himself led them through the gate. His sword took out one of the guards while Sweyn killed the other. The villagers leapt to their feet and raced away from the wall of warriors who hurtled towards them. We had the luxury of not having to kill indiscriminately for fear of being killed. These people were not armed. A couple of men ran to their huts for weapons. The rest ran towards us. They were so intent on escaping that they did not look up until it was too late. They saw this line of ten mailed and hooded warriors and fell to their knees sobbing for mercy. One of the men who had sought a weapon feebly swung it at Egill who casually decapitated him. That was the end of their resistance. Only four men had been killed the rest were our prisoners.

"Tether them together!"

I remembered what it had been like to be a slave and I said to my men, "Try to keep families together. They will be less trouble. Tie the men's feet as well as their hands."

While my warriors did that I went into the huts to see what they had hidden. Most Saxons liked to bury their valuables. I entered the nearest hut and I moved the bedding. I saw freshly turned soil. I took out my dagger and loosened it. I found a box which although crudely made, had a solid enough hasp. My seax broke it easily enough. Within were a few precious stones, some small pieces of silver and a metal cross with the figure of the White Christ. I tucked it beneath my arm and left.

Cnut grinned when he saw the box. "Lucky Dragon Heart eh?"

"No, my friend, but I know where to look. Move the bedding and seek soil which is not compact. They like to bury their treasures."

It only took an hour or so to strip the village of all that was valuable. As we left, it was the Ulfheonar who, once again, led the way. We had no need for secrecy on the way back and I took us by the most direct route. We were close to the sea, for we could smell it when I spied the walled settlement sitting high above the river on a small knoll. Haaken saw it too. "That looks to be better defended."

"And if a place is well defended then it must have something to defend." I turned to look at my men. All of them were laden with the fruits of our raid. There would be no opportunity to investigate this hill top enigma; not until we had divested ourselves of our treasure and our captives. It was no more than five miles from the village we had raided. When we returned home I would seek answers from the prisoners. We would return to raid but this time we would have a better idea of what to expect. The hardest part was loading the animals. I took the slaves for my boat was smaller and Prince Butar had more room for the animals. Of course, he would also have a harder task to clean up after them. Luckily the voyage was a short one and we reached home before the sun had set.

Chapter 11

We had tied up and taken off the animals and slaves by dark. It had been the most successful raid ever for we had lost no men and gained many animals and slaves. There were too many slaves for us to use and we would need to sell them. There was a good market across the sea in the land of the Cymri on the island of Mona. Olaf would sail there and sell our surplus. We could afford to be choosy. Before we let Olaf take them away we questioned all of the adult slaves about the mysterious settlement. There were only five or six of us who could speak Saxon and it took some time. We discovered that it was what the Saxons called a monastery where priests, male and female lived. They were revered by those who lived around the area and even the Saxon kings paid homage and tribute to them. The result was that they had many rich objects within their walls. We also found that some of these priests were warriors too. This explained the defences. When Olaf returned we would raid again and this time we would be seeking treasure.

As I counted out my share of the treasure and animals we had secured I realised that I could afford to buy weapons and mail for four more warriors. None of the Ulfheonar needed my charity but some of the newer, poorer warriors might. I decided to purchase four swords and helmets first. Snorri and Scanlan both needed them and I could decide which other two would benefit. When I had enough I would buy the mail shirts. A warrior dressed in mail feared no man so long as he knew how to fight and I would make sure that all of my men knew how to fight.

Our raid emboldened all of us. Prince Butar called me to a meeting with Jarl Erik and Jarl Harald. They had both raided the Hibernians but had lost warriors and not gained as much treasure. They had not acted together and both had met with resistance. Had they coordinated and attacked one place from two directions I think they would have succeeded. Jarl Harald appeared to have lost more men and captured little. He was not happy and looked jealously at the slaves and animals we had secured. They were both intrigued at our description of this monastery.

Jarl Harald looked to be almost sulking, "From what you say one boat could capture all from within the monastery."

Prince Butar frowned, "That is probably true but why are you looking so unhappy about the prospect of easy hunting? I did not make you raid the Hibernians. I did not kill your warriors."

From his face, I could see that the jarl regretted showing his feelings so openly. "I know, Prince Butar." He sighed, "I suppose that I just wish to raid this place and know that I will not be needed to accompany you. You will be able to gain all the treasure yourself."

My step father spread his arms wide. "I did not say that I would be raiding this monastery. My warriors made much from our raid and we do not need to raid again but you would need help to find it." Harald's face lit up. For my part, I thought that Prince Butar had dealt too kindly with the outburst. "First, we need to ask, who would like to raid this monastery?"

Only Jarl Harald spoke. The rest of us knew that he wanted this prize himself. "I will say now that I wish to go with my oathsworn."

Prince Butar looked at me and I gave the slightest shake of the head. Jarl Erik smiled, "I lost four warriors and this raid against priests will not regain the honour my men seek. We will plan a different raid." He looked at me, "Perhaps I will ask Dragon Heart and the Ulfheonar to come with us. The gods seem to smile on him and give him good fortune. I would like some of that good fortune."

"Whenever you wish it, my brother, I will come with you but I am not so sure about the luck."

This made everyone around the table laugh and the atmosphere changed. "It was you and the Ulfheonar who found the monastery would you go with the Jarl?" The question from my step father was harmless. Had Jarl Harald spoken the words then I might have been suspicious.

"I will go with Haaken and Cnut. The rest of the Ulfheonar can train my new warriors. I still have unfinished business with Tadgh. My priority is to find him and kill him but I will show Jarl Harald where this monastery is."

The looks on their faces told me that they had thought I had forgotten his treachery. I had not. I had merely hidden my feelings deep within me.

Harald's ship, *"Crow"* was bigger than mine and had twenty oars on each side. He chose his crew from his best warriors. Cnut, Haaken and I were given an oar. Some men might have thought it insulting. This was not my ship. I did not mind. It did a warrior good to row. It gave him discipline as well as reminding him that he was still a warrior, even if he did steer the ship. What concerned me was the smug superior look on Jarl Harald's face. He appeared to take delight in the fact that I had to row.

We left at night; Jarl Harald was keen to attack at dawn. Normally I would have objected but we had scouted out this place already and I did not think there would be any obstacles we could not overcome.

We landed at the mouth of the estuary. There was no moon; it was pitch black and the world felt empty. Jarl Harald had his own ship's boys to watch the ship. We took our bows with us for we didn't know if there might be sentries for us to take out. I led my Ulfheonar to the north. I had an image of the walls in my head. Jarl Harald and his men trotted behind us. After the debacle that was Hibernia, they were relying on the luck of Dragon Heart.

When I smelled the smoke of their fires I halted and waved the others to wait. This was the time for the Ulfheonar to do what they did best-disappear. The three of us slid up the slope towards the walls. We were thirty paces from each other. When I came to the ditch before the walls I stopped. There was something not quite right about the ditch. The side before me looked to be very steep. I gingerly lowered myself, somewhat ungainly, down the sides. When my foot struck something hard and sharp then I was glad that I had been cautious. The bottom of the ditch was filled with spiked stakes. The other side appeared gentle but I still went slowly. It was gentle but it had been slicked with water and something else which was slippery, possibly oil. I used my seax and my dagger to drag me up the muddy morass to the walls.

The palisade was made of thick tree trunks and was higher than me. This was designed to keep people out. I managed to walk along the side of the wall until I heard voices. I pressed myself into the wood. I still held my dagger and seax. I could defend myself if I had to. They were talking in Saxon and I gathered from the drift of conversation that they were priests. I heard mention of something called a bishop and then the voices faded as they moved away.

I had enough information for Jarl Harald and I slipped back down the bank being careful to avoid the spikes at the bottom. Cnut and Haaken waited for me and I waved for them to follow me. We soon reached the waiting warriors. Although we were far enough away not to be heard we still whispered. Sound travelled long distances at night.

"There is a ditch around the walls and it has spikes in the bottom. The bank is slippery and the walls are high. There are sentries who are patrolling. They had something worth guarding within those walls."

I saw Jarl Harald licking his lips and grinning almost in anticipation of capturing it.

"I saw that they have four men at the gate but there is no ditch there." Cnut just reported those things that I had not seen.

"Could we attack the gate?"

I shook my head, "It would alarm those inside and they would be able to defend it or even escape."

Cnut nodded, his head glinting in the moonlight, "They have another gate at the rear."

Jarl Harald turned to his warriors, "Ulf, you take ten warriors and wait by the rear gate. Cnut will lead you there." He looked at me. "Can you and Haaken get inside and kill the guards?"

Haaken nodded, "We could."

"We will wait by the gate. If you could open the gate then we will have this monastery and all its treasures."

As Haaken and I returned to the walls I now knew why Jarl Harald had not been successful. He let others do the difficult tasks. Jarl Erik or my stepfather would have offered to do one of the harder tasks and not wait for someone else to do it for them. I hoped that we could succeed but he was relying on just two warriors.

The return was easier for we knew where the traps were and we could help each other up the bank. Once we reached the walls Haaken stood with his back to the wall and I stood on his cupped hands. I peered over the wall and saw the two sentries I had heard; they were at the far end and talking. I tapped Haaken on the head and he pushed his hands up. I slipped over the top and then reached down to haul Haaken up. He used the wall to support his feet and he slipped over too. The sentries were still at the far end of the platform some fifty paces away. They appeared to be looking at something in the woods beyond. We slipped our bows from our shoulders and each notched an arrow. I aimed at the sentry on the left. I used his spear as a guide. I whispered, "One, two, three." On three we released our arrows. There were two soft thuds and then the two men disappeared over the side of the wall.

Slinging our bows, we drew our swords and ran towards the gate. There were two men on the gatehouse and they were looking out to sea. All the sentries had made the classic mistake of staying in the same place and looking at the same spot. It cost them their lives. The two on the gatehouse heard our footfall and turned. The one closest to me swung his sword. My shield was still around my back and so I used my mailed hand to push the blade away as I stuck him with the sword. He screamed as he died. Haaken's opponent had stepped back to yell, "Vikings!" That was all that he managed to get out as Haaken ended his life.

We raced down the stairs to the gate. Two more sentries stood with spears. I saw the spear head jab towards me. I could have allowed it to hit my mail for I could see that the head was crudely made but that was not a good habit to get into. I jinked to one side and brought my sword down on his neck. I left the other to Haaken and began to lift the bar on the gate. It was halfway off when I was pitched against it by the arrow which thudded into the shield on my back. It took both of us to lift the bar and open the gate.

Jarl Harald's men flooded in, their bloodcurdling screams filling the night. Haaken and I stepped back to allow them through. It was not a battle, it was a slaughter. The priests fought hard, with whatever they had to hand. There was neither honour nor glory killing these priests and so the jarl's men subdued them and the women who wailed and cried. One or two of them tried to attack the warriors with their nails and they were knocked to the ground by men who had no time for such things. I was disappointed in Jarl Harald and his men. Prince Butar would have captured more for they were not warriors. I did not think I would want to come raiding with Jarl Harald again.

Cnut joined us. "We caught a few trying to escape but there was another door, a side door and we saw three of their priests escaping."

"Well, that could not be helped. We did what was asked of us."

As dawn broke to the east we saw that Jarl Harald's men had only suffered minor wounds. Apart from the sentries we had killed there were just five dead priests and the rest we gathered in a forlorn huddle. There was excitement amongst the jarl's men. They had found much treasure as well as animals. They were about to discard the books of the White Christ when I restrained them. "They are valuable."

Olaf the Lame looked at me sceptically. "Are you sure Dragon Heart? There is no gold in them and they are just words and pictures on deer hide."

"Trust me, Olaf, they are each worth more than all the gold and silver you have collected. They can be sold in Frankia or even here in this land and you will receive a king's ransom."

Jarl Harald had heard the last part and his greedy eyes widened. "You keep them safe for me Olaf the Lame or you will be Olaf the eyeless!" He looked at Cnut. "I hear some escaped?"

"Yes, Jarl Harald. They had a secret door in the walls of the northern side."

He frowned, "What did they take I wonder?"

I had an idea how to find out. "Haaken and Cnut, come with me and talk about anything. I want to get as close to their priests as I can."

They both nodded and began jabbering about what they would like to do to the women priests we had captured. I saw the younger ones huddling closer together as the two fierce looking warriors approached. An older, stern looking woman was sat next to an equally old, tonsured priest who had a wound to the head. She was cleaning the wound. They began to talk in Saxon. I pretended I was listening to Haaken and Cnut but I was, in fact, eavesdropping.

"Did Brother Cuthbert escape?"

The old priest tried to nod and I could see him wince. "Yes, he and Brother Garth and Brother Aiden."

"Good, then the crown is safe."

"Aye and more importantly they can bring the warriors from the fort."

The woman suddenly noticed me and cast me an evil look. I was not afraid of a spell of the White Christ. I had heard enough. "Come let us find the jarl."

When we discovered him, he was beginning the process of moving his treasure. "We may have trouble Jarl Harald. Those three priests were going for help. There are warriors in a fort close by."

I could see him calculating how to get the captives and the loot back to the ship. It was only a couple of miles but it would take some time.

"Could you three find them and stop them?"

"We could try." I wondered why I had kept the knowledge of the crown hidden from Jarl Harald. At the time, I could not possibly know but it was the Weird Sisters once more weaving their webs and embroiling me in the heart of them.

"We will load the captives. If you have not returned by the time we are ready we will wait just off the coast for you." He pointed to the west. I could see that our wellbeing was of no concern to him. I could have refused to go and risked being caught by the Saxons but I had given my word that I would help the jarl. Next time I would be more cautious about giving my word to another.

The three of us secured our weapons and headed for the secret door. Now that it was daylight their tracks were easy to see. These priests were not trying to hide their escape route they were just trying to get to help with the crown. They followed the trail which headed north. I did not know how fit they were but I knew that we were Ulfheonar and could run down a wolf. We would find them.

We had been running for a few hours when we suddenly saw some game birds rise noisily into the air. We knew what that meant in an instant. We took our bows and each notched an arrow. Cnut moved to the left and Haaken to the right. We moved slowly through the wood. I thought I heard voices and I held my hands up. We all stopped. I had heard voices and they were speaking Saxon. I moved closer to catch their words. It was the priests and they were telling the newcomers of our raid. I had no idea how many men were there but the relief in the priest's voices suggested that they were allies of some description.

I waved the others forwards and I saw, in the clearing six hunters and the three priests. The hunters looked to be warriors rather than villagers. I glanced left and right and saw that the others were in position. We raised our bows. There would be no spoken signal but when I heard Cnut's arrow being released I let mine fly. Three of the hunters dropped like stones. I dropped my bow and drew *Ragnar's Spirit*. I ran into the clearing, swinging my sword as I went. The hunter thrust his spear at me. I twisted my shoulder so that the spear ran along the links of my mail and I continued the swing of my sword. It sliced through his middle and jarred on his backbone.

One of the priests ran at me and I grabbed his shoulder and threw him forward. The next spearman sank his weapon into the surprised priest expecting it to be me and I stabbed the spearman. I heard a scream behind me as the last two were slain and then there was silence in the bloody clearing. They were all dead.

I waved Cnut to check up the trail while Haaken and I made sure that they were dead. While we were doing so we relieved them of their valuables. The oldest priest was carrying a sack. I opened it and found a crown for a queen. At least I assumed it was for a queen for it was quite small. I felt a little shiver race down my spine when I saw a blue stone in the middle which was exactly the same colour as the wolf's eye on my amulet. They had been made by the same person!

When Cnut returned he shook his head, "There was no one else."

Haaken said, "But there will be when these six are missed."

"Let us go then and find Jarl Harald." We retrieved our arrows partly because they were valuable and partly to obscure our identity. I knew that warriors such as we attracted more attention than most and the Saxons would move heaven and earth to get to us. The bodies were shoved beneath bushes. They would be found but not until they organised a serious search. By then we would be safely aboard Jarl Harald's boat.

The journey south was harder than the one north had been. We had been up all night. We had rowed to the mainland and, since daylight we had been running after the priests. We moved much slower. To my dismay, I saw the sun setting towards the west and we were still a mile or so from the estuary. If we arrived after dark we would need to signal the ship somehow. We pushed on even harder and ran through the pain barrier. We made the estuary while the sun was still a golden glow in the west. We had made it early. But there was no ship, the *"Crow"* had flown and we were trapped on the mainland where every man was our enemy. I had a sick feeling in my stomach. I knew that there was another place where they could meet us but I heard a voice in my head telling me that we had been abandoned.

Chapter 12

The estuary was empty. "Perhaps he is waiting off the coast as he said he would."

I looked at Cnut, neither Haaken and I believed that for a moment but we had to give him the benefit of the doubt. "We might as well walk there anyway but let us be more careful now about tracks." Expecting the ship to be there we had moved as quickly as we could after the ambush. Now we needed to hide our presence from those who would be pursuing us.

As we moved west, trying to find solid ground and avoid breaking trail I ran through all the possibilities we might have to return home. We were not far, as the crow flies, from our island home but we needed a boat and, as we had travelled east to reach this land, we had seen no ports and few boats. The nearest place was forty miles south at the Dee. That would take two to three days and I was not certain we could evade capture for that long. By the time we reached the sea, the sun had set and the water was devoid of ships.

We sat, forlornly on the beach. We hoped that the jarl would return for us but he should have been there. This place held no danger for him. We also sat there because we were exhausted and we could go no further without something to eat and some sleep.

Cnut flourished a cooked bird of some description. He had taken it from the dead hunters and it was, no doubt, intended for supper. After we had eaten it and washed it down with the last of the water from our skins we felt better. We found some bracken to make a bed and a shelter of hawthorn and ivy. It would keep us warm, and help us avoid prying eyes. We were too few to set sentries and we lay, relying on our senses to wake us.

As I drifted off to sleep I thought of the connection between the crown and my mother's wolf amulet. She was no longer around to ask and I regretted the time I had wasted not finding out more about her origins. I knew that she had lived in the land of the Cymri but that her people had originally come from the ancient land of Rheged which had been raped by the Saxons. This crown was unlike anything I had ever seen the Saxons use. I had only glimpsed it before I had stuffed it in my satchel but I thought were intricate lace dragons. If so what did that portend? My dreams were filled with images of my mother and flying dragons. I did not sleep well and would have woken had anyone come close. I awoke stiff and cold but we were unmolested.

Dawn was just breaking far to the west and the sea remained annoyingly empty. There was little point in waking the other two and I watched alone. When they emerged from their green cocoons they stared, as I had done at the shipless sea.

Cnut stretched, "So what is the plan?"

Haaken joked, "Perhaps we could walk on water."

I smiled, "Until we can do that I would suggest we find a boat to steal." I pointed south. "Let us cross the estuary and put as much land between us and the ambush as we can."

It was not the best of plans but it was the only plan I could come up with and we set off. The hunger which gnawed at our bellies would only get worse. We would not be able to afford time to go hunting. Although it had been an uncomfortable night we had rested and moved much quicker as we headed back to the estuary. Once again, we had to ensure that we left as little sign of our passing as possible. They would be hunting us.

We made good time once we had waded across the ebbing river and climbed up onto the southern bank. The land before us was a large plain with one or two knolls to break the monotony. We headed south west towards the coast. The land worked in our favour. An enemy would not have a good vantage point to spot us. We would be hard to see. There were a few woods, copses and hedgerows. We used those whenever we could but, inevitably, we had to risk the open land occasionally. It was when we were out in the open that they spotted us. Cnut's sharp eyes saw them even as they spied us. There were ten of them on hill ponies.

I calculated that we had been travelling without food for eight hours or so. If we continued to run then we would become weaker and they would win. I saw, just two hundred paces away, a small wood and a piece of slightly higher ground. It was not much but it was better than the open.

"Let us go there and make a stand."

They nodded their agreement and we reached the wood when the horsemen were still a good two hundred paces away. I think they thought that we would try to outrun them and were happy for us to waste energy. When we halted, they urged their ponies on.

We slipped our bows from our shoulders and each notched an arrow. I kept watching them as I did so. They were armed with a sword, spear and a small shield. Some of them wore a leather helmet. They outnumbered us and that was all. I released an arrow which smacked into the shoulder of the lead rider, pitching him from his saddle. Cnut and Haaken did the same and were rewarded with an arrow in a pony and another in a rider's leg. If they had had someone who could give orders they would have withdrawn and used their superior numbers to encircle us but they seemed to be over excited. They had three of their hated enemies and were probably already telling their fellows the story of their success.

They did one thing correctly, they spread out and charged us. I loosed one more arrow which scored a red line down a pony's flank before I swung my shield around and drew my sword. We stood close together so that our shields overlapped and we held our swords above them. They came at us from all sides. Haaken and Cnut smashed their swords against the ash shafts of the spears and they shattered. I yelled, "Brace!" We all planted one foot firmly behind the other and took the hit of the first ponies. The brave beasts tried to turn. They were trying to go uphill and the metal studded shields would have looked like a wall of wood to them. As I stabbed forwards at the Saxon who leaned towards me with his spear, Cnut sliced into the throat of his pony while Haaken did the same to the second one. There was a jumble of dying screaming animals and the line halted. Now was the time for us to take charge and I yelled, "Ulfheonar!"

We leapt over the dead and dying and hacked at the warriors who had not expected us to attack. The dying pony allowed me to jump up and take the head of one warrior. I landed next to a rider on a pony and I pushed with my shield and the weight of my armour. The rider and pony fell to the ground and I skewered the rider before he could escape. Cnut and Haaken had not been idle and the others fell to their swords.

"Grab those ponies. They will save our legs."

While they caught the remaining ponies, I went around the Saxons to make sure that they were all dead. One was alive, barely, but he had enough breath to curse me in Saxon. "Priest killers!"

I nodded and spoke to him in Saxon, "You were brave warriors and I will see you in the Otherworld. Would you like me to put your sword in your hand for the journey?"

He laughed and blood trickled from the corner of his mouth. "I will be with Christ in Heaven and you will not, barbarian!"

There was no pleasing some people. I would watch him die if he did not wish a warrior's death. Then I remembered the crown. "What is this?"

His eyes widened when he saw it and he spoke without thinking, "The crown of the Queen of Rheged!"

I nodded, "Thank you." His face screwed up to curse me again but he had used the last of his life force and he fell dead.

The others had returned with four ponies. "The others fled."

"It appears we have the crown of the Queen of Rheged here. I suspect the Saxons and the priests of the White Christ wished to use it to confirm their rule of this land." Putting it away I said, "Check the bodies and let us leave this place quickly. There may be others."

We left the bodies as I did not know the rituals of the White Christ. They were a strange people. They did not wish a warrior's death. Why did they fight? How would they get to their heaven? Their loss was our gain and we rode swiftly towards the coast. We reached it by late afternoon and headed south seeking a settlement and, hopefully, a boat.

Cnut's sharp eyes picked out the houses at the same time as Haaken's nose sniffed out the wood smoke. We halted, "This is not the time for war. Take off your helmets and sling your shields. We will try to pay for our passage home."

Haaken gave me a strange look. "Why?"

"We need a boat and we need to get home." I sighed, "Haaken, just try it my way. You can slaughter them all if I fail."

He nodded affably and I heard Cnut chuckle. Haaken was predictable. "Here, take my helmet and wolf cloak. I would take off the mail shirt but I fear I might need it. Wait under cover of yonder beech. When I wave then come, slowly, to the village."

I led the pony towards the village. It was undefended and, thankfully, had six or seven small fishing ships drawn up on the beach. The pony I led neighed and it alerted the fishermen who came out armed with a pathetic assortment of implements. There was one sword. I had left the others behind for I spoke Saxon and they did not. As I expected they initiated the questions.

"Who are you, stranger?" Their weapons, poor as they were, were all pointed at me.

I smiled, "I am one of King Eardwulf's oathsworn. I am here with two companions who are tardier than I." I leaned forwards, putting my throat perilously close to a rather rusty pitchfork. "We have been sent on a secret mission."

Thankfully the weapons were lowered a little. My tongue and my smile had disarmed them. Their leader, a man with skin which looked like leather and arms like knotted rope put his sword aside and asked, "What can poor fisher folk do for warriors?"

"You can sail us across to the island of Man."

They burst out laughing, "Are you mad? Have you been bewitched? The Vikings have Man and they will eat your heart and use your empty skull as a drinking vessel."

"Even so I am sworn to go there and retrieve a treasure taken by Viking raiders." I paused and looked around as though someone might be listening. "The crown of the Queens of Rheged."

They had obviously heard of the treasure. The headman stroked his beard and greed flashed into his eyes. "We would like to help the king but we are poor people."

"I can pay you."

He smiled, "What with, you do not look to have anything with you to trade."

"We have four ponies." I could see that I had almost persuaded him. Ponies could be used for many tasks, dragging boats to the beach, transport, even food. "And this." I took out one of the seaxes we had taken from the dead warriors."

His eyes lit up, it was a far better weapon than the one he had. He held out his hand. "We will take you. When would you go?"

"Night would be best. We would like to land unseen."

He nodded. "That is sensible. How will you escape them when you have the treasure?"

"The king is sending a ship." The thing about a lie was that once you started, it was hard to stop. "I will go and see where my men are." I stepped back on to the trail. "As I thought, they are resting." I waved, "Come on you sluggards."

The headman headed for the beach. "Come, the tide is almost right now."

When Haaken and Cnut rode up I gave a slight shake of my head and put my finger to my lips. I waved at them to follow me. They both exchanged a worried look but then complied leaving the three ponies to be taken away before the exorbitant price could be renegotiated. I smiled to myself. The ponies had not been mine to trade nor had the seax. It was worth the price to get home safely. I kept hold of the seax as insurance. Cnut handed me my helmet and my cloak. I murmured, "Keep silent."

The headman was already in the boat and two of his people were holding it steady. He frowned when he saw the size of the men and their armour. "They are heavier that I thought. We will have to balance them carefully. You sit next to me and put them one in front of the other in the bottom of the boat."

Climbing in was easier said than done. I found it easier to take off my shield and put that in the bottom first and then I hauled myself up and over. The boat tipped alarmingly but the men in the water held it. They grinned at the look on my face. Cnut came alongside and I pointed to the front of the boat. Once he fell into the bottom the balance was much better and Haaken had the easiest time of all as he clambered to the middle.

The fisherman wasted no time in hoisting the triangular sail and the boat leapt forwards into the setting sun. Despite the small dimensions of the boat, there was enough freeboard for us to feel safe although I would have preferred the security of *'Wolf'*.

"I will drop you at the first empty place on the island that I can."

"That suits us."

He gestured at my two companions. "They do not say much do they?"

"They swore an oath that, until they have recaptured the crown they will not speak."

That seemed to impress him. "Why do you all have the cloak made of the wolf skin?"

"It will help us to hide once we are among the heathens."

That was almost a mistake for he suddenly asked, "Where is your cross?" He lifted his wooden cross from beneath his tunic.

I shrugged, "We had to leave them behind. We need to pretend to be Norse. If they found a cross on us then they would know we were from Northumbria and King Eardwulf's men."

He laughed, "You will never pull that off. You are not big enough. They are all giants I hear."

"We will see." The stories told by the Saxons of the Norse have always made me smile. Our ships are always longer and bigger than they were in reality and there were always hundreds of us. This idea that they were all giants was also a myth. The truth was that a hundred raiders was a large number but we were efficient. We left few behind to tell the tale. I suppose the ones who remained had to believe that we were as numerous as the fish in the sea and, somehow, superhuman.

Once we left the shelter of the land the small boat began to rise and fall alarmingly in the crests and troughs of the sea. The waves through which we were passing did not appear to be that big but to the small boat, they were. In the middle of the night, our fisherman gave us some dried, salted fish. It was chewy but it satisfied the hunger pangs for we had not eaten all day. We had our own water skins and we emptied them. We would be able to refill them on our island.

As dawn broke behind us I saw the dark shape ahead that was Man. The fisherman began to reef the sail and I looked at him curiously. "We don't want to be seen. This way we are harder to spot." He pointed ahead, "There is a place at the corner of the island where there are no people. It is a long way from their villages but it is where I will drop you."

He was not to know that I knew exactly where that was and, short of sailing into Hrams-a, it was perfect. Our island home looked all the more welcoming arriving in such a small boat. It seemed bigger and more substantial. I recognised the hill ahead. The fisherman did not know that, just over the crest, was my fort. Perhaps I would have a tower built to watch over this secret way into my island.

Cnut crouched in the bow as the boat began to slide along the sand. He leapt over the side and stood in the water holding the bow. As Haaken joined him I gave the seax to the fisherman. "Thank you."

"He stuffed the blade into his belt, "May the Lord protect you and help you do the king's work."

"He will."

As soon as I left the boat it bobbed up; it was lighter than it had been. The three of us pushed it and, as the fisherman hoisted the sail, it soon flew east, back to his home.

Once ashore Haaken slapped me on the back. "How did you get him to bring us so close to home?"

"He chose the place. He said he wanted it to be a lonely and deserted place."

"And how did you get him to bring us in the first place?"

"I told him we were on a mission from the King of Northumbria to get the crown of Rheged."

"Once again Dragon Heart has more than his fair share of luck."

Cnut shook his head, "It is not luck. Have you not noticed my friend that he makes his own luck and does not take what is given to him?" The dawn's early light picked out his face and I could see it was stern. "And I would like to hear Jarl Harald's explanation for leaving us on that beach."

I had liked Jarl Harald at one time and I was unwilling to think badly of him, "There may be a good explanation. We do not know. Come let us get home for I am starving."

Chapter 13

We headed around the headland towards our home. I was pleased when we were challenged by Ulf. As soon as he recognised us he shouted to wake the village. "Dragon Heart is back!"

Most of my people would already have been waking anyway but they rushed out of their huts as soon as they heard the cry. I wondered what Jarl Harald had said to them. Egill and Olaf were the first to reach us. "We were told you had been captured."

The three of us exchanged looks, "Who told you that?"

"Why Jarl Harald of course. He said you pursued some priests and he went to pick you up but you were not there."

Cnut said, quite simply, "Then he lies."

That was a serious statement to make but we knew the truth. That would have to wait for another day. My family came out of my hall. Maewe held Arturus while Erika waddled over to me. She threw her arms around me, "I knew you were not dead. I could feel it. The baby knew it too; she was peaceful."

"And we are returned so there is no harm," I held her at arm's length, "but that is the last time I serve aboard another ship. From now on I sail with Ulfheonar only; with men that I can trust." I did not say it quietly and my warriors all cheered. As I went to my hall I could see my men asking Cnut and Haaken what had happened. Neither would lie nor exaggerate and my men would become angry at the casual way we had been abandoned.

Scanlan helped me take my byrnie off. It was the worse for wear. The salt water had spotted it with some rust and it would need cleaning and then firing with the charcoal again. After I had changed and while Maewe and Seara prepared food for me I went with Scanlan and Aiden to see Bjorn. It was like seeing a younger version of his father. He had the same intense eyes and the same knotted arms. He gave a slight bow, "I am pleased that you have returned Dragon Heart. This place we call home would not be the same without you."

"Thank you, Bjorn. My mail needs some work. Will you show Aiden and Scanlan how to clean it and protect it with the heat and the charcoal?"

He nodded, "It is some time since I did this. It will be good to have two assistants."

I handed him a small dagger I had taken from one of the dead Saxons. He shook his head. "I need no payment from you. I owe all that I have to you."

"If I do not pay for the work then Thor will be angry and the mail might fail. Besides the Saxon I took this from is dead. I have no use for the blade." He reluctantly took it.

I wolfed down the food the women had prepared and answered Erika's questions between mouthfuls. "Prince Butar knew you were not dead too. But why did Jarl Harald leave you there? It makes no sense."

I had to agree with my wife. It did not seem like the man I knew. I liked the Jarl. I knew Jarl Erik better but I had not seen this treacherous and unreliable side to the jarl. Like Erik, he had sought sanctuary with us after fleeing our homeland. He had proved himself by fighting alongside us when we drove the Saxons from the island and he had been to Hibernia to punish our enemies. This seemed like a different person or someone who had been changed. Had he been bewitched? Perhaps some witch in Hibernia had cast a spell on him. I would not leap to conclusions until I had spoken with him.

We are a small island I know but I am always amazed by the speed at which news travels. By noon we had a visit from Prince Butar and the ever present Eurwen.

"I am pleased the news of your death was exaggerated."

I shrugged, "We were never in danger." I explained to him about our pursuit of the priests and how we had disposed of them. "We returned to the estuary while it was still daylight and reached the meeting place before the sun had set. I cannot understand why the jarl was not there."

He looked at me carefully, "Are you not angry?"

"Not until I have spoken with him. He may have a good explanation."

"And if not?"

"Then we will have more than words."

He nodded his understanding. Then he laughed, "And I hear you persuaded a Saxon to bring you here to steal a crown we do not even possess."

"That is not quite true." I went to my satchel and took out the crown. Erika had not seen it and I had not examined it properly. My examination had been hurried and in poor light. The light through the door made it sparkle and seemed to light up the blue stone.

"That is true beauty, my husband."

"According to the men we chased it is the crown of the Queen of Rheged." I saw Prince Butar stiffen and he held his hands out. I gave him the crown. "What is it, father? You look as though someone has walked over your grave."

He looked at it carefully and then said, "The wolf token, where is it?"

I took it from around my neck and handed it to him. He examined both stones carefully. "This stone came from the same mine. There is more than happenstance at work here." He handed them both back to me. I gave the crown for Erika to examine while I replaced the wolf around my neck.

"What do you know of your mother's people?"

"Little enough. Had I known she would be taken from us so untimely then I would have asked questions but I thought to wait until my son could hear his grandmother's wisdom too."

"That is true. None of us know how short the Norns will cut their threads. Well, your mother and I spoke of many things and this was one of them. Your mother was not a Saxon. She was captured south of the Dee. Nor was she Welsh. Her people were an ancient people from the north of the land." He pointed out of the open door to the north east. "Less than half a day's sailing from here. It was the land of Rheged." He allowed that information to sink in. "Your mother was not of royal blood, she made that quite clear but it appears that the line of the house of Rheged had died out. She came from the family of the lord who led the warriors protecting the people. There were still men who protected the land. They were called knights and were armoured riding powerful horses, not little ponies. They kept their people safe within the land of the Welsh. Your grandfather was a warlord, the last warlord. When your mother was captured the last warriors of Rheged were slaughtered when the Welsh king betrayed them. I think the crown came from that last battle. Your mother said that the crowns of the kings of Rheged were always taken into battle. The blue stone confirms it." He took a bracelet from his arm. "This was your mother's and it too has the blue stone." He paused, "There is another connection too. The warriors fought under the banner of a dragon and they called themselves the Wolf Warriors. You were meant to find that crown. The threads are complex but they lead to you."

This was almost too much to take in; a dragon banner and wolf warriors. This was beyond me. I muttered. "Then perhaps I should thank the jarl for his desertion."

Erika snorted her derision, "From what you have told me you had this crown before he deserted you. You won it but Prince Butar is correct, my husband, you were meant to find this precious object."

I shrugged. "I will speak with him first." She handed me back the crown. "If they had this one then there may be other pieces. I wonder where those priests were going with it?"

Prince Butar rubbed his chin reflectively. "There are two of the women priests here. Jarl Harald gave them to your wife as your share of the treasure."

For the first time, I became angry. "There was a huge amount of treasure and slaves. Even if he thought the three of us were dead then our families deserved more than two slaves!"

"I dare say when he returns from his raid Jarl Harald will make amends."

I stared at Prince Butar. "He went away raiding so soon?"

"Almost as soon as he had reported that you were lost. He went to the land of the Welsh."

"Then he did desert us. He must have sailed away as soon as he loaded his ship."

Erika stood and stretched her back. "His wife, Hilda, is very ambitious. She wants finer things than Jarl Harald has. Perhaps he has ambitions beyond Man." She waddled from the room. It would not be too long before we had another baby in the house.

When we were alone Prince Butar said, "Your wife is wise and may be correct. Jarl Harald has built his warriors up so that he now has more than any of us and his ship is the same size as *"Ran"*.

"I would not want war over this."

"We may have no choice in the matter. My warriors, as well as Jarl Erik's, were unhappy about his actions and I know, just from walking through your men just now, that they are ready for a fight."

I shook my head, "That is what the Hibernians and the Saxons would love. I will think on this. I am intrigued about these crowns of Rheged."

"What would you want them for?"

I had no real idea but the fact that my mother and my grandfather had protected them made them even more valuable in my eyes. "I would want them because they are a connection to my mother and the family I never knew."

He nodded, "A good enough reason. Come, I am intrigued too. Let us find these Saxon priests."

Erika had the two women making butter and cheese. They were jobs which needed someone to do them every day. They were also simple enough jobs once the slaves were shown what to do. Both were younger women and their hair had been cut very short. Apparently, that was what they did with younger priests. They both looked unhappy with their new situation.

"Deidra and Macha, you can stop work for a while. This is your master and he wishes to speak with you."

One of them recognised me and spat out, "You were one of the raiders. You killed the abbot!"

I remembered the anger of some of my fellows when I had been captured. I should have punished her for her reaction but I could understand her feelings. I smiled. "I need some questions answering and you two would be the best placed to answer them." The one who had recognised me was the one called Deidra and I could see from the thin slit of a smile that she would be reluctant to cooperate. Although I could get what I needed from Macha I wanted confirmation from a second source.

I put my face close to that of Deidra and spoke quietly. "You have not been harmed here. You have not been molested. Nor will you be for that is not my way but if you do not give me the answers I wish then I will sell you to the Hibernians and I know that they will enjoy two pretty girls such as you." Her widening eyes told me that she understood.

"Now three priests left the monastery with a piece of jewellery. Where were they going?" Macha's face was one of pure terror. The image of lusty Irishmen pleasuring themselves on her young body was just too much.

"They were going to the fort of Prestune. The crown was supposed to go to the monastery of St. Cuthbert."

The sagging shoulders of Deidra told me that the young girl had spoken the truth. I lifted Deidra's chin. "And where is this monastery?"

She murmured something so quiet that I could not hear. I shook her and she said, louder. "North of our monastery; the one you destroyed. It is on the coast and close to the place of the lakes. I have never been there so I do not know exactly."

"And this fort affords protection to both places?" They both nodded. "Good then carry on with your work and I will not sell you. Work hard and I may even find you, good husbands."

Prince Butar and I left the dairy and he said, "I will return home. When Jarl Harald is back on the island I will convene a meeting of the jarls. This grievance should be heard in public and in a calm manner. If Jarl Harald is ambitious then I do not wish him to use this opportunity to start a war."

"I will do whatever you wish."

"I know and you have an old wise head on those broad young shoulders."

I went into the house and played with Arturus for a while. He was still in the habit of taking a nap and when he did I took the opportunity of seeking out Scanlan and Aiden. Amazingly they were still with

Bjorn. The armour looked perfect and my sword shone. The two of them looked as though they had been bathing in charcoal but their white teeth grinned through their blackened lips.

Bjorn nodded, "They are good workers. I have told young Aiden that if he wishes to learn how to smith I will teach him. It is as good a skill as that of a warrior."

"I know." I looked at Aiden, "Would you like that?"

"Only when I am not serving you, my lord."

"And that is a good answer. Come the three of us will bathe. You need to become clean again and I need the sea to bring me peace."

The invigorating sea did indeed make me calm and peaceful. It also washed away the last of the blood and the salt from the past few days. As we made our way back to my hall I felt a new man.

Erika greeted me. "The Ulfheonar wish you to eat with them in the warrior hall this night." She was a wise woman and could see that I was torn. My men would not request this unless it was important and yet it was my first meal with my family. She shook her head, "Go but just eat. I do not want you falling down drunk."

I felt indignant. I was always the Ulfheonar who was sober enough to put the others to bed but I knew what she meant. I kissed her. "If our daughter is half as wise as her mother…"

The hall was filled that night, not just with Ulfheonar but every male warrior in the village. Even Bjorn was there. I wondered what was at the back of it. I saw Cnut and Haaken at the head of the table with a space between them. As I walked in the hall erupted into a wall of noise as they banged their hands on the table and chanted my name. It was embarrassing.

When I reached the seat Haaken said, "You may wonder why you have been invited here, Dragon Heart, and there are a number of reasons not least the fact that Egill and Sweyn have both been hunting and actually managed to bag enough for us to feast. I fear it will not happen again in my lifetime so we thought that we ought to celebrate."

Everyone laughed at the two warriors who took the banter in good part. The food and the ale flowed but I was mindful of Erika's warning and I was careful. After the pies and the roasts, there was the usual lull while we all drank and made room for the next course. Strangely a silence descended almost as though it had been arranged that way.

Cnut stood, "Dragon Heart, we were abandoned to die in the land of the Saxons by a jarl without honour. We are your oathsworn and we have decided to teach the jarl and his cowards a lesson. We will not allow this to continue."

Everyone applauded and Cnut sat down looking very pleased with himself. I stood and smiled back at them. "This will be a fine trick if you can manage it."

Poor Cnut looked confused, "What do you mean?"

"Have you learned to walk on water?"

"Well no."

"Then how do you propose to get to Wales which is where Jarl Harald is at present raiding?" The whole room deflated. I had seen this before where warriors whip themselves up into a blood frenzy. Had Jarl Harald not been in Wales they would have stormed over to his settlement and a blood bath would have ensued. "Thank you, Cnut, and the rest of you but I can still make my own decisions. I will hear what Jarl Harald has to say. He is a jarl and deserves the opportunity to speak and explain his actions. I would do no less for any of you."

I heard Haaken shout, "He has no answer!"

"Mind reading now old friend, eh?" He subsided. "Prince Butar will convene a meeting of the jarls and we will ask for an explanation. Then and only then will I make my decision but I am more than capable of fighting my own battles."

They all sank into their seats and looked as sad as could be. "However, I can tell you that as soon as this matter is resolved then I intend to raid a monastery in Northumbria. It promises great treasure. I would prefer to take all of you so don't take it into your heads to do something you will regret."

That brightened them up and when the next course was brought they all became their old selves. Cnut and Haaken were intrigued. "Is this a different monastery?"

"It is and I have discovered that there is more treasure where the crown came from," I told them of my mother's connection and what I had found from the priests.

"This is the work of the sisters again. They are spinning their threads."

I nodded. "And now I see that the finding of the crown was as important as lightning striking my sword. There are higher forces at work."

I spent the next few days working with Scanlan and Snorri. They had both improved in the past weeks and were well on the way to becoming warriors. Poor Aiden watched wistfully from the side. He had enjoyed working with Scanlan in the forge and now he was excluded.

A messenger came from Prince Butar; Jarl Harald had returned and I was summoned to Duboglassio. Cnut and Haaken insisted upon coming with me. In fact, all of the Ulfheonar wished to attend but I forbade all

110

but Cnut and Haaken. "I do not want to be responsible for destroying this island. I promise I will do all that I need to do."

They were satisfied that I was taking two comrades but I saw them all sharpening weapons at the forge. There was much anger.

We took ponies to make the journey quicker. I was pleased to see that there were many more families farming along the road to Duboglassio. I did not know them all but occasionally I would recognise the face of someone who had once lived in one of the villages. This was truly a perfect place for us and I thanked all the gods again for directing us here. I was quiet and did not speak much with my friends because I was thinking of Rheged. My mother had been taken not far from where we rode. It was close enough to be there in a morning by boat. Her journey had been a circle and I knew that it was not an accident. It had happened for a reason and that reason was to bring me here. The question was, what was I to do now that I had returned? Was I to complete the circle and return to the land south of the Dee? Or was the circle to take me back to the land of Rheged in the north? I realised that I had never set foot in that land although I had seen it many times as I sailed up and down the coast.

As soon as we reached the town we were whisked to Prince Butar's Hall. He and Olaf greeted me with huge smiles. "It is good to see you again."

"I thought we would have been staying in the warrior hall."

Prince Butar and Olaf exchanged a guilty look. "No, that will be too crowded and besides you are family."

I shook my head, "Cnut and Haaken are not family. You want me here because you do not trust me."

"That is not true. You have given your word but I wish to avoid bloodshed before we meet and there is enough bad feeling as it is." His face pleaded with me. "Please, do this for my sake and the memory of your mother."

"Very well." We took our weapons into the large room used by the guards for the hall. We knew the others well and had fought alongside them. All of them were vitriolic in their condemnation of Jarl Harald. I still could not fathom his motives but, if what my stepfather had said was true, then he was building up his war band and there had to be a reason for that. You needed to be either wealthy or successful to have a large retinue and Jarl Harald was neither. Then I thought back to the other raids we had been on; he had always stayed on the island to protect it. It was only latterly that he had tried to emulate Erik and me. A glimmer of an idea crept into my mind. Perhaps I did know what motivated the jarl.

The meeting was held in the area Prince Butar used for eating. Each jarl was allowed two men to advise him. I sat between Cnut and Haaken. Erik and his two warriors were on the left of me and Prince Butar to the right. Olaf was next to him so that there was a space for Jarl Harald. He was late. The rest of us chatted. We were all old comrades and I had fought alongside all of the men in the room. We were comfortable in each other's company. I had been friendly with Jarl Harald but now I remembered things which jarred. He always seemed to be a little distant with me. I thought about him in battle. I had not seen him draw his sword at the monastery. This was a puzzle but slowly the pieces were dropping into place.

When they finally did arrive, he had with him two warriors I did not recognise. They had not been on the monastery raid. Both scowled at the assembled jarls and oathsworn. Jarl Harald assiduously avoided looking in my direction. I watched him carefully.

Prince Butar stood. "We are gathered here today so that certain issues can be resolved." Every eye was on Harald who seemed distracted. Prince Butar was becoming annoyed; I could see it in his stance and hear it in his voice. "Jarl Harald you said that when you left after the last raid that Dragon Heart and his two companions were lost."

"Why is he here? He is not a jarl. And why does he have the ridiculous title of Dragon Heart? He is Garth the son of a slave."

If he had wanted to light a fire in the room he could not have chosen a better means. Everyone else was on his feet clamouring and shouting. I saw a sly look exchanged between Jarl Harald and his two companions. My fears were now confirmed; I knew exactly what he was doing and I remained silent.

Eventually, my step father restored order. "Dragon Heart is here because he is a jarl in all but name. I offered him the title but he said he was not ready. Answer the question."

He shrugged, "I waited."

I felt Cnut move forward and I restrained him. I stood and looked him directly in the eye. "You lie."

I could see from the triumphant look in his eyes that he thought he had won. He had not. I knew he wanted to appear to be the one transgressed against. "There is only one way to settle this. Combat to the death."

My stepfather and the others smiled. They did not know what I did; the jarl would not be fighting. I had never seen him fight. I had never seen him lead. One of the two mercenaries next to him would be the one to fight me and when I was dead the jarl would claim Hrams-a. He would own half of the settlements and, with a larger army, would take over Man. I did not know how long he had been planning it. I suspected not long for it was only after the failed Hibernian raid that he changed. A horrible thought entered my head. I hid it in the dark recesses. I needed all of my concentration now.

"And of course, Jarl Harald, because I am not a jarl then you cannot fight me. You will nominate a champion." The smile was wiped from his face and a scowl appeared. I had spoiled his surprise. "And of course, it will be one of these two animals you have brought with you." That really angered them and I saw their faces fill with hate.

Prince Butar looked at me as though I was a witch. Then he looked back at Jarl Harald. "Is this true?"

"That I will not fight with him because he was a slave who should never have been made a warrior? The answer is yes. And I have the right to do so. Of course, he can forfeit, leave the island and I will have the settlement you so generously gave him."

The room erupted again. I took the opportunity of speaking to Cnut and Haaken. "Keep your eyes on those two. I do not trust them."

Cnut said, "I have seen them before." He paused, "They were with Tadgh in Hibernia."

I looked over and saw that he was right. I did recognise them and the thought I had had before reappeared; Tadgh was at the back of this. He must have met with the jarl when he raided Hibernia. Now I could see the change in Harald. Tadgh had always been able to get others to do his work for him.

The prince regained silence. He stood and glowered at the warriors around the table. When it was calm again he said, "And if I do not agree to this…"

"Then perhaps it is time for a new leader."

I could see men going for their swords. I stood and shouted, "Enough! I will fight with whichever of these animals the jarl wishes me to but when I kill him jarl, what then?"

I could see that the thought had not crossed his mind. He had been persuaded that Tadgh's man would kill me. "Why I…"

"Let me explain it a little better than the snake Tadgh did. He told you that if I lost you would have Hrams-a. So, if you lose…"

"I won't."

"If you lose?"

"Then I will leave Man for it will either be my island or I will have nothing to do with it." Jarl Harald was not the cleverest of men and Tadgh's arguments had supposed that we would have begun fighting already. I knew that the next hours would be the most dangerous for me and my people.

I was happy and I smiled. It was out in the open now. I knew what I would have to do. If I won then Jarl Harald would leave and we would be safe from internal treachery. I would have to win or my family and everyone that I loved would lose their homes and possibly their lives. I was fighting for Man.

Chapter 14

Prince Butar came to me while the area for the combat was being cleared. Cnut and Haaken were with him. "Let me make you a jarl now, my son. Harald is no fighter."

"I know which is why I must defeat his champion. Harald will lose face with his men and we will achieve the same object. Harald is working for Tadgh."

I had surprised my step father. "How do you know?"

"We recognised the two warriors he has with him. They were in Hibernia." I turned to Haaken. "Get back to Hrams-a and bring *'Wolf'* and a crew." I saw the question rising in his throat. "I think that Harald or Tadgh, or both will try a surprise attack here. They have the leaders of the island all together without their warbands and if we were killed…" I let him finish the sentence in his head.

"I will return quickly and I will send our people to the hill."

I thanked the gods for sending me Dargh. He and his warriors would protect my family. Jarl Erik joined us and I could see that he was fuming too. "What a treacherous snake and to think I sailed with him."

Prince Butar told him our news and that annoyed him even more. "I will send for my ship and men too."

"I would leave them where they are for the other trick may be to attack our homes while we are here. If they come they will come by sea and my ship can trap them. Besides we have the best warriors here already." I pointed to Olaf who was storming around with his two oathsworn. Olaf was old fashioned and this treachery was beyond his comprehension. Jarl Harald had broken his oath and there was no punishment strong enough for that.

He came over to us. "When you have killed his man, make sure you kill him too. He has no honour and does not deserve to live." I nodded and he put his gnarled old arm around me. "Ragnar will watch over you. The gods will not allow you to die." I hoped he was right but I knew how precocious and unpredictable they could be.

Cnut and I went to my room to don my armour and weapons. He smiled as the byrnie slipped over my shoulders. "It is lucky you had this cleaned and repaired. And you had *Ragnar's Spirit* sharpened. Tell me you did not know of this?"

"I knew, or perhaps felt, that something was wrong but I did not know what it was."

Cnut rummaged around in my war gear and brought out a sheepskin we used to protect my sword. He ripped it in two and then stuffed each piece under my mail shirt and over my shoulders. "What is this for?"

"He is bigger than you and he has a skeggox with a spike. It will take the force of a blow and yet will not weigh you down. Do not underestimate this animal. He has a cunning look about him. I did as you asked and watched the two of them. They are planning something."

"You mean a trick like they pulled when I fought Tadgh?"

"It could be but they know we will be watching for that. Watch his eyes and remember he has two hands."

I nodded and stuffed a seax down each of my leggings. My shield had been repaired and strengthened but this would be the first combat I had used it since it had been damaged. This would be a sterner test than I might have planned for it. Finally, Cnut placed my helmet and mail cowl over my head. I touched the wolf token at my neck. Now that I knew of its history it was an even more powerful symbol of protection. I came from a line of wolf warriors. The Saxons had a word for this, *wyrd*.

We left the hall and walked out into the sunlight. The warriors and jarls were in a circle. I had learned the name of the warrior I was to fight, it was Tucsem and he was waiting with eager anticipation. He had, like me, a well-made shield and, as well as his sword he had a skeggox which had a wicked spike where the beard should be. It looked as though he had had the weapon specially made. He would know how to use it. I had never even seen a weapon like that let alone fought someone wielding one. There would be skill needed to use such a weapon and, perhaps, he had tricks which only he knew. I would learn much this day if I survived.

As I passed Prince Butar he slapped me on the back. "You will beat him and remember your mother and my father watch over you. Be true to your heart." I moved towards my foe. Everyone was well out of range.

I adjusted the shield on my left arm and I turned my sword in my hand; the balance was perfect and it felt right. Cnut had been correct; this man was a hand span taller than I was and a little broader. He could strike from further away. His skeggox was also longer. I would have to find a way to get inside his swing. It was then that I saw his gloves. Not only were they mailed, they had spikes on the knuckles. His hands would be deadly weapons too. As I approached, I looked to where the second warrior was. He was directly behind his friend but, more importantly, closer to the gate. He would have to wait until the combat was over and either I would be dead or able to do something about it. His position was not an accident. Jarl Harald stood close to him.

Tucsem grunted and then grinned at me. He had many teeth missing and his mouth looked like a mountain cavern. "I will enjoy killing you, little man. Jarl Harald has promised me your pretty little wife. She will soon find what it is to have a real man between her legs."

I knew that he was trying to provoke me. Even if he did kill me he would never have my wife. The Ulfheonar would avenge me. "Why? It is well known that those who follow Tadgh prefer the company of a little boy's arse."

My barb proved more effective than his. I also had confirmed that Tadgh had sent him. He moved deceptively quickly for a big man. He swung overhand with his spiked axe and, had I not spun away, my helmet and head would have been in two parts. As I turned around I saw that his swing had been so powerful that the blade was in the hard ground. As he pulled at it I slashed at the back of his leg and saw my sword come away red.

He screamed in pain and turned to face me. "You will find out what kind of man I am when this spike meets your body."

He had turned the weapon around and he swung it in a flat horizontal arc. The spike almost tore my shield from my arm. If I had not held it as tightly as I did I would have lost my shield. He did not give me the chance to recover and he tried to punch me with his own shield. Instead of standing up to him I allowed myself to be turned around and I let him close with me. His face appeared just above my left shoulder. I pulled my head back and butted him in the face. The force was so great that his nasal bent as his nose erupted in a mess of blood and cartilage. He was forced to step back.

I went on the offensive. I feinted with my sword and when he put his shield up I punched with the boss of my shield. I stamped down on the foot of his injured leg and he had to step back again. All the time he was moving backwards he could not swing his deadly weapon. I punched with the hilt of my sword and heard him wince. He showed his cunning by twisting and leaving his foot before him. I tumbled over it. I was going to fall anyway and so I rolled. It was as well that I did. Had I just fallen then his spike would have impaled my leg. He swung it as I dropped. As it was I was helpless on the ground and he roared towards me. I swung my sword along the floor and he was forced to jump. I took the opportunity of getting to my feet. That is harder to do in mail armour than one might imagine and he closed the gap and smashed his axe down on to my shield. It was such a mighty blow that my arm was numbed. I was not even sure if it wasn't broken. I stepped back to get my breath and to work out my next move.

I could see that his nose and mouth were still bleeding but the puddles on the ground came from the wound to the leg. I needed him even more tired and to lose even more blood. I feinted and stepped away. I moved quickly to the right as he swung his axe. I darted in with my blade and stabbed at his knee and he had to jump back. All the time the blood oozed from the first wound. I could see that he was desperate to finish this before he tired. I was tiring too but I did not have a bleeding wound to my leg. The strap would hold the shield in place despite my damaged arm.

He swung his axe again in a mighty arc. He aimed to split me in two. Instead of countering with my shield I swung my blade. I had fast hands and this time it paid off. I caught the haft half way down. Not only did it stop the axe from hitting me it also gouged a slice from the ash shaft. For the first time, I saw fear in his face. He stepped back and I swung my sword in an arc towards his middle. He grinned as he stepped back I saw it in his eyes; he thought I had made a mistake and his axe came crashing down towards me. I could barely feel my arm and so I put my shoulder behind the shield. The axe head struck the shield but my shoulder with the sheepskin padding took the blow and not my arm. The weakened shaft shattered. The head dropped to the floor and I heard my supporters cheer. He grabbed his own sword. We were now on an equal footing. We both had swords and if he was a good swordsman he would have used that first.

He was moving much slower now but I could hardly hold up my shield. Each movement sent waves of pain through my left arm. He saw that and quickly swung overhand. I was not fast enough and the sword smashed down on to the rim of my shield and my shoulder. I heard the mail rings crack and break. I put that from my mind as I slashed sideways and struck his already injured leg just above the knee. He crumpled to one knee and I hacked down at his neck. He brought the shield up but not quite quickly enough and the edge went through his mail and into his left arm.

He limped backwards. He was now desperate to keep me away from his left side. I saw that and I feinted to his shield side and when he turned to meet the blow I spun all the way around and *Ragnar's Spirit* sliced through his mail and into his spine. His lifeless body fell in a heap at my feet. Even with the cheers ringing around my ears I raced towards the gate. Tucsem's companion and Jarl Harald were racing for the gate. "Stop them!"

Warriors went to grab weapons but the two men lifted the bar on the gate. Harald showed himself to be the coward that I knew. He raced out of the gate towards the rest of his warriors who were emerging from his ship. I took in that the harbour guards lay dead but that they had briefly halted Harald's men. I stabbed down at Tucsem's companion. He fell to the floor. "Bar the gate!"

Cnut and Olaf were right behind me and they managed to secure the gate as the warriors hurled themselves bodily at it. I heard Prince Butar shout, "To the walls!" Then he was at my side. "That was bravely done."

I nodded, "There are two ships out there and I think that I saw Tadgh."

He nodded, "And we have but forty warriors here."

"We just need to hold out until Haaken returns. Then we can attack them."

I heard a gurgle next to me and saw Cnut pulling his sword from the neck of Tucsem's companion. "And that was too kind of me. I should have let him bleed out." He looked at my mail. "You have split the rings."

"Aye but your sheepskin protected me. I cannot feel this arm though."

"You have fought enough. Let us do this now."

I shook my head. "They need to see me on the walls." If Tadgh and the others thought I was dead it would give them heart and we needed them to be delayed until help could reach us.

Cnut nodded, "You are right but I will guard your side until the others arrive."

I could see Tadgh and Harald. They were both well to the rear and looked to be arguing. Their men were drawn up before the walls and I could see that there were almost a hundred of them. It was two drekar crews' warriors and big ones at that. I could see their frustration. They must have counted on two things: defeating me and then opening the gates before those inside knew what was happening. It would have been a massacre for most of those watching were without armour. I could see that the guards at the harbour had killed some of the attackers but they had merely slowed them down.

I looked up at the sun as I tried to calculate how long it would take Haaken to reach us. I guessed that he would have reached Hrams-a by now and would be dividing the warriors between the fort and the ship. I wet my finger and held it up. The wind would be in his favour so we could expect him in an hour or perhaps two. Would we have an hour?

The warriors had hacked down the mast from **"Ran"**. They intended using that as a ram. If I had had the use of my left arm I could have used my bow but I would have to rely on the dozen or so bows which were within the walls. It was woefully inadequate. Their arrows bounced off mail, helmets and shields. These were not archers; they were warriors using bows. The renegade warriors made a wall with their shields. The mast was not heavy and they could easily manage both. One or two warriors pitched and fell as arrows struck them but it did not slow them down.

Jarl Erik saw the danger. "Oathsworn! To me!" With his twelve brothers in arms, he descended to form a welcoming wall of warriors behind the gate. They would break it down. We knew that. Our task was to thin them out. The rest hurled rocks down on the men as they swung their improvised ram. I took one of the spears which were stacked by the gate and hurled it to strike a warrior between the shoulder and neck. He fell, spurting blood. I hit the next one in the arm and then they raised their shields. It meant they could not see before them but they knew what was there; a gate. I heard a crack as the bar holding the gate began to weaken.

"Come Cnut, they know where I am now. Let us go and give aid to Jarl Erik."

Prince Butar counselled, "Keep him to the rear Cnut. I can see that he is still injured."

If I just watched and they were all killed then I would die anyway. I was injured but so long as I wielded my blade I would fight. I would have to rely on my sword skills and not my shield. Jarl Erik grinned when he saw me, "We are safe now boys, we have Dragon Heart with us. Take care, brother, I would not be the one to tell my sister that she is a widow."

We stood so that I was on the extreme right of the line. My weaker shield arm would be protected somewhat by Cnut. We saw the bar crack a little more and the heavy gates flew open. The mast came through and the warriors at the front lost their balance and fell at the feet of Erik and his oathsworn. The first six died wriggling on the ground as they were skewered from above. As the others tried to clamber through the gap and over the dead they exposed themselves to our swords from underneath. It could not last for they outnumbered us but it delayed them until I heard someone shouting to remove the mast. The mast had been our ally; it was slippery with blood and made their footing hazardous. We stepped forwards into the gap which had been the gate. We just fitted from wall to wall.

When the warriors saw that I was in the front line they charged at me. Cnut and Sweyn Ulfsson, one of Erik's oathsworn, hacked and chopped at the spears as they were thrust at my face and then they despatched the weaponless warriors. One spear actually made it to my helmet but the mail and the metal cowl defeated it. I sensed a movement below me and saw a warrior with a dagger trying to crawl closer to us. I knew not if he was wounded but he was dead when I impaled his head with my sword.

Someone on the opposing side began to use their head and I heard the order for a wedge. They would burst through our perilously thin line. Prince Butar must have heard the order too for he shouted for those within to bolster our line. I felt the reassuring presence of a shield behind me and a spear appeared between Cnut and me.

It was my brother in law, Jarl Erik, who would be the point of their attack for he was in the middle. The warrior who led them had a weapon like the one wielded by Tucsem. I hoped that Erik's shield was sound. I knew the power of that weapon. The bodies before the gate prevented them from running at us which helped but the impact was still a shock. I saw the skeggox come overhand towards Erik's head. I hoped he would get his shield up but the oathsworn next to Erik chopped across with his sword and severed the arm which threatened to end Erik's life. Erik finished the warrior off and then I had no time to be a spectator. I angled my shield to protect both Cnut and myself and I braced myself against the gate post and the man behind. Holding *Ragnar's Spirit* before me I watched as the first warrior ran straight at me. His sword was aimed at my head. I ducked slightly and twisted my head to one side but I never took my eye from him. He impaled himself on my sword. He hung there for the briefest of moments, his lifeless eyes staring accusingly at me before the weight of his body dragged it from my blade. An axe came towards Cnut and my arm could not lift the shield to protect him. I swung my sword overhand and I heard the bones crunch as it sliced through his arm. The warrior who stood next to him took advantage and stabbed at my middle with his spear. I felt it tear the links and then it became entangled in the leather and woollen garment I wore beneath it. I twisted my sword as I brought it back and it sliced across his unprotected throat.

There was a slight respite as they pulled back to reorganise their ranks. I saw that three of Erik's oathsworn were dead and the men who stood in their stead had no mail. We were about to be severely tested. The next attack would, in all likelihood, succeed and they would break through us.

Suddenly I heard a shout from the rear of their wedge and then Prince Butar shouted down, "It is *'Wolf'*, the Ulfheonar are here!"

I knew that Harald would know how few men we had but he would not know how many other warriors were aboard my threttanessa. When we heard the order to withdraw then we knew we had won. Jarl Erik's blood was up; he had lost close friends. "Slaughter them!"

We lurched forwards after them. They were trying to turn and flee at the same time. It was almost impossible. Their tight formation worked against them and we found unprotected backs and fallen men to slaughter. It did, however, delay us and I could see the warriors pouring aboard the two drekar. They both dwarfed *'Wolf'*; Haaken would be able to do little about their escape. He did the next best thing; he placed his ship so that they had to pass by the length of his boat to escape. He had every warrior loosing arrows as the two ships tried to pass him and escape. They managed to do so but I knew that they would have had many casualties on board.

There was no cheering for we had lost too many good men. I left Erik and his men to despatch the wounded. I returned to the settlement. My arm was in agony. Cnut was close behind me and he helped me off with my shield. Pulling my byrnie off was excruciating and when that was done we saw that the arm was purple and angry. "That, my friend, is broken. Luckily it looks as though that man mountain did you a favour and gave you a clean break and no broken skin. I will get a splint for you. Sit over there and do not move it."

I gave him a weak smile. "I couldn't if I tried."

Prince Butar sought me out. I could see the worried look on his face. When he saw my arm he just said, "Broken?" I nodded. "You were lucky. I am sorry about Jarl Harald. That was a misjudgement on my part. I was so desperate to have allies on the island that I never questioned what drove the man." He shook his head. "I was blind."

"Not so. It is only now that I can remember that he never led his men and always remained at the rear of any attack. Besides he may have just been a weak leader had he not met Tadgh. That is the sisters at work."

"You are right."

Cnut arrived with two clean pieces of timber. "I measured them against my arm." He put a piece of wood between my teeth. "Hold his shoulders, Prince Butar; I will have to make sure the ends of the bone are together before I tie it." He carefully and gently put four linen strips under my arm. I almost screamed when he did that but I knew that the next pain would be worse. I closed my eyes and prepared as he placed the two pieces of wood on top of the linen and next to my arm without actually touching the purple mess. I heard him say sadly, "This will hurt." And before the words were out he gripped my arm and moved the ends of the broken bones slightly until they married. The pain was such as I have never borne before. If I hadn't had the stick in my mouth I would have screamed loud enough to be heard in Hibernia.

I opened my eyes and saw that Haaken and the Ulfheonar were there watching. Cnut began to tie the linen and then snapped, "Don't stand there like drips in a summer shower, tie the other strips tightly." Haaken did as he was ordered. "Keep that still." He took out another piece of linen which he tied around my neck and then slipped under the arm to support it. The sling made it easier. "You will have to avoid moving it and I would imagine that sleeping will be hard. But you are, at least, still alive."

I reflected that I had emerged better than I might have hoped.

Haaken said, "Where will they go?"

Prince Butar stood and looked to the west. "I would imagine they will head for his settlement first."

Jarl Erik had arrived, the blood still clinging to his armour and sword. "He cannot stay there."

"No, but he will want to take as much as he can."

"Then let us stop him. We can be over to the other side of the island in less than a couple of hours. We can stop him taking his animals for a start. I want to punish the treacherous bastard."

The prince nodded. "Take your men and the Ulfheonar. You need speed."

After they had gone the prince said. "And you can get to bed. You need rest." I shook my head. "I need to be with my wife and my family."

"I can understand that but a journey on a pony would kill you. If you insist upon going then you will go in a fishing boat. The journey will be easier."

I did not argue. He disappeared and when he returned he nodded. "You are a fool but I can understand why you need to see your family."

The prince led me to the harbour where four of his men waited. They were fishermen and not warriors. "I will send your armour by cart. I assume you will want your sword?"

I nodded and gave a weak smile, "I may not need it but I will feel safer with it close to hand." The men were amazingly gentle as they helped me aboard. Even so, every jar and knock sent waves of pain coursing through my body. My stepfather was right. It was gentler, so gentle in fact that I fell asleep. I was awoken by Erika kissing me, "Now you will stay here until you are fully healed. Your warrior days are over until you are fit once more."

Chapter 15

I was restricted to my bed and Scanlan stood guard to make sure that I did not move. Cnut was right; the pain at night stopped me sleeping for the first four nights. It took draughts of a distilled liquor which Seara made to help me to sleep.

The Ulfheonar returned after two days. They were in high spirits. Haaken and Cnut sat and told me of their journey to Harald's lair. They had caught some of his people driving his animals west. Those settlers had swiftly changed allegiance. The families had not managed to evacuate all of their goods and belongings. Harald had been so confident that his plan would succeed, he had failed to think of the consequences of failure. They would be able to start a new life but it would be without the bare necessities of life. Jarl Erik took over the settlement and immediately began to fortify it. We were learning that the greatest danger to us came not from Saxons or Hibernians but our own people.

Once I found that I could sleep my life became tolerable again. I persuaded Erika to allow me to walk around Hrams-a and to speak with people. There was a buzz about the place. I had defeated a giant. His stature grew with the telling of the story. I knew who to blame for that, Cnut. He had told Haaken who had written a saga which made me sound like Thor himself. No matter how much I protested they merely thought I was being modest. It made them feel better about the treachery. We had emerged with honour and the goods which Harald Two Face, as he was now known, had left behind.

Bjorn was repairing my armour while Snorri and Scanlan repaired my shield. As autumn approached it was obvious that I would not be raiding again this year. They all had plenty of time to make them not only good but better than they had been. I had planned a raid to recover the rest of the jewels of Rheged but I knew that would have to wait. I could not inflict a one-armed leader on my men. We were too few to carry passengers. Instead, we traded. We had much metal from the battle and much treasure from Harald's lair. Haaken and Cnut went with Olaf to Frankia to buy more sword blanks. They returned with Rolf, Erik Redhead and Ham the Silent. The count had returned to Cologne and their services were no longer required. They were three new men who stepped from my drekar. They were clean, well armed and each had a short byrnie. They were nothing like the vagabonds we had met in the alehouse in Cologne.

When he saw me nodding in approval Rolf gave a half bow, "Sigismund was most appreciative of our efforts and rewarded us well."

"Did you not wish to stay?"

"We are warriors and not nursemaids; besides we heard stories of you when we walked Sigurd to the shops and back. You are the champion all wish to defeat. You have slain giants even when fighting with one arm. Even when you fight dishonourable treacherous men you win. We would serve you." He looked worried, "You did offer to take us did you not?"

"Of course." I pointed to the warrior hall, "There is your new home."

I knew that they would, eventually, become Ulfheonar but I also knew that we needed warriors. The Ulfheonar had special skills but we needed warriors who could protect our homes and help us to raid. Jarl Erik had raided the Saxons again to steal their grain. Although he had been successful he had lost more men than we could afford to lose. Warriors, especially good ones, were at a premium.

When winter finally came we were comfortable with plenty of food and security behind our newly refurbished walls. We had lost men but we had stocked up with what we needed to survive the winter. The winter would be a time of building, training and planning. Scanlan and Snorri were almost ready to become warriors. We were assimilating the new warriors and I had planned how I would recover the rest of the treasure of Rheged.

Just before the first frosts, Erika gave birth to our daughter, Kara. Erika gave her the name. "She is pure and I can see greatness in her already."

I smiled, "I am just pleased that she has the right number of everything; fingers eyes, feet..."

Erika gave me an irritated shake of the head, "Men!"

It meant that I grew closer to Arturus. Aiden had proved to be the perfect friend and guard for Arturus. He watched over him as though he was a precious object. He proved to be patience personified and would play with Arturus long after everyone else had thought of a reason to be elsewhere. My arm healed slowly which proved to be a good thing. It meant I could not use it. I watched Aiden and Arturus and I watched Snorri spar with Scanlan. I could not interfere, as I know I would have done had I been whole. I could not show them how it was done. I had to use words to make them better swordsman and I had to listen to my son speaking to understand what he meant. Perhaps the injury was sent by the gods to make me a better warrior and a good father. It worked.

My arm began to itch when the weather turned wet and windy. Erika and Cnut agreed that it was a good sign but both were also in agreement that I should not use the arm. Instead, I had been using my right arm regularly and I had fought practice bouts with Haaken and Cnut. Although I always won I suspect it was because they went easy on me. I had had to learn to be more skilful with the blade and that was no bad thing either.

By the time the winter nights began to shorten, not by much but enough to let us know that the worst would be over, we were planning my expedition to the land of Rheged. My men had built another drekar. I had become quite rich with the trades I had made and we needed a second. We had enough warriors now to man two of them. I would not necessarily take both of them for it would be useful to leave one patrolling the island and watching for enemies. We had just finished the sea trials when a storm wracked ship limped into Hrams-a. It was a fellow Viking from Orkney. He and his men had been caught in a storm far to the south of us and lost half of their oars. The wind had almost driven them on to the shores of Hibernia. It would have meant a savage end had they not managed to turn the ship and find Man.

The captain was Gudrun Sweynson and he had sailed from Orkney to Frankia to trade. We had all been surprised at that and were unable to hide our feelings. You did not travel that distance until it was summer and the weather was kinder. Gudrun was a rough old warrior and I liked him; he laughed. "I know. You would think when you get to my age you would know not to travel those seas in winter but we had a good year and kept harvesting until the nights became longer. The journey was perilous and we found ourselves stuck in Frankia when the river froze over. Still, we made a good trade and your port is a haven for traders such as us."

"Aren't there any places where our people offer sanctuary to fellows such as you?"

He spat into the fire in the warrior hall. I was glad I had not taken him home, Erika disapproved of such things. "You would think so, wouldn't you? No, some of them are worse than others. There is a nest of vipers just south of the river which leads to Frankia and there is a large band of pirates there who prey on all ships; even those of their fellows. They are treacherous and every warrior I have met curses Tadgh and Harald Two Face."

A chill crept over me and I saw that Cnut and Haaken were equally concerned. "This Tadgh, does he have a limp?"

"Aye, he does. He has the look of a Saxon about him." He paused, "Why? Do you know him? Is he a friend of yours?"

When we all burst out laughing he looked offended. I held my hand up. "Please take no offence. I have fought with both of them and it was me who made him lame." Haaken then told the story of our encounters.

Afterwards, Gudrun shook his head. "The Weird Sisters have been spinning, have they not. I can see now that my coming was necessary. You will go after him?"

"I will, but not yet. I have something else to do first but you have now given me another reason to find their lair and end this once and for all."

The sea trials for my new ship were fraught with difficulties. We had named her *"Bear"* and she proved to be as bad tempered as a bear woken from a winter sleep. It took us many days to balance her correctly and to rig her sail. The weather did not help and there were gales which curtailed trials and huge seas which stopped us sailing altogether.

Olaf the Toothless had chuckled, "This will be a good drekar. Already you know how she will perform in every sea and she has told you of her problems now. The gods smile on you, Dragon Heart. Do not worry she was just not ready to be born. Now she is."

I was not so sure but I put the thought from my mind. Having fitted her out I needed to captain and crew her. I sat on the beach with Cnut and Haaken watching as the carpenter fitted her dragon prow. "It is a fine ship."

I nodded, "You are right Haaken. Would you like to captain her?"

He laughed, "That is what I like about you, Dragon Heart, you do not beat about the bush. I am honoured but no, I am Ulfheonar and I sail with you."

Cnut shook his head while smiling, "And do not ask me. I suspect that all of the Ulfheonar feel the same."

"Then whom do I choose? The other warriors I have are young and lack the experience we need."

Haaken chewed on a piece of grass and watched as *"Bear"* was finally finished and the dragon head, painted green and red shone in the late afternoon sunlight. "There is always Rolf. Since he has arrived he has shown himself to be a good leader and the men like him. He is older than most of us."

I had already thought of Rolf but wondered if some of the warriors who had been with me for some time might take offence at being commanded by a new comer. I had hoped for an Ulfheonar but I was touched that they would all wish to take a bench with me.

Cnut convinced me, "Ask him. He may not want to or be able to."

And so, I sought out Rolf. That evening I took him to the new ship. I gave him no reason save the opportunity to view her.

"What do you think of her, Rolf?"

"I like small ships. They are nimbler and the crew get on better. They are easier to balance. Aye, she is a good vessel."

"You had one yourself, did you?"

"My first ship. We lost her in a battle with Frisian pirates and then I sailed in a big ship such as Prince Butar's. It was a fine ship but I preferred my first. It must be like a first love. You may have other women but you never forget your first."

"Would you be able to captain her for me?"

He looked genuinely shocked. "But you barely know me. Suppose I should turn out like the one known as Harald Two Face?"

I smiled but it was a smile without warmth. "Then you would share the same fate as him and I would hunt you down and kill you."

He knelt, "I swear I will serve you unto death."

"Thank you and I believe that you will keep your word. As captain, you get five shares and the crew one each. I assume Erik and Ham will serve with you?"

"Aye, they are as keen as I am to get back to what we do best."

"I do not think that we can crew her completely yet but you should have sixteen or eighteen warriors."

"You will not split the men equally between the two boats?" It was a question without a hidden meaning.

"The Ulfheonar are all sworn brothers." I shrugged, "I offered *"Bear"* to them but they declined. They would rather serve on my ship."

"It is what I have heard. Men wish to follow you. I can see why."

By the time the first spring flowers were blooming on the hillside we were ready. Dargh and his ten men were ready to defend should a raider come and we had another ten men who worked in the village. Men like Bjorn would protect my family. All those who toiled in the village were also warriors who could fight any raider who was foolish enough to chance his arm at Hrams-a. Now that Jarl Erik held the western side, Olaf the south and Prince Butar the east, we were well protected and beacons would be lit if anyone came again. We had learned our lesson the hard way, with the lives of those we loved. We would not be found wanting a third time.

Snorri and Aiden were to accompany me but I left Scanlan at home. Maewe was with child and I knew that she would wish him to be close by. I gave him my old shield and a spare seax. "You have earned this trust. Watch over our families."

He knelt and touched the scabbard of *Ragnar's Spirit*. "I will my lord."

It was strange the way everyone but me wanted me to be a lord. I was not ready and I would only accept the title when I felt that I was ready.

We left Hrams-a under cloudy, damp skies, but the winds were propitious and that was more important. We did not rush across the water. Rolf and his crew were smaller in number and not used to their ship. I would rather we all reached our destination together than piecemeal.

The rain became heavier and the boys had to bail continuously to keep the rower's feet dry. When Rolf's ship began to drop astern I ordered the oars stacked and set all of the men to bailing. Gradually *"Bear"* drew closer. The inclement weather helped us as it hid us from prying eyes ashore. I was not sure if they had rebuilt the monastery at the estuary. If they had then we would be seen. I intended to moor in the river. According to the prisoners that was half way between the fort at Prestune and the monastery of St Cuthbert.

We reached the river in late afternoon. I saw no sign of occupation but, as soon as we touched the shore I sent Egill and Olaf to investigate. Rolf arrived soon after. "I am sorry about that my lord. The new timbers shipped a little more water than I had expected and we had to bail quite hard."

"I thought it would be something like that. I will take my crew north to the monastery. You and your crew can make good your ship but both ships need guarding. There are Saxons a few miles upstream."

Rolf looked disappointed not to be going on the raid with us but he was experienced enough to know that my orders made sense. Egill and Olaf came back down the slope. "There is no one there; just the gnawed bones of the dead."

I wondered why they had not buried their dead. The Christians liked to honour their dead in that way. "We will be back tomorrow. I would place a sentry on the hill and he can give you warning." Rolf raised his arm in acknowledgement. I suspect he would have done that anyway but, until I knew the man better, I would continue to make things explicit.

Snorri was excited to be coming but his face dropped when I placed him at the rear of the column of warriors. I didn't really have time to explain but it was his first raid and so I did. "We are Ulfheonar and we are good at what we do. You are not even a warrior yet. When you can track and trail as well as any of these then you can lead until then you follow and make sure that we leave little sign of our passing."

He looked contrite, "Yes Dragon Heart."

Haaken led the way. He had a nose for finding enemies. The trail we followed went close to the coast. The problem was it would, occasionally, emerge from a small wood and we would be on an exposed beach. I could not see any way around it. We spied the monastery. It was on top of a small cliff surrounded by beaches. It was still early afternoon and I suspected there would be priests working in the fields and we would be spotted.

"Haaken, take half of the men and work your way north."

"How will I know when to attack?"

"Have the men hide themselves fifty paces from the walls and you will hear our cry." I would use the same plan which had been so successful so many times.

He was satisfied and he silently led the warriors off. We worked our way closer until we were just a hundred paces from the gate. We found a ditch and a hedgerow. We were invisible and yet we could see the gate through the gaps in the undergrowth. It was fortunate that we had hidden for a column of brown robed priests with farming implements trudged past our hiding place. They were, seemingly, oblivious to our presence. They all looked weary. Cnut nudged me and drew his finger across his throat. I shook my head. Although I could see what he meant, there were just ten priests and we could have slain them easily, I wanted Haaken in position. The priests had tried to escape with the jewels the last time. I did not want to give them the chance to do so again.

I heard a bell tolling within the walls and a short while later another four priests came driving some sheep before them. So far, we had only seen males. This appeared to be a different type of monastery. There might be no females here. I scanned the walls and the gate but I saw no armed guards. There were just priests who appeared to act as gatekeepers.

When the gates closed we knew that the priests were all within the walls. The sun was setting slowly behind us and I waved my men forward. There was no defensive ditch, just a drainage channel and it would not cause us any problems. As we moved forwards I began to wonder at the wisdom of storing such relics as crown jewels here. There was no defence unless there was something I could not see. I would tread warily. With our black cloaks and the sun setting, I knew that we would be hard to see. I noticed that there appeared to be no sentries. As we neared the walls I heard singing coming from within the walls. I knew that the followers of the White Christ did this often. Perhaps that explained the lack of sentries.

I reached the gate. I could see that it was barred from the inside but the wood on the gates was not a tight fit. I slipped a seax between the gates and began to lift the bar. It was heavy. Sweyn and Cnut saw me struggling and they helped me to push it up. Suddenly there was a crash as it fell from its resting place. We pushed the wooden gates open and shouted, "Ulfheonar!" The cry was to alert Haaken rather than announce our arrival.

Once through we could see the buildings were neatly laid out. There was a large, well lit, central building with a cross outside. That would be their church. The other buildings were evenly spaced within the stockade. Some must have been alerted by the noise for a number of priests burst from the church. One of them ran back inside as we hurried to get to them before they could escape. The ones outside grabbed the stacked farm implements from the outside wall and bravely launched themselves at us. It was foolish for they all fell to the blades of my men. We did not need to kill them but disarmed them and ensured they would not attack us again. When we reached the church, it was empty. There was another door at the far end and they had fled that way.

None had gone to any of the huts which suggested that they had treasure with them. Suddenly I heard a cry ahead of, "Ulfheonar". Haaken had arrived. When we reached the rear gate, there were three huddled bodies lying on the ground and six elderly priests looking forlornly at their comrades.

"Have you searched the bodies yet?"

Haaken nodded at his men. "They are just starting."

I saw that the oldest priest had a golden cross about his neck. I put my sword beneath his chin. "Where are the crowns of Rheged, old man? Where is the treasure you guard?"

He seemed surprised at my Saxon but he smiled, "Where you will never get it Norseman. It is safe behind the walls of the fort. They will guard it with their lives. You can do what you will with us; you will never have that treasure."

"It is not your treasure to steal, priest."

"No, it is the symbol of the pagans and so long as we have it then God will win and you pagans will perish and die."

I laughed, "You old fool. I am a young man yet I know that God always wins. The only difference between us is that you have only one god to call upon." I turned to Egill. "Tether them but do not harm them." I took the golden cross and tucked it inside my tunic."

"Nothing here, Dragon Heart."

"Let us go back to the ships then and decide what to do next."

We had collected a fine haul of precious metals and jewels. Oleg had even found himself a leg of mutton which he had tucked into his bag. I was the only one disappointed for I had wanted the jewels. I was also disturbed by the lack of religious books. Most of the monasteries seemed to spend all their time writing down the works of their White Christ for others to read. It was a mystery to me for you could just as easily tell the stories and you did not need to read to do that. This monastery appeared to be different from the others.

When we reached the boat, I ordered the priests to be tethered aboard *"Bear"*. I gathered the men around me. "It seems the real treasure is in the fort just up the river. Cnut, take three men and scout it out. We will attack at dawn." He nodded, pointed to the men he had chosen and left. I turned to the waiting Rolf. "You will leave half a dozen of your men here to watch the ships and the priests. The rest will come with us. Your warriors will get some action."

We ate and I made sure that the men who had been to the monastery rested. Rolf and his warriors were more than happy to stand a watch. I could not sleep for I was too busy wondering if I would get the treasure and if it was worth the lives of my men. This time we were going against warriors and we could not afford to be gentle. Some would die, that was inevitable.

Cnut and his scouts arrived back a few hours later. "The fort is six miles upstream. It is mainly wood but they have used some of the Roman stones to make a tower and to make the walls stronger. There is a ditch and this time it serves a purpose."

"How many men?"

They looked at each other. "It is hard to say. It was dark. We counted six sentries."

I nodded. We could take those out with arrows but the number inside worried me. Cnut saw my dilemma, "They are Saxons. They have not fought us before. They will not stand against us for long."

Haaken couldn't help adding, "And the alternative is to turn and go back to Man with our tails between our legs."

I had already made up my mind but my two friends had convinced me. We would try.

We made good time running swiftly through the flat land which ran alongside the river. We could all smell the Saxon settlement long before we saw it. I did not think that the Saxons would flee when we attacked and I did not wish to dilute my warriors. We would all go in together. They had cleared the land around the ditch but only for a distance of thirty paces or so. Our bows would strike easily at that range.

I had asked the others to scout before but now I crawled to the ditch and peered in. I needed to see what we would face and make my plans accordingly. There were no spikes and they had been careless and discarded their rubbish in the bottom. It was not as deep as it should have been. When I looked at the wall I saw that, although it was only made of wood, it was high. We would have to have two warriors lift a third on his shield. We had to clear the walls of sentries first and I knew that getting men inside would not be quick.

When I returned to the warriors I outlined my plan, "Sweyn, take eight men and silence the sentries with arrows. You need to do it at the same time and there should be no noise."

"It will be done." He gathered his men and spoke to them. One came and stood near us for there was a sentry just above us. I saw him counting. He began to draw back, still counting. Suddenly the arrow flew from his bow and the sentry put his hands to his throat before falling into the ditch.

I clapped Harald on the back and led the men forwards. Olaf and Egill held a shield for me and I stepped on to it and then sprang up to the top. I quickly looked for any sentries but they all lay dead. I put my arm over the wall and felt Olaf take hold of it. I leaned back and he began to climb up the wall. When he reached the top, he did the same for Egill while I ran to the steps. We had to take advantage of every moment of silence.

I finally reached the bottom and I was joined by Cnut and Rolf. I pointed to the warrior hall. It was a stone building and looked old enough to have been built by the Romans. That was a problem as I had no idea what the inside would look like. We had rarely been in such buildings. We would have to go in and trust to luck. A dozen other warriors joined us, including a grinning Snorri. I unsheathed my sword and hefted my shield around to my front. Waving the line forward we hurried to the door. Surprise was our greatest weapon. I held my finger to my lips. I wanted silence. A noise would only alert them. I wanted us to be as ghosts in the night.

When I reached the door, I checked that I had warriors behind me and then, throwing the door open, I stepped inside. I was struck by a wall of heat and the smell of unwashed warriors. A fire at the far end threw some illumination on the scene and I could see that there were many warriors. This was a powerful fort. Before I could do anything, a man who had been four paces away filling the night bucket saw me and shouted, "Vikings!"

His prompt action cost him his life. Even as I killed him I was moving on to the next warrior. We had no time to lose and we raced in hacking, stabbing and killing the half-dressed men who threw themselves at us furiously fighting to save their fort. More and more of my men flooded into the hall and it became a maelstrom of bloody combats. Our armour and our weapons made the difference. The Saxons were brave but they were half asleep and half dressed. Soon the hall was filled with the dead and the dying.

I looked around and saw Rolf. "Rolf, get to the gate and secure it. Haaken and Cnut come with me. The rest of you start collecting their weapons and give them a warrior's death." I saw Olaf's surprised look. "I know they are Christians and do not need it but they fought well and deserve it."

When I reached Cnut and Haaken I saw that Snorri was behind me. I was about to chastise him for disobeying orders when I saw his ashen face. "I killed two men, Dragon Heart." I then remembered that this was his first time.

"You did well, come with us."

There was another stone building close to the warrior hall. When we reached the door, I saw that it was locked. There was an axe lying nearby and I gave it to Cnut. Within a few strokes, the door was open and there, cowering behind a bed was a priest. This was a young priest, little older than Snorri. I put my sword to his throat. "Tell us where the treasure is or you die."

He almost burst into tears. He pointed to the door behind the bed. Cnut opened it, looked in and then said. "It is empty."

In a petrified voice, he stammered. "Th.. th.. there is a trap door. It is where the Romans kept their coins."

Haaken lit a candle and the two of them found the hidden handle and opened the trapdoor. They held the light and peered down. Haaken gave a whoop of joy. "There is treasure here. Come on Snorri, give me a hand."

While I watched the terrified priest the other three brought out boxes of coin and other valuables but my heart sank when I saw that there were no jewels, no crowns and nothing that was from Rheged.

"Where are the crowns? Where are the Rheged jewels?" I was not my normal calm self. I knew that I had become obsessed by these crowns and had to have them. I found I was shaking him hard. He began to weep and I could see that I had gone too far. He was terrified. I forced myself to calm down and I released him. I gave an apologetic half smile to reassure him. "I promise you shall live and I will not enslave you if you speak the truth."

He nodded, seemingly persuaded by my words. "They were taken away a week ago by the bishop and King Eardwulf's men. They took them north to the monastery at Hexham."

"How far away is it?"

"It is a hundred miles north. It is on the old Roman wall."

I could tell that he was speaking the truth. It was a blow but at least I knew that they existed and I would find a way to get there. "How many crowns are there?"

"There were five until one was taken some time ago. There is the king's crown and the crowns of the three princes. There is a mace from Byzantium and a golden Roman helmet."

I smiled; I now knew more than I had before. "Tell me about this monastery. Is it guarded and how far along the wall is it?"

"I have never been there but I think the monastery is in the big town. The monastery is half way along the wall and I think the wall is a hundred miles long." He smiled and reminded me of a puppy who has done something good and expects a treat for doing so.

"Stay here until we leave and then go. Find a new life for yourself. All the rest are dead."

"All of the warriors?"

"All of them. Thank your White Christ that Dragon Heart was in a kind mood this night."

We had plenty of time to head back to our boats for there was no one left to follow us. We had lost five warriors and we carried their bodies with us. The arms and the treasure made this a very successful raid but I tasted ashes. I did not have the treasure I wanted. My men were of a different mind. They were singing my praises as the leader who would make them the richest of warriors.

Chapter 16

The elderly priest had a smug look on his face as we sailed home. He had seen my disappointment. He knew that the jewels had been taken away. I suppose his main disappointment was that we had not been slaughtered by the fort's defenders as he had hoped and predicted.

We reached home by the middle of the next afternoon. It had taken some time to balance the boats. We did not need speed, we needed care and we did not want to capsize because of a badly loaded boat. I was just grateful that the *"Bear"* had a small crew and could carry more. There was great rejoicing at Hrams-a. We had returned quickly with much treasure and we had returned with most of the warriors.

Erika saw my disappointment and she did her best to cheer me up. She had Maewe and Seara cook me my favourite foods and went out of her way to keep me amused. As we lay in bed she asked me why I was so disappointed.

"I did not get what I wished for. The crowns are still missing."

She laughed, "No they are not. You know where they are."

"They might as well be on the moon. Hexham is in the middle of the country; the middle of Saxon country! How would we get there?"

"I did not say it was easy I just said that they were not lost. Of course, if the task is too hard for you I will understand."

I smiled, in the dark; I knew what she was doing and she was quite correct. I did know where they were. My next job was to find out how to get there. It was still early in the year. I had plenty of time to plan and to find out all that I would need to know.

"You are right, my love, now let us see if we can make a brother or sister for Arturus and Kara."

After we had divided the bounty I took stock. I was now very rich but I did not know what to buy next. Haaken and Cnut had no such worries; their money was frittered away in less time than it took to acquire it. They both bought better mail from Bjorn but the rest went on things that they ate or they drank. Snorri managed to buy a decent helmet from Bjorn. I think our blacksmith did the best out of the raid for every warrior wanted a sword or a helmet and the lucky ones, like Rolf who had a lot of money to spend, had mail byrnies made. All of this meant that they were content for a while which allowed me to consult with Olaf and Prince Butar about Hexham and how I might get there.

In the end, it was the two slaves we had captured who proved the most help. They had both adapted well to the life in Hrams-a. They were well treated by Erika and confided in Seara that their new life was, in many ways, better than their old one. Ironically, they thought that they had more freedom. They told me that we could sail up the river close to the wall and only have a forty-mile journey to get to Hexham. It was the best news I had had in a long time. My dream could still be a reality. They had heard of the monastery which was as important as the one on the other coast, Lindisfarne. It suggested that we might make a good profit from this raid even though it was the most dangerous one we had undertaken.

I met with Rolf, Cnut and Haaken to tell them what I intended. "We will sail north. The female priests tell me that the estuary is the biggest north where we acquired the first crown. We just sail north until we find it. We can sail up the river and hide the ships amongst trees. There is a Roman road and a Roman wall which leads to Hexham. We can do this."

Cnut and Rolf both nodded but Haaken shook his head. "And they will just let us go there, steal the crowns and then not try to stop us?"

"Of course, they will try to stop us. This is why we are meeting now. I want your ideas on how we escape."

"We will need horses or ponies."

"Good, Rolf. Now how do we get them?"

"Steal them!"

I knew that was a good idea but I also knew that a band of Norse warriors stealing ponies and horses as we crossed the land would attract the kind of attention we were trying to avoid.

"We will need to buy them otherwise they will alert the whole of the land that Norse raiders are about."

Cnut laughed, "And you think that forty or so warriors turning up on their doorstep would not be noticed."

He was right, of course, and then, like a flash of sunlight on a cloudy day, I saw the answer. "We use Scanlan and Aiden. Scanlan is Saxon and he could buy them without attracting any attention at all."

Rolf raised his eyebrows. "You would trust a slave when he is out of sight?"

Cnut nodded and I said, "I would trust Scanlan. When you come to know him, Rolf, then you will understand why."

"We cannot buy enough horses for a large warband."

"I know Haaken. I am thinking of leaving half of the men on the route for protection. I am certain that we will be pursued and having other warriors along the way will increase our chances of avoiding detection."

They looked sceptical. "And you would leave some guarding the boats. The warriors you are able to take get smaller with each breath you take."

"You are right Haaken but I am only taking one ship. It is not as if we have to bring back a great quantity of treasure. We will be able to carry it. We will take extra crew and that will give us greater speed if we need it. This way we risk just one boat. If we fail then our people will still have warriors and a ship."

"Then you are thinking of capturing the treasure with just twelve men?"

"I was thinking more like ten."

Even Cnut who normally agreed with my every word shook his head. "That is madness."

"Think about it Cnut. We have raided two monasteries. How many warriors did we lose in the attacks?"

"None?"

"Was that because we had overwhelming numbers or because the priests are an easy target?"

"They are an easy target."

"Danger comes when we try to escape for they will pursue us with warriors and that is when we will be aided by smaller numbers. A small group can hide and vanish."

Haaken sat back and smiled. "You have made your mind up anyway. I do not know why you asked our opinion."

"Because when I explained it to you I explained it to myself and I refined the plan." I looked at him. "You need not come, Haaken. I only intend to take those who wish to come."

The normally affable Haaken suddenly became angry, "I am not saying I wanted to be left behind! I am your oathsworn and I will be with you on this mad escapade." He smiled again, his anger dissipated, "Besides, who else can make your saga?"

Scanlan was delighted to be going with us. He felt it made him more of a man and less of a slave. I took Rolf and his two warriors as well as six others who begged to join the Ulfheonar. All of the Ulfheonar wished to be part of this adventure. They all knew that it would be worthy of a saga by Haaken as well as a chance to spit in the face of the priests of the White Christ. They all knew that the objects we sought were pagan and that the Christians would, eventually, transform them into objects of worship in the shape of a cross. We were doing the work of the gods and we would be rewarded in Valhalla.

We left Hrams-a at midsummer. That was the riskiest part as far as I was concerned for it meant more daylight for us to be seen. However, it also meant that the farmers would be busy working to use every hour of the day and that might help us. Whichever way you looked at it we were taking a risk. I still did not know why my heart kept telling me to do this. My mind told me that it was a mistake. I had to go with my heart.

Perhaps we had not made the right sacrifice to Ran, I do not know, but the weather and the winds were against us from the start. The summer winds, which normally came from the south west bringing warm conditions, perversely came from the north bringing icy blasts and forcing us to row. The extra crew came into their own and the balance of the boat was better in the choppy, icy sea. It meant the voyage was not as bad as it could have been. We were also able to change rowers and keep going for longer but it took us a whole day to reach the start of the wide estuary we had been told to seek.

When we found it, we knew we had the right place. It was as wide as the estuary of the Dee and the Dunum. This was a big river. We saw high mountains to the east. Some of them looked higher than the ones we had left before we had sailed west to find our new home on Man. The land intrigued me. It looked beautiful and yet there was something else which attracted me now. This was Rheged and the land of my ancestors. I was going home. It may have been that Ran was trying to help us. We reached the estuary after sunset. We were able to row up the river and find a sheltered bend with shady trees for our berth.

My men had rowed hard and were tired. I took Snorri and Aiden with me as I went to scout out the land which lay around us. I needed to know if there were people nearby. We clambered over the side to explore the northern bank. The river had a wide flood plain and the ground was quite marshy for at least three hundred paces. That was good. It would be unlikely that anyone would stumble upon us. I let Snorri lead for he was smaller than I was and had a good nose. He eventually found us a path and we headed west. It was not a well used path, it was more like the kind hunters or fishermen might use. After four miles of trudging through the moonlit land, we spied a farm. It was not large but it had a stockade around it. The idea of creeping in there and slaying the occupants came to mind but then I thought better. These people might be descendants of the men of Rheged. It was just one farm and was far from the river. I turned around and we retraced our steps.

When we reached the ship, I saw that Haaken and Cnut had stepped the mast and disguised her with branches. It would not fool anyone who was close to the ship but that was a risk we would have to take. She would not be seen unless someone came to the bank of the river and the guards would be able to deal with them. After a brief nap, I could hardly call it a sleep, we left. Erik Short Toe remained behind along with Ragnar Eriksson and five other warriors. I took the Ulfheonar along with Rolf and his men.

Scanlan and Snorri walked in the middle of the column with Aiden. My warriors would protect them. Cnut led and we headed east. By the time dawn broke, we were on the slopes of a steep hill. We could see, in the distance, the Roman Wall curling away east and we knew we were on the right road. The trees and the dips occasionally hid it from us but, by keeping the sun to our right we knew we were always heading east.

Once we started to climb I sent Egill to the right and Harold Blue Eye to the left. They scouted parallel to our course about a mile from us. The land was, surprisingly, devoid of any human life. There was game a plenty but no houses and no people. Wood smoke can be detected from a long way away and there was none. We reached the wall when the sun was high in the sky. We stopped to eat some of the cheese and bread we had brought. It would last us another day and then we would have to forage. As we ate I looked at the wall. It was impressive. It was as high as me and four men could have marched along it. We did not risk that as it would expose us to being seen from a long way away. Egill had joined us and he reported a Roman Road to the south. We could have risked that as it was flatter but this way was safer and the way was not particularly hard. The land around the wall, especially to the south, looked ripe for farming. I had not even seen one sheep. Why were there no people here? Far from satisfying my curiosity, this adventure was drawing me further into the land. I needed to know more about Rheged and the ones who lived here.

Each step next to the wall increased my admiration for these ancient soldiers. At one point, they appeared to have tried to make the wall climb a cliff! It twisted up a cliff that I thought a goat would have struggled to climb. They must have been a tenacious people. Once at the top we could see the land stretching away to the north. There it looked less hospitable and appeared to be covered with gorse and bracken. Harold had to walk with us for there was a sheer drop to the left and he could no longer watch our flank. As the sun dropped lower in the sky we saw the remains of a huge fort. It was enormous and seemed to grow out of the wall and tumble down the hillside. The gods had been cruel on the journey across but now they answered our prayers by giving us shelter and security for the night.

I sent some of the men to fetch water from the lake which ran next to the cliff while others went hunting. It was not a great catch but they managed a couple of squirrels, a hare and a couple of game birds. Had we had a pot they would have made a good stew but we had to roast them and they were a little tough. It was, however, a change from bread and cheese and therefore even more welcome. We now had enough food for an extra day.

As we watched the stars high above us Rolf stated what was in all our minds. "We have seen no ponies yet."

"I know. If we have no ponies then we will have to think of something else." I was much calmer and philosophical about this dilemma than my men were. I could sense the agitation and worry in Rolf and Cnut when they spoke. I was certain that the land would help us. We were doing something for the ancient people of this land and I knew that they would not let us down.

"I am thinking that this would be the best place to have men waiting for us. By my reckoning, we have about twenty miles or so to go. There may be another of these on the way but we cannot count on it."

Haaken nodded, "It would be a good place and the cliff path will also hold up anyone who pursues us. Now you have to decide who will stay and who will go."

I smiled and lay back to sleep. I had already decided who I would take, Scanlan and Aiden of course, Haaken, Cnut, Egill, Olaf, Harold, Sweyn, Lars, Oleg and Gudrun. They were Ulfheonar and had been with me the longest. Rolf would resent being left behind but he had already shown me that he was a leader of men. I would have a safe place to return to.

The next day there was marked contrast n the faces of the men. The ones I had chosen walked tall while the rest had a hangdog look on their faces. Poor Snorri was the one who looked the most hurt. Aiden was not even a warrior and he was going with me. He did not know that the plans I had made needed both Aiden and Scanlan.

The land began to descend to the west and, alarmingly, we saw more farms. There were now just a handful of us which made hiding easier. A whistle from Egill warned us of any danger. When we heard it, we hid. For the second time that day we heard his whistle. There was an old Roman tower crumbling and half destroyed by time close by but it would hide us. We scurried into its walls and hid. I did not worry about Egill he would be able to hide. I heard the Saxon voices as they tramped along the side of the wall.

I caught snatches of their conversation which told me that King Eardwulf was beginning to move west. There were just four warriors and we could have killed them easily but I did not want our presence known. These four were exploring the wall for defensive structures. If they reached Rolf they would have a shock! After they had passed we emerged from our hiding place and continued, very cautiously towards the east. The wall seemed to plummet down to the river and we found another fort which spanned the river. This would have been an even better place to secrete Rolf and his men but it was handy to know where it was. From what I had heard from the Saxons this was largely unexplored country for them. We would be on an equal footing.

After we had crossed the river and begun to climb east I was aware that we were getting close to Hexham and we needed directions. Eagle eyed Egill spotted the farm and the horses as we walked along the side of the wall. We halted and hid in some woods.

"Scanlan now is the time." I handed him a purse with coins. They were Saxon coins taken from the monasteries and would not arouse suspicion. I pointed towards the farm. "Take Aiden and go to the farm. Tell them you are a horse trader and wish to buy horses. Haggle but you will have to pay them. Find out where Hexham is. Tell them that you are going to try to get horses from there."

The two of them left us. This was the part I hated. I preferred to be the one taking the chances. I didn't like the idea of either of them coming to harm. In addition, the acquisition of horses was vital to our plans.

"What will you do when you have these crowns?"

"I do not know. At the moment, I am just protecting them from the Saxons. I owe it to my ancestors." Haaken's question was a good one but I had no good answer to it.

It seemed an age but eventually, I heard the sound of horses. We waited until Scanlan and Aiden appeared next to us leading the four horses. Scanlan shook his head, "From the price we paid these must be horses which can fly!" he shook his head in disbelief. He had been a poor farmer before he had been a slave and the thought of paying large amounts of coins for animals was beyond him.

"And Hexham?"

"We are almost there." He pointed to the south east. "It is south of the old road but the farmer says there are few horses there, just monks and warriors."

I felt the hairs on the back of my neck tingling. Warriors meant that there was something worth protecting. "Did he say how many warriors?"

"No."

"Well, we can now leave this wall and head towards our destination." I looked at the sky. "We still have plenty of time before sunset. Let us eat and then move on." We wolfed down our cheese and bread. We had eaten the last of our supplies. Putting Aiden on the back of one of the horses we led them along the trail which led to Hexham. We had not gone far when one of the horses neighed. I knew nothing about the beasts but Scanlan did.

"There are other horses around."

I helped Aiden dismount. "Egill, go and find the horses." I turned to Scanlan. "Do you still have coins?"

"Aye and this time I will haggle better."

"Spend what you have to." I smiled, "In any case, we will be passing this way on our way back. If we have time we could get a fairer price from our greedy farmer friends on our return journey. Swords can be very persuasive."

Egill was back almost instantly, "In that field on the other side of the hedgerow are three horses. They are smaller than these. There is a farm at the top of the hill."

"Go, Scanlan, we still have time enough."

While we waited I examined the horses. They had no saddles but each had a rope halter. It would not be comfortable riding them but we would be able to outdistance any pursuit.

Cnut broached the question which had been lurking at the back of my mind. "Suppose these warriors outnumber us?"

"They may well do. I think tonight the Ulfheonar use stealth. We become true wolves. We get rid of the guards, even if it takes us a long time but we must do so silently. We do not know how many others live close by this place do we?" I could see the doubt on his face. "I chose this war party because I trust all of you. You will all know what to do when we have to."

Cnut shook his head, "You make it sound so easy and yet I know, as we all do, that this is an almost impossible task."

Haaken chuckled, "And they make the best sagas, don't they? Throw in a dragon or two and we can all die happily."

"For the sake of my wife and family can we save immortality for another night?" The horses neighed again and then Scanlan and Aiden reappeared.

Scanlan was smiling, "That was a better trade. I think the other farmer robbed us."

"It doesn't matter. We have acquired seven horses now. If some ride double we have enough for us all."

We knew that we were close to our destination which made the next couple of miles even tenser. The ground began to drop away and we found ourselves coming to the edge of a large forest. Egill raced back holding up his hands to halt us. "I can see the town. It is a mile away, no more."

"Scanlan and Aiden, tether the horses here. Find some water, they will need it and then guard them. The rest of you, come with me." Once we reached the edge of the forest I could see, in the fading light of this summer evening, the land stretching out before us. It was flat farmland and I could see why they had eschewed the hills. Why farm where life was harsh when you had a verdant valley like this one so close to hand? I could also see why they had built the monastery where they had. It dominated the landscape. That also explained the warriors. Some Saxon lord claimed ownership of this land and the soldiers would impose his will. The monks had merely taken advantage of the arrangement.

The tolling bell identified both the time and the site of the monastery. It was just north of the town. As with the others, it was protected by a palisade. The lowing of cattle and bleating of sheep told us that they had animals within. That might even help us.

We watched the gates as the last of the priests entered. This time there were warriors. Two guards stood at the northern gate and we assumed there would be the same number at the south. These were warriors and not just armed villagers. They had axes and shields as well as helmets. I even saw the glint of warrior bands on the hilts. The lack of mail did not mean they were inferior to us just that their role did not necessitate mail. We saw two men patrolling the ramparts. The church was easily identified by the small bell tower and the cross. There looked to be more buildings here than at the other two. Would this one prove to be luckier?

With just ten of us, I did not want us separated. We kept together. Our shields were over our backs and we held our swords before us. The slope which led down to the walls of the monastery was dotted with bushes and we made our way down through them using each one for cover. The gates were slammed shut and we waited in the bushes to see where the guards were. The two we had seen on the ramparts were augmented by another two. With four walls to guard them meant one to a wall. This created problems as there would always be one sentry watching out when we approached. I intended to strike as early as possible. The bells meant that the priests would be at their prayers and then they would have their food. This was the time when they would be occupied and, hopefully, at their least vigilant.

We waited until the sentry had left the middle of the wall and then ran the last fifty paces to shelter beneath the wooden timbers. The walls were as tall as me and then half as tall again. Olaf and Oleg held the shield at knee height and Lars crouched upon it. He had a wickedly sharp dagger in his hand and he was an accomplished warrior with a blade. He waited until the sentry was level with him and then he tapped

Oleg on the helmet lightly. The two men stood and raised the shield above their heads. Lars lightly sprang over the wooden walls and within a heartbeat had his arm fastened around the mouth of the sentry while his dagger slashed his throat. He hurled the body over the palisade and continued the march the sentry had been making. In the dark, we hoped they would not look too closely at their fellows.

We moved around to the next wall. Lars would keep away from the other two sentries while we disposed of the third. This time it was Gudrun who stood on the shield. Although not as skilled with a knife as Lars he was one of the strongest Ulfheonar. His grip was such that the sentry had no chance of moving. I think he pulled so hard that he broke the man's neck but it mattered not for his throat was cut too.

He reached down and hauled Cnut up and then Haaken. We went around to the gate. This part was the most dangerous moment. Lars and Gudrun would have to deal with the other two sentries with Haaken and Cnut poised to help them. The rest of us waited helplessly by the gate. We could see nothing. If we heard anything then it would all be up with us for we would be discovered. It seemed an age but then waiting always does. I knew that Scanlan and Aiden would already think that we had been away for hours. We heard not a sound from within.

When the gate finally opened I saw all four of my men. Their smiles told me that the blood they bore was the Saxons and not their own. We moved swiftly through the gate and barred it again. We had to find the remaining warriors and kill them silently. If anyone came out we wanted them to see the gates closed, as they would have expected. The town was just a little too close for comfort.

I did not think that we would find them in the church. We searched elsewhere. There appeared to be a long building which looked like a warrior hall. I led the men there. Sweyn watched our backs with an arrow notched in his bow. We waited outside and heard the laughter of men. We had no idea how many there were within. We stood with drawn swords and I counted down with my fingers.

We burst through the door. It was a Saxon warrior hall. There was a fire in the middle and the men were seated at a table drinking. There were ten of them. Surprise was all and I leapt towards the one nearest man who was reaching for his sword. He was fast and he managed to smack my sword away as it plunged towards his middle. He had no armour and I did. I also had a mailed glove. I punched him on the side of the head, stunning him. It gave me the chance to prepare my sword to swing down. He was groggy when I struck his sword; it shattered in two and the blade continued down to sever his throat. I spun around as I felt a movement behind me. The warrior who had launched himself at me with the spear had almost stuck me. I chopped down on the haft and the head fell to the floor. He was a huge man and he leapt at my neck with two hands that looked as big as a shield. I fell over with him on top of me. I could not move *Ragnar's Spirit* which was trapped beneath us and I felt myself slowly blacking out. "Filthy Viking! Die!"

He would have been better to shout a warning to the priests but he was too intent on my death. I slipped my hand down to my leggings and grabbed my seax. I was losing consciousness as I ripped it up and into his heart. I lay there for a moment or two letting the blood enter my own head as his life blood left him and oozed all over me. When I stood they were all dead as was Lars who lay there with an axe embedded in his back. We would take him home with us but first, we had to find the treasure.

As we left the warrior hall I sent Gudrun to one gate and Harold to the other. I whispered, "No-one escapes!"

The rest of us headed for the church. We could hear those within intoning chants and responses. I did not think that anyone would leave early which gave us the chance to see if there were any other exits. "Olaf, go around the building. See if there are any other ways in or out." After he had gone I said to the others, "These are priests and they will not fight. Keep your weapons ready but do not kill. We need for them to cooperate. Perhaps they will value their lives rather than some pagan treasure." In truth, I did not want to kill them. I had not enjoyed ending the lives of the priests we had killed before. Ironically the ones who we had taken now seemed happier. Even the old priest from the monastery of St. Cuthbert appeared to be a happy prisoner although in his case it was because he thought that he could convert us all.

Olaf returned. "This is the only door." He grinned and he looked even scarier than he normally did. "Lambs to the slaughter."

"Do not kill unless you have to." He looked disappointed. "Let us go!"

I stepped into the candlelit church. There were no more than fifteen priests there but there were two warriors. I could see their mail. They were all chanting and had not heard or felt us enter. I waved my men down the sides of the kneeling congregation. I moved swiftly towards the warriors. I was aware that Haaken and Cnut had followed me. I held *Ragnar's Spirit* above my shoulder in both hands and I focussed on the nearest warrior who was kneeling at the front on the left. The other was on the right.

There was a shout from a priest as I passed him. He threw an arm out to stop me and Cnut's sword slipped into his throat. The warrior at the front heard the noise and, with amazing dexterity, whipped out his sword to face me. Had I not had my sword ready then it might have gone ill. As it was I brought it down savagely and his head rolled to the floor. I heard a scream behind me and, as I turned I saw Haaken withdrawing his sword from the second warrior's chest. I stepped to the front table which had a cross on it and some of the lace my wife so admired. I turned and roared, "Silence! I am Dragon Heart and I give you my word that if you do as I say you will neither be harmed nor taken as slaves." I spoke in Saxon and it seemed to take them by surprise. I waited until they were all quiet. "All of the warriors are dead and your lives are in my hands. If you die it will be because you have willed it and I believe your White Christ frowns on taking your own life."

I saw some of the priests looking at each other when I said that. They assumed that all Vikings were ignorant of their religion. I was not ignorant I just did not agree with it. I saw a young priest who looked as though he had just wet himself from the puddle between his legs. I walked over to him and pressed the tip of the sword to the end of his nose. He was not to know that it was almost impossible to kill a man quickly with the sword there but it had the effect of focussing his attention on the shiny and sharp blade. I spoke to the priests as a whole but my question was aimed at the terrified young man before me. "I come here for one thing; the jewels and crowns of Rheged. They do not belong to you. They are pagan and I want them."

I could see the older ones exchange looks and the wet priest flicked his eyes to look at the priest behind me who still knelt.

"I can see you know of what I speak. Tell me or this young priest dies." I allowed a heartbeat for them to react and then I added, gently, "This is not one of your relics, it is a pagan relic. Is it worth the death of one of you? It will not make them a saint and it will not make them a martyr. It will make them dead and foolish."

Despite wetting himself the boy whose nose touched my sword was brave and he closed his eyes and began to mouth a prayer. His fingers caressed the cross at his neck. I would not like to kill the boy but I would.

The priest behind me said, "Leave Brother Michael alone. We have what you seek. Take it and go." He stood and took a chest from under the table which bore the cross. I nodded to Cnut who opened it. He took out a crown held up four fingers and then nodded.

"Thank you. I would have hated to kill such a brave youth." I pointed to Cnut, "Take the chest. Tie the priests up. Haaken, see if there are any horses. Olaf, collect the warrior's weapons."

My men were experts at tying men so that they could not move and within a short time they were all secured. "I expect you will all be rescued soon. Next time leave pagan treasure where it belongs, with us pagans."

As I left the church I checked that they were all tethered. Once outside I saw that Haaken had found two horses. They may well have belonged to the mailed warriors we had slain in the church. "Put Lars on one and the weapons and chest on the other. Haaken, you watch the horse with the treasure. Now let us go east."

Oleg looked at me, "East?"

"We need to make them think we are heading for a boat to take us east. It will not buy us much time but every moment is precious."

Chapter 17

Once we left the gates, which we closed, we headed east along the well-worn trail which led to the settlement. We did not try to hide our tracks and when one of the horses decided to relieve itself I was delighted. We could not have left clearer signs of our route. It would be obvious we were moving east and the lands of the Norse. We headed into some woods which were to the north of the settlement and then began to make our way north east. When Egill found some bare rock, it was the perfect place to change direction. Leaving Egill to make a false trail east we turned north over the rocks and, after fifty or so paces, when the rocks ran out, we turned due west. Egill soon caught up with us. We now pushed on towards the forest where Scanlan and Aiden waited for us.

I was worried that they had been captured when I did not see them immediately but the two figures ghosted from the woods once we halted. I was impressed, they had been hidden well. We mounted the horses and I took Aiden with me. We had to ride some of the horses double but that could not be helped. We made our way west through the thick forest. It was slow going as the horses carefully picked their way through the thick trees. There was silence. Any animals which might have been in the forest scampered away when they heard the footfall of the horses. As we began to descend I knew we were close to the river and the Roman fort. We heard the rushing of the water and then the bridge and the fort loomed up. I felt relief that we had reached our first way point. We could rest a while. After we had dismounted and led the horses down to the water for a drink Gudrun and Harold came to speak with me.

"We will not make it home if we have to take Lars' body with us."

"He died well as a warrior should and his body is in Valhalla now."

I was surprised that his two closest friends should say this. "You would have us abandon his body here?"

Gudrun shook his head. "We will not abandon him we will send him home. The river and the sea will watch over him until he reaches his home in the fjords." Harold nodded his assent. "There are trees nearby. We can put him on a raft and send him to the sea. He was born to the east of here. The sea shall have him."

It seemed that the other Ulfheonar were of one mind. It made sense. It would mean that we had an extra horse and that might make all the difference. It did not take long to fashion a crude wooden raft and tie Lars and his sword to it. We descended to the river. It was dark and it was noisy. His two closest friends lowered it into the water and spoke their words and then he was gone. Strangely that act seemed to give all the Ulfheonar more confidence that we would escape.

"He will watch down on us. This is good. It was not right to have his body bouncing up and down on the horse." Olaf could be remarkably thoughtful at times; normally he was a doer and not a thinker.

We still had many miles to go and even Rolf and our comrades were hours away.

The long summer days meant very short nights and the sky was lightening behind us when we heard the dogs. My plan had been nullified. It didn't matter that we had tried to lead a false trail; they were on to us now. In fact, our attempt to delude them had cost us time and distance. We would now have to hurry. The trail was not a good one and we risked injury to man and beast. We pushed the horses on but we were moving uphill with some horses carrying double weight. We were moving faster than we could have walked but the Saxons and dogs behind us would be running.

"Egill and Scanlan, lead the men. I will ride at the rear with Haaken and Cnut."

The three of us were the most experienced of the warriors and we had the best mail. Haaken cast a look at Aiden who still rode before me. I shrugged, "Aiden will be a warrior like Scanlan one day and besides if we have to fight, he can hold the horses."

He looked up at me with gratitude written all over his face. "I will fight master." He touched the hilt of his dagger. "I am not afraid."

"I know you are not." He was a brave boy and he reminded me of me. I had had the same attitude when I had been enslaved. I was glad that I had left him free.

The horses were labouring up the slope and I wondered about walking them for a while. I dismissed the thought for it didn't matter about the horses. We were saving our legs and our energy. I now knew that we would have to fight to defend our crowns.

"Master, why did they put Lars on a raft and throw him and his sword into the river?"

"He had a warrior's death and they gave him a warrior's burial. When I die they will put me aboard '*Wolf*' and set fire to her. That will be a fine burial."

He seemed appalled at the concept, "But she is a good ship. Why destroy her?"

I laughed, "Hopefully she will be old when I die and need burying but I thank you for your kind words about my ship. I like her too."

Suddenly the dogs seemed much closer. I urged on my horse and said to Sweyn. "No matter what happens to us you push on to Rolf and keep the treasure safe." He glanced at me and then nodded.

Haaken looked behind him and then ahead. The fort and the ambush were still at least three miles away and the land rose steadily. "There is nowhere close by to lay an effective ambush. The land rises and is quite open." Ahead we could see the others quite clearly and the land was open before them. "We will just have to fight them and slow them down."

Cnut pointed ahead. There was a wide swath of open land before us. "If we stop there then we can use our bows. This is steep ground here. They will have to slow down. The rest will help the horses."

It made sense. "Good. Aiden can you hold the three horses?"

"Of course, and I can fight if I have to."

"If you have to fight my brave little Irishman then we will be dead so do not wish to fight just yet. For the sake of *'Wolf'* eh?"

He laughed as we dismounted, "Yes, master."

"Now take the horses along the wall a little and sing to them. It will keep them calm."

By the time we had taken out our bows, I could see the four enormous dogs and the first of the Saxons. They were spread out and the ones at the fore were lightly armed. I could just make out, some way behind, the forty or so warriors who had shields and helmets. We needed to get rid of their dogs and their scouts first. I heard Aiden singing. He had a lovely voice and he was singing the song of *Ragnar's Spirit* which he had heard Haaken singing. It was a good song and the horses stood calmly as he sang. It helped me too for it reminded me of Ragnar and the day I was touched by the gods.

The dogs were eager to get to us. We waited until they were thirty paces from us and then loosed our arrows. Three died immediately but the fourth made up the ground faster than we had thought. He launched himself at me, his slobbering jowls and teeth so close to my face I feared he would swallow me whole. He was a large dog, as big as a small horse and he knocked me to the ground. I jammed my mailed fist into his mouth to stop him biting and then punched him hard on the side of the head. He whimpered and fell to the ground at my side. I had my sword out as I stood. He growled at me and prepared to launch himself once more. He died on the end of my blade.

Cnut and Haaken had thinned out the scouts who were trying to loose arrows at us. I felt a crack on my helmet as an arrow pinged off it. If he had been a good archer I would have been dead. The main Saxon band was still some way off; lumbering up the leg sapping slope. "At them!"

There were just four scouts left and they were taken aback when we charged them. Two bravely tried to hit us with arrows but a man has to have nerves of steel not to be affected by a Viking charging at him. The arrows flew harmlessly over our shoulders. The two brave ones fell to our swords while those who used discretion fled to the protection of their friends' shields. I did not need to give orders and we turned to run to our horses. The slope was steeper than I had thought and we were out of breath when we reached Aiden. I thrust him up and then climbed on to the back of the beast.

As I looked down the slope an arrow whizzed past my head. They were less than fifty paces away. "Ride!"

The horses had been rested and the arrows flying around them were just the incentive they needed. There were now no dogs to worry about but it would be obvious to any pursuer that we were heading west. I had estimated forty or fifty men following us. I hoped that Rolf had created a good ambush or our treasure hunt could end on this high, lonely and windswept outpost of the old Roman Empire. The ground dipped a little ahead of us and I could no longer see the rest of my riders. That brought me hope. Egill would be able to give Rolf warning of our arrival.

We were drawing away from the Saxons. When we dropped down the slope they became hidden from view. That meant that they could not see us either. We rode as fast as we dared but the trail had many rocks which had fallen from the wall and we did not need to be unhorsed so close to the enemy.

I was relieved when I recognised the twist in the wall. I remembered that it marked a place four hundred paces from the Roman fort. The Saxons were now a hundred paces behind us and they could see us once more. When they reached the next crest, they would see the fort. The crest was almost the undoing for our horses. They had carried mailed men further than they ought to have. They began to labour and to stumble. I could clearly see the fort but not my warriors.

"Keep going as though we are passing the fort and continuing west."

Cnut's voice was nervous, "Where are the others?"

"If we cannot see them, then neither can the Saxons. They will be there; believe me." I knew they would be there but like Cnut, there was that slight doubt in my mind.

There was a gap in the wall where there had once been a gate and we thundered through it. I could see no-one. The track passed the wall and the small turrets and towers which lined the northern wall. To our left and the south were the barracks and buildings the soldiers must have used. The fort had been built on a hill and it followed the curve. Once we reached the top of the hill I glanced over my shoulder. The Saxons were rapidly approaching the gate. As we dropped down I lost sight of the Saxons. Suddenly I heard Scanlan shout, "In here, master!"

There was a half-ruined building to my left and I wheeled my horse through the narrow gap, rapidly followed by Cnut and Haaken. Scanlan and Egill were there with the rest of the horses. We dismounted and drew our swords. Rolf would need our help. "Where is Rolf?"

"He and the others are on both sides of the trail. You passed them." Egill was grinning childishly at the idea that they had hidden themselves so well that Dragon Heart had not seen them.

"Then lead us to him."

Egill took the three of us out of an opening in the opposite wall and we moved along the shell of the building. After a few paces, I saw my warriors crouching behind the low walls. I also saw the Saxons hurtling through the fort eager to get to grips with us. This would be the first test for Rolf and I hoped he was up to it.

Suddenly the first of the Saxons pitched forward with an arrow in his back and then my men erupted from their places of concealment to fall upon the surprised and shocked Saxons. We leapt over the wall and into the fray. *Ragnar's Spirit* bit into the shield and then the arm of the Saxon who rushed towards me. His left arm dropped and I finished him off. I heard a roar and a Saxon wielding an axe ran towards me. My helmet and mail marked me as a leader. The axe sliced down and I barely managed to deflect it with my shield. I weakly hacked at him as I fell to the side. The tip of the sword cut his leg as he passed but I knew that it would not slow him down. His axe was a two-handed affair and he had no shield but he had a much longer reach. As the axe whirled above his head I darted in and flicked the end of my sword at him. It clanked off his mail. This was a warrior who could afford good armour. All around me my men were all engaged in their own individual combats. There would be no one to help me.

He changed the arc of his swing and as it looped down towards my shield I stepped back. One of the new warriors, Sweyn Sweynson was just stepping forward to finish off his own opponent and the axe hacked into his helmet and the side of his head. Sweyn's death saved my life for I stabbed under the arm of the Saxon as his axe head became entangled in the dying Sweyn. I saw my blade emerge from his neck and he fell to the floor. As I struggled to withdraw my sword another Saxon stabbed at me with his spear. I barely had time to swing my shield around to take the blow. I just managed to get my sword out when he threw the spear at me. It caught me on the side of the head and made my head ring. Before he could get his sword out I swung *Ragnar's Spirit* and his head flew along the ground. I was out of breath and my head was still ringing. As I looked around I saw that we had won. There were ten or twelve warriors running away, towards the east, and the rest lay dead. We had won but I saw too many of my own men lying dead to celebrate. I knew that we had alerted King Eardwulf to our existence. We had raided his lands three times now and stolen valuable treasure. We had killed his priests and his warriors. He would now know he had an enemy to the west.

Rolf and the warriors who had been further up the wall walked towards us despatching wounded Saxons as they came. I could see that three Ulfheonar were dead. I had lost four of these most valuable and loyal warriors capturing the crowns. Was my desire for the treasure of Rheged the reason they lay dead? There would be time, later, for such recriminations. I had to try to get us all back to *'Wolf'* safely.

"There is some good mail here. Strip the bodies of all that is of value." As, after every such battle, there was a balance between the good that came from it and the losses. We had lost eight men in total. I made a decision. "Oleg, gather wood. We will send our comrades to Valhalla with honour."

He nodded as he strode to the bushes and trees which line the far side of the old wall. "Well done Rolf! That was a fine ambush. I did not see you and I was looking for you."

He gestured at our dead. "There were more than I anticipated."

"Aye and me too. They only had a handful of warriors at the monastery. There must have been a warrior hall and fort nearby."

He gestured east. "So, there may be more?"

"I would think so. We have bought time; that is all."

He looked at Egill and the others as they stripped the bodies. "The men you took with you have had no sleep. They will be tired."

"I know. We will have to rely on you and your men. At least we have horses to carry the captured weapons and the wounded." I had already noticed warriors limping or holding limbs which had been cut. We had not escaped unscathed. When the horses were loaded and the warriors had donned the captured mail we stood around the funeral pyre. Each warrior was laid with his sword in his hand. As the flames licked around the base of the pyre each of us remembered the dead. We quietly told them that we would meet again in Valhalla and they would be remembered.

I made Aiden mount one of the horses. He was not happy but I pointed out that he was so light as not to slow down the horse and I needed someone mounted. The other riders were the four warriors who had leg wounds. One of them was Snorri. It was not a bad wound but it had taught him a lesson. Cnut had seen the blow and had chastised

Snorri. "You are not an Ulfheonar and you are certainly not Dragon Heart. Use your shield to protect yourself. You could have avoided the wound."

Snorri respected Cnut almost as much as he did me and he was contrite. "I am sorry. I forgot."

"Aye well you may have another warrior band to add to your sword but if you are dead then there is little point in showing the world how brave you are. Be a warrior for a long time, Snorri, not just one battle."

Secretly we were all pleased with the way that young Snorri had handled himself but Haaken and I both knew that the difference between success and failure for a young warrior could be the width of a hair.

We had twenty-five or so miles to go to reach our ship but it was downhill. Rolf left a couple of warriors close to the path down from the cliff in case the Saxons came when we were trying to get the terrified horses down the ridiculously steep trail. It took us longer than I would have liked but the rearguard reported no enemies close to us.

I had a nagging doubt in the back of my mind. There was a road just a mile or so from the wall. It ran parallel to our route and the Saxons could move much quicker along it. I did not know where it finished but the Saxons would. I sent Olaf and Oleg ahead as scouts. They would have to sniff out the Saxons.

We soon left the wild and rocky land behind us. Rolf had been right, we were exhausted. I felt my eyes closing. The others who had raided the monastery would be feeling the same way. I forced myself to stay awake. I began to use my mind and keep it occupied. I looked ahead to see where the trail went. Suddenly I saw five or six wood pigeons take flight and rise into the sky as though alarmed. "Halt! Aiden, Snorri, Scanlan, stay with the horses. Guard the treasure and the wounded."

Rolf and Cnut ran to me. "What is it?"

"We have not seen Oleg and Olaf, have we?"

"No, but that is a good thing it means the enemy are not ahead. They would have let us know." Rolf was no Ulfheonar and this way of fighting was not natural to him.

I pointed to the pigeons now roosting in an ash tree. "Then what made those birds move?"

"Olaf and Oleg?"

"They would have been further down the trail. I smell an ambush. Rolf, detail three men to stay with the horses. Tell them to count to a hundred and then move down the trail slowly." He nodded and hurried off. "Cnut, get the Ulfheonar."

Rolf returned and the Ulfheonar reached me. "Haaken, take Rolf and half of the men and go to the right of the trail. I will take Cnut and the other half to the left. I think there is an ambush ahead. If I am wrong then feel free to mock me but at least then you will all be alive."

Cnut said seriously, "If you say there is an ambush then there will be one. You can see things which are hidden from others, Dragon Heart. Ragnar speaks with you still."

I drew my sword and pulled my shield around. I had to be ready for whatever came my way. The undergrowth to the left was thick and the ground was uneven but it made perfect cover for us. I was mentally counting one hundred. The problem with waiting in ambush is just that, the waiting. The Ulfheonar are very good at this. I hoped that the Saxons ahead were getting nervous and hearing every little noise as an enemy. We would make no noise. We advanced silently and stealthily through the undergrowth moving leaves and branches of the bushes as little as possible. I knew that the Saxons if they were there, would be nervously waiting for us to appear. Their eyes would be focussed on the trail. They would be waiting to sink their sword into our flesh.

As I peered through the blackthorn bush I saw the first warrior, his back was to me. I turned and nodded. Cnut nodded back and turned to Gudrun. I continued through the undergrowth. My black armour, helmet and cloak made me hard to see, even in daylight. My men would not strike until we had reached the end of the ambush. We would ambush the ambushers.

We passed the bodies of Oleg and Olaf. There were five dead Saxons around them. Their swords were in their hands. They would be in Valhalla. The number of wounds showed that they had fought long after they had been mortally wounded. They had given their lives for their comrades and we would not forget them.

The Saxon ambushers were not even looking in my direction. They were just watching the trail and listening for the clip clop of the horses. I counted six warriors and then I stopped. In my head, I was up to eighty. Soon the horses would come down the trail. I turned and looked at the warrior I would kill. He had no mail but he had a long sword almost as long as mine. I could choose my target. With his back to me, I chose his right side. I would slice upwards and he would die. I glanced to the left and saw the next Saxon. He had mail and an axe. I would take his head. As I counted down to one hundred, I drew my sword back. The others were all counting as I was. I pulled *Ragnar's Spirit* back and stabbed as hard as I could upwards. My sword entered his side and, before, he could scream, entered his heart. He slumped to the ground. The warrior next to him sensed my presence but by then I had withdrawn my sword which was slicing towards his neck and there was nothing he could do about it.

I watched as the next warrior in the line raced towards me his sword held ready and his shield protecting his chest. He swung his sword at my head. I dropped to one knee, stuck my shield before me and, as his blade sliced harmlessly above my head I slew him. I could hear the screams of the dying and the clash of arms. We had foiled their ambush but could we escape with our lives?

I knew that there were no Saxons behind me; my men were too good to allow any to survive and I headed down the trail aware that the horses were trotting down behind me. Three warriors suddenly materialised before me. I held out my shield as they all hacked down at me. The trees and bushes prevented them from outflanking me and they got in each other's way. Although they all struck my shield, it held. I jabbed forwards and felt my blade sink into the soft middle of a warrior without armour. As I withdrew the sword I punched forward with my shield. They were not expecting the blow and one fell backwards. I ignored him and brought my sword overhand to slice through the helmet and head of the warrior before me. The warrior on the floor was struggling to rise. I stamped on his face and then stabbed him in the throat. They were all dead.

I peered west. There were no more warriors before me. I found myself breathing heavily. The long night had taken it from me. Behind me, I saw the Ulfheonar ready to go into a shield wall if needed. As Aiden and the horses trotted by I pointed my sword to the opposite side of the trail. We slipped through between horses. There we found the men led by Rolf and Haaken surrounded by Saxons. They must have had more men on one side. The Saxons had forced the survivors into a small circle and were advancing towards them. Their backs were to us and their focus on the men they thought they were about to slaughter. We showed no mercy and soon there were just the dead and the dying before us.

Cnut banged his shield and shouted, "Ulfheonar." The chant was taken up by all of the warriors. We had won and we had survived.

Chapter 18

The Ulfheonar had emerged from the ambush with their lives. Oleg and Olaf were the only losses amongst the Ulfheonar but only Rolf and his two men survived from the ones who aspired to be Ulfheonar. It had been a brutal encounter. All of the Saxons perished but I mourned Olaf and Oleg who had been with me since we had conquered Man. We could train new men but we could not replace old friends. The horses were, once again laden with the weapons and we built another pyre.

"The Saxons may see!"

"I know, Rolf, but if there are any Saxons close to us they would have to be suicidal to face us now. The bodies of their dead mark our trail. We will honour the dead and we will send them to Valhalla."

Snorri and Aiden were both distressed at the losses we had suffered. I could see that they were visibly shaken. As the bodies were consumed by fire I took them to one side. "Those warriors are happy now. They fulfilled their oaths and they died with their swords in their hands. They will be with Ragnar and the others waiting for us to join them. You two need to decide quickly if you can make that sacrifice. If not, there is no shame in not being a warrior. None of the dead would change places with you. All of them killed our enemies and will be celebrating in Valhalla."

They both wiped their eyes and Snorri said, "But lord, they are gone and we will never speak again."

"You will when you go to Valhalla."

Scanlan came over and put his arm around Aiden's shoulders, "Lord I would fight next time. I like not running away."

"You obeyed my orders. You did not run away. You shall fight, Scanlan, for I know that you are a warrior."

When the fires had died away we trudged down the trail towards our ship. It was getting towards dusk when we drew close. I felt such relief to reach it that I almost kissed the hull. I knew that I had to be strong. I was the leader. I could not think about the dead. I had to think of the living. The weapons and the treasure were placed below the deck. Cnut and the others raised the mast.

Scanlan came to me. "These horses have served us well. Could we not take them home?"

I looked at him and I knew that doubt was written all over my face. "Could you get them aboard and keep them calm on the crossing?"

He nodded, "We have fewer rowers and there is more room." He gave me a resolute and determined look, "And if I cannot I will slit their throats myself."

I was dubious but I owed it to him for his service. "If you can then do it but you and Aiden must watch them on the voyage. We only have a few men to row and Ran may be against us again."

The young all conspired to help Scanlan. Snorri and Aiden coaxed each animal aboard on a rough gangplank. Cnut kept shaking his head as he watched whilst raising the mast. Eventually, all of the horses were aboard and the three of them held the ropes which tethered them as though their lives depended upon it. Even Erik Short Toe helped.

We pushed off and began to row west. At first, the horses were calm but once we struck open water and the boat began to bob up and down they became distressed. Suddenly Aiden began to sing. I knew he had such a pure voice but I did not know it was powerful enough to be heard above the sounds of the sea and the ship. It worked and the horses began to calm. The rowers also seemed to pull better and I found myself in a better place. When Snorri joined in with the singing it was as though the gods had smiled on us and was making our journey home easier. My thoughts turned to those who had died, Lars, Olaf, Oleg and the others. I knew that they were happy; they had fulfilled their oaths and died well. We had succeeded and I wondered what King Eardwulf would make of it. We had erupted into his land and left a savage scar. His response would tell us much about the man. From what I had seen of Rheged, it was a land worth fighting for. There would come a time when we would land and stay. We would build as we had on the Island of Man and then we would measure King Eardwulf as a warrior.

The journey home was in direct contrast to our outward journey. The winds blew from our quarter and the sun shone. We were truly blessed and we knew it. When we saw the shadow that was Man I was tempted to sing myself. I had the treasure of Rheged and we had given the Saxons a bloody nose. Life was good.

The sentries on the tower must have been watching for us. The whole of Hrams-a appeared to be waiting too as I ordered the sail to be lowered and the oars raised from the water. It was a proud moment and, at the same a poignant and sad moment. There would be widows who did not know that yet. We had much treasure and the dead would be rewarded along with the living. No amount of treasure, however, could compensate for a dead warrior.

As was traditional, I stepped ashore first and was welcomed with a cheer. This time we did not let the men off; we had livestock who would need to be coaxed ashore. Aiden and Scanlan proved to be masters of the horses and they were happily led ashore. I looked at the bottom of the boat, Erik and Aiden would have a dirty job clearing up after the horses but I knew there would be farmers desperate to trade for the pungent gold that the animals had left. As for the real gold, we had not removed it from its chest. That was a pleasure which would be savoured. I left Haaken and Cnut to bring the box and I raced to greet Erika. Leaving home was always hard but the return made the absence worthwhile. As I hugged her Arturus gripped my leg tightly. I was home.

After we had eaten Haaken and Cnut joined me in my hall for the opening and examination of the box. The crowns, all four of them, were of a similar design to the queen's crown we already had. The main difference was the lack of a blue stone. It was obvious they were all a set and yet why just the one blue stone amongst them all? It was a mystery. We also found golden objects which the priests had stored there for safe keeping. I removed them from the chest as they would be shared between my warriors as a reward.

After Cnut and Haaken had taken the gold to distribute amongst the men Erika and I lay in each other's arms. "Well, my love, have you rid yourself of the need for adventure and travelling?"

I nodded, "I have. I shall stay at home and watch our children grow. But…"

She laughed, "I knew there would be a 'but'."

"No, I just meant that I have warriors to train and some time," I tickled her, "a long time in the future, I would like to return to this land. It has possibilities. It is even richer than this island."

"Ah, the wanderlust…"

"Not so much wanderlust as a desire to make life better for our people. All of them." I had no title as jarl but I felt responsible for the people in Hrams-a; even the slaves like Scanlan and Maewe.

Prince Butar arrived a few days later to view the crowns. He was as impressed as I had been. "And now what do you do with them?"

I had to confess that I did not know. "I am not sure but I think that, for the moment, I will just keep them safe. I think the followers of the White Christ would have melted them down to make another of their golden crosses. Some day there may be a kingdom of Rheged again." I shrugged, "Who knows." I looked him in the eye." I did this for my mother."

"I know and it was a noble thing to do. She would have been proud of you." He chuckled, "She would have been angry with you for risking your life but that would have passed." I nodded; he was right. "And Erika tells me that this land you passed through was fertile and green?"

"It was. I think our people could make a good home there."

"At the moment, we are too few but it maybe for the future."

We put the crowns back in the chest and placed it in the secret place we had built beneath the floor of the hall. Erik had not come for he was preparing his ship to go trading. Prince Butar, too, was planning on visiting Frankia. The success we had had meant that we could afford to travel to Frankia, and Sigismund, where we could trade for those objects we could not make. The horses we had captured meant that we could now trade for a plough. We could grow our own grain. Bjorn had said that he could make one but he would prefer to have a good model to copy. It made sense and we did need more sword blanks. The warriors who had died had taken their swords to the Otherworld with them. We had more warriors who would need to be well armed. We still had warriors who arrived in ones and twos having heard that our island was a place of sanctuary for those who were Norse or Dane. We made sure that none were like Jarl Harald.

Rolf came with us when we went to see the two ships off. His work as a bodyguard had given him an insight into how Sigismund and Sigurd worked. He also gave Prince Butar tips on the right value of trades. I did not think that we would be robbed by the two traders but any knowledge would help us to benefit.

The two ships were not to be fully crewed. They had bulky items to trade. It was about this time that we began to consider having a trading vessel instead of a drekar. The drekar could still escort and protect but the trader could hold more goods. That would be for the future. Olaf stayed on the island and did not accompany his old friend. He looked old and he looked tired. I think that my stepfather was happy that Olaf was staying behind. His home would be safer with Olaf and Dragon Heart watching over it.

Eurwen came to stay with us. She was delighted for Kara was a giggling gurgling baby and more fun to be around than the noisy and active Arturus who loved playing with his wooden sword and fighting with Aiden. It was a wonderful couple of months. I was able to make my home and my fort even stronger. We were able to train even more warriors and the glorious summer promised us a bounty from nature that would keep us well fed all winter. It was a good time. It was also the time of babies for not only Erika but also the wives of most of the Ulfheonar fell pregnant. Once again, the women all said that the babies would be the dead Ulfheonar reborn. For myself, I was not too sure but it was not an unpleasant thought.

The only cloud in that glorious summer was the appearance of Irish pirates. Since we had met with the High King there had been peace but two ships appeared off the western coast of our island. The warriors left by Jarl Erik rode to me to tell me that the two ships had been seen lurking off the coast. I sent word to the other two towns and we prepared *'Wolf'* and *'Bear'* to deal with them if they came too close. The towers we had built were now manned all the time as we watched for their reappearance.

Although they did not reappear for a few days we knew that something was wrong when two fishing ships and their two-man crews vanished. They were good fishermen and the weather had been clement. I summoned the Ulfheonar.

"We will find these pirates and discourage them. Rolf, I want you and the other warriors to keep watch in case this is a diversion to allow them to attack Hrams-a. We will seek them out."

"But there are two of them."

"And they are pirates. *'Wolf'* can out sail and outfight anything that floats. I might worry about taking on a drekar but these crews will be ill disciplined. I suspect that when they see us they will turn tail and run for home. You can keep *'Bear'* here in case we miss them."

I was wrong. I had become too confident because of our success. I took Scanlan and Snorri with me as I wanted help with the steering and Snorri was a competent sailor. Scanlan had become a skilled archer and I wanted his ability to aid us in case they were set to fight us.

I made sure that our men left their mail behind. It made the ship lighter and I did not think that we would need it. As the fishing boats had disappeared from the east coast I took my ship to the west. My sentries on the towers had not seen the pirates pass them. We deduced that they had to be sailing towards the southern end of the island.

We passed Jarl Erik's stronghold and I took us close enough to wave to the sentries on his ramparts. Had there been a problem they would have alerted us. I did not often travel down this side of the island and it was gratifying to see the new huts springing up on the hillsides and the white dots which showed the flocks of sheep. We had come a long way in a short time and it made me more determined than ever to stop the pirates from spoiling our life style. They would need to be taught a harsh lesson and find easier victims to torment.

We saw the Hibernian pirate ships as we edged around the southern headland. The two pirates were closing with the smallest port on the island. Olaf the Toothless had made it well defended but I knew that he had the fewest warriors of any of our settlements within its walls. They were mainly fishermen. The ships had not yet landed but it would only be a matter of time before they did so. Ran was with us and the wind was behind us and helping to move us quickly towards the two enemies.

"Ulfheonar, the Hibernians are attacking Olaf and his people. Row as though your lives depended upon it. Scanlan and Snorri take your bows and aim for the men at the stern of the ships."

Although they only had two bows I knew that they might get lucky and, in any case, it was hard to concentrate when arrows were raining down on you. I estimated that the two ships had forty or so men on each of them. "Erik, come here!"

Erik Short Toe ran the length of the ship from his position as bow look out. "If I am able, I aim to board the ships. You will have to steer. First, I want you and Aiden to lower the sail. I know that it will be hard but I believe you can do it. Then have Aiden bring me my helmet."

He stood proudly, "We will not let you down, Dragon Heart."

The two ships had seen us and were hurrying towards us. I had given Olaf and his people a reprieve, albeit brief. Now I had to try to defeat them. They had kept their sails up which was a mistake. It would impair their sight and make them less manoeuvrable.

I shouted to my men, "I intend to make them think they can surround us however I intend taking us down the side of the ship to our left. When I give the order, I want the rowers on the left to stop rowing. I will lay us alongside and we will board them."

They cheered and, as the noise carried across the waves, I wondered what the Irish would make of it. I gradually pushed the rudder over. I did it slowly but I was aiming my ship at the boat on the right. I could see that they were rowing as hard as they could. Scanlan and Snorri's arrows were falling short but as soon as I closed they would have good targets. Erik and Aiden stood next to me. Aiden held my helmet.

"Left bank, stop rowing!" The oars on the right propelled us hard left and it seemed that the Irish ship would plough into us. "Right bank, up oars. Left bank row for your lives."

As the oars came up I pushed the rudder hard over. The left oars bit into the water and we began to arrow towards the side of the Irish ship. I could see that they would not hit us and they had no idea where we were. Their sail hid us from view.

"Stop rowing and get your weapons. Egill, Gudrun, ropes!"

Our hull ground down the side of the pirate and the oars of the pirate ship were shattered. I heard screams from the pirates, many of whom would have had their arms broken by the impact. I glanced beyond the first ship and saw the second one desperately trying to turn into the wind. It would take them some time. I donned my helmet. "Erik, hold us close!"

Egill and Gudrun had thrown the two ropes with hooks attached. One bit into the wooden rail at the stern while the other tore through a pirate's arm, before digging into the wooden side. Ignoring the danger of the two hulls which were grinding next to each other, I leapt over into the pirate ship. I crashed down onto some of the injured rowers. I heard a sickening crack as one of the pirates had his leg shattered by my jump. I swung *Ragnar's Spirit* in an arc and two pirates felt its blade rip into their unprotected chests. My men had no mail with them but their leather tunics would give them some protection from the Irish weapons. I raced to the stern. I saw an arrow pitch the steersman over the side and another warrior fell clutching the arrow in his neck. There was no control over their ship now. The captain had a long curved sword and I made my way directly for him. He made the mistake of swinging at my head too early. I ducked and stabbed him in the top of the leg. He screamed and threw his head back. I pushed him over the side and into the water. The arterial blood spurted in a dramatic arc as he fell.

I looked down the length of the ship and saw my men ruthlessly butchering all who were before them. These were pirates and not oathsworn warriors. Many of them leapt over board and the rest were despatched.

"Haaken take Snorri and two others secure this ship. The rest of you back aboard *'Wolf'*!" I could see that the second ship had managed to turn. She was heading for our unprotected stern.

I reached Erik and grabbed the tiller. It needed critical control to do what I intended. My crew were well trained. As soon as they reached their benches they took their oars and awaited my orders. The second pirate ship had still to lower its sail which was flapping against the wind. It was slowing them and not helping them. Cnut ordered his rowers to push us off.

"Left bank, back water!"

The ship began to turn. It seemed to take forever but the second pirate ship had slowed. Even so, it threatened to strike us amidships. "Right bank, row". As soon as Cnut's men began to row the ship seemed to spin in the water. *'Wolf'* was a lively and responsive ship. "Left bank row!"

The ship leapt forwards. I had to time this well or my men would be swimming to land. As we closed I judged the time correctly. "Left bank, ship oars." As they all obeyed I pushed the tiller over and, as with the first ship, we ground down the side of the ship and the oars were shattered. The captain must have anticipated the manoeuvre for there were fewer screams and I saw that some of the men had withdrawn their oars. I wondered how it would go this time when Scanlan's arrow plunged into the throat of the captain. The steersman jerked the rudder to the right in panic. The right side of the ship still had oars and the ship moved at an angle to us. As it did so the wind caught the sail and the pirate ship began to move west.

"Lower oars!"

I was about to order a pursuit when I saw that they were not turning. They were fleeing. The death of their captain and the capture of their other ship had put a damper on their enthusiasm. It would take time to raise the sail and by then they would have gone.

"Well done men. Let us go and see our prize!"

They cheered as they rowed. We had captured our first ship. We split our crew and rowed both ships towards Olaf's town. He stood there toothlessly grinning as we tied the ships up. He put his once powerful arms around me, "Old Ragnar would have been proud of you today. That was clever sailing. You did well."

"I think Ragnar must have been with me today or they were poor captains."

"A little bit of both I would say. Come, let us clear out your prize and see what she has for us."

Sadly, the first things we found were the belongings of the fishermen. Of them, there was no sign and we could only imagine their fate. It made the task of throwing the dead pirates into the harbour more palatable. The crabs and the prawns would feast well. The pirates had a box containing many coins and their bodies yielded swords and daggers. The goods were an unexpected bonus. I had done what I had intended. I had driven away the pirates. Olaf's sentries who continued to watch the fleeing pirate had reported the ship continuing to sail west. I did not think they would try the same thing any time soon. They had lost a ship and two captains. When Prince Butar and Erik returned I could look them in the eye and tell them I had done my duty and protected the Island of Man.

Chapter 19

We had suffered only minor wounds in the attack. It was as I had thought; the pirates had not been trained as well as my men. The shattering of their oars and the speed of our attack had meant they could not respond quickly enough. Of course, Scanlan's arrows had helped and I decided to get him a good helmet from Bjorn. The captain of the ship had one which could be adapted. We also had another ship and that was always useful.

Erika was just delighted to see me returned unharmed. She never showed that she was upset when I left but I could see the relief in her eyes each time I returned.

We named the new ship *'Hawk'*. She was more like a bear and was a little lumbering but we had one of those and it did not do to take a name away from a ship. We had no captain yet but, until Erik and the prince returned from Frankia, then we did not need one. Events were turning out well for us and we were certain that the gods smiled on us. As the nights grew a little longer and we began to gather the harvest in we began to plan our celebrations for harvest time. When our ships returned we would make the feast one to remember.

Sometimes the Norns like to play tricks with you. They are like Loki and smile at you while preparing a disaster. That was what happened to us. The sentries on the tower signalled a ship approaching. It was Jarl Erik. His ship was, like mine a fast vessel and we assumed that *'Ran'* would be close behind. When *'Man'* docked I could tell from Jarl Erik's face that disaster had struck us.

He came directly towards me and his face told me the tale without words. When he spoke, I felt my heart sink to my boots. "We were ambushed on the way back when we were heavily laden with goods. It was Tadgh and Jarl Harald. They had four ships and they launched themselves from a hidden bay. Prince Butar's ship stood no chance and she was sunk. We saw some survivors; they were captured on the beach. One of them was Prince Butar." He dropped to his knee. "I am sorry brother; I have lost your father."

My mind was filled with so many thoughts that it was hard to think straight. I forced myself to breathe slowly. "Did you see him killed?"

Jarl Erik looked surprised at the question, "No. He was led away with the others."

I nodded. I understood Tadgh. He was baiting a trap for me and he was using my stepfather. He knew that I would go. "He is alive and we must go and rescue him."

Erika's hand went to her mouth. "This is Tadgh! He is doing this to get to you. You cannot trust him!"

I held her hand, "I know, my love, but this is Prince Butar and I owe him everything. I have to go."

She threw her arms around me. "I know but it does not stop the sickening feeling in my heart when I think of that viper!"

I whispered in her ear, "I must plan but I will make sure you and our people are protected."

She nodded, her heart too filled with emotion to risk speaking. She led Arturus and Eurwen away. Both of them had the confused look of a child who has wandered into an adult conversation which they do not understand.

I led Erik to the warrior hall. I did not need to speak with any of the warriors; they just followed me. Once inside I sat at the seat normally occupied by Prince Butar. I was his heir and, until he returned, I would have to make the decisions.

"As you all now know Tadgh has captured our prince and is setting a trap to capture me." I smiled, "I am not in a mood to satisfy him but I will rescue Prince Butar." The men all cheered and banged the table. I held up my hand. "However, I am not leaving Hrams-a undefended." I turned to Haaken, "You have followed me always and you and Cnut are the warriors I trust the most in the entire world. I want you to command here while the rest of us go to Frankia."

Haaken, who was normally affable and easy going, jumped up. "Leave Rolf here; he is a good leader. I am Ulfheonar."

"And that is why I must leave you. And remember Rolf knows Frankia better than any man on this island. I need his knowledge there." My eyes pleaded with my oldest friend. "Do not make this harder than it is. If I do not return I know that you will care for my family better than any man alive."

I saw the acceptance in his eyes and he bowed his head. "I will obey you, my friend."

"We sail tonight with just two ships. Haaken, you will need to tell the others of the events for we are in danger until we can affect a rescue. This island is now under siege until we return."

As I left the hall Scanlan and Snorri ran to me. "My lord are..."

"Yes, I need you both. You have shown me that you are skilled archers and brave to boot. I will need your skills before too long."

My parting from Erika was tearful. Her brother and her husband were sailing into a trap and she did not know if she would ever see either of us again. I know that I was lucky in my choice of wife. She would care for our family and our people whilst we were away. We boarded

'Wolf'. Cnut made sure we had plenty of supplies and Scanlan made sure that we plenty of arrows. We had extra crew so that we could double bank the oars. I wanted as swift a voyage as possible. The thought of the tortures which Tadgh might be inflicting on Prince Butar made my heart go cold. We sailed on the night tide and Ran was with us for the wind blew hard from the north. Perhaps the fact that her namesake had been sunk made her favour us for the wind blew us all the way around the island the Romans had called Britannia in the fastest voyage I had ever experienced. It was like trying to hang on to a maddened, stampeding horse. Disaster loomed large with every rock but somehow, we survived and, each morning we could see *'Man'* in close attendance. Jarl Erik would not let me down.

The ride became a little calmer once we crossed the open water to Frankia. Jarl Erik had told me that Tadgh had used a river further south than the mouth of the Rinaz. We had always sailed close to the coast of Frankia as it avoided the lands of the Saxons. There were some inhospitable islands off the coast and we usually steered well clear of them. A storm had forced the two ships to sail between the islands and Frankia and that was when Tadgh had struck. On the voyage south, I had been planning my response to the kidnapping. I would use the islands as a base. I was not so stupid as to sail into Tadgh's lair and expect to survive. I would use the skill of the wolf. I would use the Ulfheonar to scout out the enemy's dispositions. Ran had helped us by giving us such a speedy voyage south. I did not think that Tadgh would expect me to make such a swift passage south. I would now use the time we had been given to our advantage.

We approached the islands from the west and I kept the islands between us and the mainland. There were six or seven islands and I chose a small uninhabited one as our base. I beached my ship and jumped ashore. We soon discovered water and Cnut and two of the Ulfheonar confirmed that it was uninhabited. Once Jarl Erik had joined me I gathered the men around me.

"You will drop me and ten of the Ulfheonar, tomorrow morning, before dawn, as close as you can to Tadgh's lair. You will return the following morning at the same time to pick us up. We will attack then and so you will need to bring both boats. I intend to find out how the land lies. We will be as prepared as possible to enable us to avoid this trap which Tadgh is setting for us. Meanwhile, I want you to build four rafts and find as much brushwood and material which will burn as you can."

Jarl Erik looked confused, "Why?"

"Let us say I have an idea to upset Tadgh's plans."

Cnut slapped me on the back. "Dragon Heart you have a mind like a bear trap."

We wore no byrnies as we slipped ashore on the, apparently, deserted part of the coast. Jarl Erik had told me that they had seen a hill fort when they stood out to sea. He assumed it was Tadgh's. Rolf had told us that there was a hill fort close to an estuary but he had thought it unoccupied. He had seen it when he had been wrecked on this graveyard of ships. The dark and the cliff masked the fort; it was invisible to us. We had to trust that we would find it. We had made our plans before we left the ship. There would be no words once we landed. We were all acutely aware of how far sound would travel at night. Cnut took his four warriors to approach the fort from the far side. We were not here to fight; we were here to spy out the lie of the land and to see what traps the treacherous Tadgh had prepared.

The wolf cloaks soon hid Cnut and his men from sight and we ascended the gentle, grassy slope. We did not know how far we would have to travel but we had all night to do so. We went carefully and slowly. Egill found the first trap; it was just off the main trail and was a piece of thin rope attached to a stick and a pile of rocks. Had we caught it then there would have been the sound of rocks falling down the slope. There had to be a guard nearby. We spotted him soon after. He was huddled close to a rock and was peering out to sea. We skirted him and headed north. Tadgh had more traps in the form of pits covered by bracken and grass. We found many of these as we ascended the slope. Our slow and methodical approach was paying off.

The wind must have changed direction for I suddenly had a whiff of wood smoke and man. We halted and moved even more slowly. Suddenly we saw the walls of the fort. It looked to be an ancient one which had been refurbished. I could see a tower and a wall of timbers. As I watched I saw a guard patrolling. Then we heard a moan. We slid along the ground like shadows of small clouds and reached a sheltered dell towards the sound we had heard. I crawled on hands and knees to peer over the end of the depression. As I looked over the lip I saw Prince Butar and ten of his men. They were tied to low crosses with their knees on the ground. The moan I had heard was from Tostig who looked to have a head wound. I felt Ragnar begin to move next to me and I restrained him and shook my head. I moved north again away from the prisoners. I had seen enough there. The prisoners were bait. I could see that their position was uncomfortable but would not kill them. They would be able to stay there for many days and not die. It was not kindness on Tadgh's part; he needed them to draw us in.

I took us on a long loop around the fort keeping well out of sight but always observing the ditch and the walls. It was well built and the slope was deceptively steep. When we reached the far side, I saw a second gate and towers. There were just two sentries above the gate. Now that we knew they had men on the hillside we watched for them and were able to avoid them.

The hill dropped on the far side and we followed the incline down. There looked to be a natural dry valley which gave the fort protection from the land side too. We followed it towards the sea. Suddenly we heard a movement ahead and we froze. I could smell human rather than animal and I slid my seax from my boot and moved forwards slowly. I saw the shape of a man before me. There was something familiar about the shape of the body. I hissed, "Ulfheonar," and Sweyn turned around. We had found the others. I signalled for them to follow us and we headed towards the sea. I saw the masts of the drekar at the same time that I heard the gentle bumping of wood on wood. We found a copse of trees which was quite close to the shore and we hid ourselves in the dense foliage. In another four weeks, it would be bare. Tadgh now had three ships but they were moored so that, from the sea, it would only look like one ship. He was laying a trap and it was for me. I had seen enough. The sun was lightening the sky in the east and we needed to be far away. I led my Ulfheonar north and we travelled in a straight line well away from the fort. We walked until the sun was up.

We needed a place to hide up during the day. I was looking for a wood when we stumbled upon a clutch of huts in a small clearing. There was no sign of life and no smoke to suggest fires. We moved cautiously into the ring of eight huts. We could see the bones and the remains of the villagers. The animals had done their worst and all flesh had been gnawed from the bones. There appeared to be children as well as adults there. I saw the hand of Tadgh in all this. We found a hut which was habitable in that it had no bones within it. I set Bjorn to watch from the edge of the village and then we shared the information we had gathered.

"They have laid a trap for us. The bait is Prince Butar and the rest of his men. They are staked out in plain view inviting rescue." Cnut cocked his head to one side with the obvious question written all over his face. "There were men watching. They have sentries and traps on the hill sides. He wants us to attempt to rescue them. The moment we do his men will fall upon us. The last thing we need to do is to free the prince."

Cnut nodded his curiosity satisfied, "And that is why he has disguised the numbers of his ships. He wants us to think he has fewer men than he does."

Egill asked the question which was on every warrior's mind. "Have you a plan to rescue them?"

I nodded. "That dry valley we used is perfect. We can approach the fort from the landward side and they will not be expecting it. I found fewer traps on that side. We will distract them and make them look to the front and we will attack the rear."

Cnut smiled, "They have four gates; one on each side. If their attention is on the captives then we can surprise the sentries."

I nodded, "We use Scanlan and Snorri to take out the sentries and we can enter silently. I have no doubt that they think we will try to get the prince and his men first. There is little point. We have to get to Tadgh and destroy him. Jarl Harald is a coward as we know and if Tadgh is dead then Jarl Harald will flee. The warriors will be leaderless. We go for the head of the serpent first."

We took it in turns to sleep. There was a stream nearby and we had water but the dead villagers took the edge from our appetite. This village would be haunted at night and we were glad to leave, in the late afternoon, and head for the meeting point. We moved as quietly as we could and used every single piece of cover that was available. So far, we had avoided detection and I did not want Tadgh to be aware that we had returned. As we waited in the darkening dusk I ran through my plan and what Tadgh would be doing. He had allowed Erik to return unscathed so that it would draw me in. He would keep the prisoners alive until we arrived. He had to have someone watching from the cliff to spy out a ship arriving. He could do nothing about the dark; his men would be blind then. That was the reason why he had the sentries dotted around the hillside and had laid the traps. His men would be listening for the sounds which would warn them of an enemy attacking at night. I had no doubt that if it had not been Ulfheonar who had scouted then the traps would have been effective. I had to get Tadgh's attention to the front of his fort and the prisoners. It was where he would expect me to attack. Hiding the ships in the islands had given us the edge and that was all we needed.

Suddenly Cnut tapped my arm and we saw the two shapes of the drekar loom up in the dark. Behind them, they towed the rafts. Jarl Erik waited for me as I waded out to the ships. After we had donned our armour I explained my plan to him in detail. When I told him how the prisoners were held his face darkened. "This time we finish it."

"Aye we do but he has three ship's crews waiting for us. You have the fewest men. You will be the diversion. I need you to draw Tadgh's warriors back here. You will need to leave four good warriors with the ship's boys. If our ships are lost then so are we." He nodded. "You will be the one who will launch the attack. We will need at least two hours to get in position. I will leave Bjorn with you for he knows the dispositions of the enemy." We clasped arms. "We do this for Prince Butar!" He nodded. "You attack and we will be watching and listening. Use the cry of Ulfheonar. It will draw Harald Two Face and Tadgh out. When Tadgh and his men emerge, you will run back to your ships as though you fear him. He will think he has won and follow you. We will attack the fort while he is away chasing shadows."

I led the forty warriors who would accompany me. Most were Ulfheonar but I had Rolf, his men, and some of Jarl Erik's as well. The jarl would have to make his fifteen men appear like an army. It was the main reason I would attack in the dark. He had been told to use our war cry. It would be like nectar to a bee; Tadgh would not be able to resist it.

Cnut led and I brought up the rear with Scanlan and Snorri. Aiden had been unhappy to be left with the ship until Erik gave him a clip about the ear. He was then unhappy about the blow to the ear. We moved with confidence for we were well away from the traps and sentries. There was more noise than I would have liked but most of the warriors with me were not Ulfheonar.

When we reached the dry valley, we began to ascend the hill. I had explained to Scanlan and Snorri what I expected of them. Their task was to kill the sentries silently and then to target the most dangerous warriors they could see. We crouched in the dark thirty paces from the walls and the gate. The two sentries were busy talking and not watching to the landward side. There was no reason why they should. Any rescuer would have to come by sea. It was their confidence in their position which would be their undoing. I am not sure how I would have prepared against an attack such as ours but I knew that we now had a slight advantage and I would use every help the gods sent my way.

Chapter 20

Time seems to drag when you are waiting. I was reliant on Jarl Erik and the tide. Suddenly I smelled smoke and I saw the two sentries turn. Jarl Erik had launched his fire rafts and they were, even now, drifting inexorably towards the three ships tied closely together. Tadgh would have to send men in that direction; he would need to save his ships. Fire was the enemy of a wooden ship. As soon as I heard orders being shouted within and the noise of alarm I tapped my two archers. The sentries fell without a sound. One dropped over the wall and the other within. There was no sudden noise on the other side and I assumed that their deaths had gone unnoticed.

We rose as one man and raced to the gate. Two of the smaller warriors were boosted over the wall and we waited for the gates to swing open. We had to step over the body of the dead sentry. The inside of the fort looked to be almost deserted. I assumed they had all gone to the far end and the main gate of the fort. I could see that the gate at the opposite end of the fort was open and men were rushing out. We moved forwards silently.

I heard the shout, "Ulfheonar!" and knew that Jarl Erik was doing his part. Two arrows flew from behind me and the two warriors who had come from a hut some thirty paces away fell dead. Rolf took his men into the huts and I heard shouts as they killed those within. We continued to move purposefully forward. As warriors ran from their huts they were slain before they could react. We had to kill many more of them before they realised what we were about.

I turned as Rolf came out of a round house. His blood-spattered tunic showed that he had slain the occupants. I shouted to him, "Fire the huts!" The turf on the roof would slow down the fire but the smoke would aid the confusion and, perhaps, disguise our numbers. As we neared the gate I could see that at least two of the rafts had found their mark and one of the ships was ablaze. It gave me some pleasure to see that it was that of the traitor, Jarl Harald. He had sought the wrong ally and was now beginning to pay the price for treachery.

The light from the inferno showed the warriors as they hurtled down the slope towards Jarl Erik's retreating men. I could not see our warriors but I assumed that Erika's brother was obeying my instructions and retreating. Our life was made easier by the fact that we had the backs of men to us and they were slain without knowing who we were. I had planned on killing Tadgh first but my plan had succeeded far better than I could have imagined. The prisoners were unguarded.

"Cnut, take four men and free the captives."

He nodded and raced off. I turned to the ones who remained. "I want a shield wall between the prisoners and those warriors."

We ran beyond Cnut and his warriors. I saw faces glance up at us with sudden hope on them but I had a more dangerous task. I had to ensure that they could escape. Soon Tadgh and his men would see the flames flickering behind them and know that we had stolen a march on them. They would know there was an enemy behind them. We now had the slope in our favour. They outnumbered us that much was true, but we were the better warriors. Skill would out. They would have to attack up the steep hill which had deterred us. Now it acted in our favour.

"Take them to safety!"

Cnut looked at me. "Where is safe?"

The enemy was between us and our ships and I had fired the fort. I shrugged. Cnut would have to improvise. I sought Scanlan and Snorri. "Go down to the ships and kill those trying to put out the fires!"

I held *Ragnar's Spirit* and waited for the onslaught which I knew would come. I glanced to my left and right. I had twenty warriors only. When Rolf and his men had finished firing the fort and slaughtering those within I would have another fifteen. I estimated that there would be forty or fifty warriors, perhaps more, charging up the hill to get us. We would be outnumbered.

I saw that Cnut and his men had freed the prisoners. None of them could move well. They had been hobbled and doubled over for days. I was amazed that they were alive still. They were our people and they would fight, even if injured. I saw that Cnut was leading them down to the water. It made sense. There was at least one undamaged ship down there. They lost at least one but their efforts had saved one. Snorri and Scanlan could be the difference between escape and death. They had to thin out the warriors saving the boats and then Cnut and his men would have to secure a ship. My job was to buy them time... and kill Tadgh.

The renegades came up the hill towards us piecemeal. The faster warriors reached us first. The faster warriors were the ones with the least armour. I knew that Tadgh would struggle to climb the hill. He still bore the scars and the injuries from our last encounter. We had to make the hill a killing zone. The first warriors rushed at us as though they would attain glory by killing Dragon Heart. I was not an easy man to kill. I had Ulfheonar on either side of me and we slaughtered all those who dared to approach. There were many of them but they had no armour and their swords and spears could not penetrate our shields and our mail. Fighting when you are below a warrior is never easy.

The second line of warriors halted as they waited for someone to take charge. I saw Jarl Harald there and I called to him. "I am surprised you are here, Jarl Harald. I thought that you like to be at the rear watching other men die and admiring the arses of the young boys!"

My men laughed and I could see that the barb had hit home. He ordered his men forward. It was a mistake for he did not lead. A man will fight to the death for a leader he respects, Jarl Harald had lost all respect and the attack was half hearted. His men did not have the heart for this. The first warrior hacked down at me with his axe and I turned my shield slightly so that the blade slid down my metal studded shield. He expected me to return the blow the same way but I jabbed forwards with all of my power and the sword slid over his shield and into his throat. His fellows fared no better. They were downhill from us and our blows stuck home with the added power of height.

Rolf's voice came from behind me, "The fort is on fire. We have no place to retreat."

I laughed, "The thought never crossed my mind. Put your men behind us. We will soon have to deal with real warriors. Tadgh comes!"

I could now see him clearly from the glow of the fires all around us. It was as though it was daylight. He was angry and was berating those around him. I suspect he was angry that Jarl Harald had attacked prematurely and he could see that his captives were gone. Had the jarl waited for Tadgh then it might have been different. I was desperate to see how Cnut was faring at the ship but I would have to leave that to him. And what was Jarl Erik doing now? All of that was beyond my control and I gripped my sword tightly. As I did so I heard a voice in my head. *'You are the wolf and you have the sword touched by the gods'.* It was Ragnar's voice and it gave me comfort. I had fought the wolf when I was not yet a man and I had won. I had fought against the raiders and saved Ragnar and my people. I was fighting a man without honour. I had to believe in my arms and my skill.

As I expected, Tadgh did not come himself. Instead, he sent his mailed oathsworn at us. It was a mistake. They had to struggle up the hill in their armour and I could see the exertion showing on their faces. They had already run down the hill after jarl Erik and now they had to come back up that steep slope. Their weapons would have to strike up at us while we could chop down on them. We would have more force behind our blows. The danger lay in them forcing us to retreat into the inferno which raged behind us.

"Rolf, have your men brace themselves. We do not move!"

I think I heard him laugh as he said, "We move only when they shift our dead bodies!"

We would hold.

They stabbed up at us with their swords and the blades slid harmlessly up our shields. I smashed down with Ragnar's Spirit and the blade cut through metal and wood to sink into flesh. Each warrior fell back bleeding. After they had lost many men Tadgh reorganised them. He made a wedge and forty warriors arrowed up the hill towards us and more particularly, towards me.

"Brace!"

I made no attempt to hit them I just held my shield before me as they crashed into us. They were strong warriors and our feet slid back a little on the ground which was now slippery with blood and guts. Rolf and his men leaned into us and the line held. I saw a warrior's face level with the top of my shield and I punched at it. My shield was studded with metal; it ripped across his face and he could not help but move back. I jammed the hilt of my sword into his eye and he fell backwards screaming. Now that I had space to swing I used the long reach of my sword and carved a swathe before me. The edge of my blade ripped through unguarded faces and heads. If we had had enough men we could have pushed them all the way down the hill but we had to be strong and just stand. I saw that we had not escaped unscathed and some of Rolf's men were now in the front rank.

Rolf himself stood on the other side of Egill. He turned to me, grinning. "Now I am a warrior once more and not a glorified bodyguard!" As if to emphasise his statement he brought his sword down to split the helmet and head of the warrior before him.

Tadgh's warriors were now wary of advancing. They were losing too many men. There was a lull and I glanced to the shore. I could see that one ship was a wreck while the second was smoke and fire damaged. The third, the smallest of the three was now forty yards off the shore and I could see Cnut on her deck. Prince Butar and his oathsworn had been rescued. We had done what we set out to do and now I had to get my men to safety but not before I had done that which I swore to do; kill Tadgh.

I stepped forwards and addressed the enemy, "Your prisoners are gone and your trap has failed. Will you now face me as a man and end this."

He too limped forward but he stood behind the front rank of his men. "You are outnumbered and you have nowhere to run to. Your men have abandoned you."

I laughed; he was pathetic and did not understand the code of the warrior. He had not been trained by Ragnar. He was an opportunist and a killer. "Once more you hide behind your men and once again they will die while you live. My men have not abandoned me. They obey my orders. You and the coward Harald deserve each other. You are a marriage made in heaven. I hope you will be happy in each other's arms."

It was an insult and, I thought, without foundation but Jarl Harald's reaction showed me that there might be some truth in my assertion.

"That is a lie!"

My men sniggered, "Then fight me and prove it. The gods will defend you if you speak the truth."

He stepped back and I saw his men look at him with disgust. Whatever happened here his men would no longer follow him. He was a leader with no one left to lead. Even Tadgh sensed the change. The warriors below us did outnumber us but they no longer believed in their leaders. My handful of men stood proudly ready to fight to the death for me and they knew it. I pushed home my advantage. "Come Tadgh. Let us save the lives of our men and fight to the death. Let the gods decide who is worthy of life."

When his men all stared at him he had no choice. His closest warriors had all been killed, either in Hibernia or the Island of Man and they had died at my hands. Those men he had sent against me had been his most loyal. It had been a gamble and it had failed. He was left with no choice; he had to fight me.

He pointed to the beach. "Down there then where the ground is flat." He knew his leg would not cope with the uneven hillside and he was giving himself every advantage. I did not mind.

"Anywhere so long as you are within a sword's length of me."

His men moved down the hill. "Rolf, make sure there is no treachery."

We moved down in a line parallel to them. I noticed that Cnut had kept the captured ship less than fifty paces from the shore. I was not abandoned. When we reached the shore, his men formed a line behind him. Had we attempted to escape by sea they would have fallen upon us. I had no intention of running. I had that which I had wanted, I had Tadgh and I could end this blood feud once and for all.

Although I had injured Tadgh's leg the last time we had fought that would have no effect on this encounter. This was a flat field on which to fight and I would find it hard to use that to my advantage. I would have to use my superior sword skills.

He limped towards me and I could see hate and anger written all over his face. This was not a good way to fight. Ragnar had taught me to be calm and to fight cold and not hot. I would seek to find his weaknesses and exploit them. He suddenly roared and leapt at me using his good leg to launch the attack. His sword smashed down from a height and I barely had time to parry the blow with my shield. My arm shuddered. The break had healed but it was still tender. I could ill afford many such blows.

I pulled my sword over my left shoulder and swung it at his head. It was an awkward blow but it meant that he was unable to use his shield. He had to use his sword or move backwards. He had to parry it with his sword and that allowed me to punch at him with my shield. It sent rivers of pain through my arm but I gritted my teeth and bore it. He was forced to step backwards. He had to favour his weak leg and I saw that he had moved closer to the sea. Wet sand can be treacherous.

He swung sideways at me and I was too slow to bring my shield down; my arm refused to react. The blade hacked into my mail byrnie and I heard rings shatter. Tadgh's eyes lit up when he saw the damage that had been done. It was a weakness he would exploit. The leather tunic I wore beneath stopped the sword from penetrating too far but it was a warning. My right hand darted forward so quickly that Tadgh, who was still busy anticipating my demise, could not parry the blow and the sword sliced through the mail he wore over his helmet and ripped open his cheek. The wound looked worse than it was but his men gasped as blood spurted.

"Look on your death, you treacherous viper."

For the first time, I saw fear flicker in his eyes. He swung again at the damaged byrnie but I had expected the move and my shield took the blow. The pain in my left arm was now almost too much. My next blow was met by his sword. I saw slivers of metal flying off from the edge of the blade. He stumbled a little and I flicked my sword out. He thought I was going for his face and his shield came up. Instead, I had aimed at his knee and he screamed as the tip entered his knee. Suddenly I was aware of a shape hurtling at my unprotected right side. It was Jarl Harald wielding an axe. There was no way I could defend against the blow. Before he could bring down the axe, I felt the wind passed my cheeks as two arrows smacked into his face, throwing him to the ground. Snorri and Scanlan had been watching for such treachery. The traitor had died as he had lived, without honour.

I heard a collective growl from the men who had followed the jarl; no one likes treachery and I could see the murderous glances they cast in the direction of Tadgh who was rapidly running out of followers. He was desperate to end it now and he swung at my damaged byrnie once more. This time I did not use my shield, I just spun around so that he struck nothing but air. *Ragnar's Spirit* sliced through his mail byrnie and into his spine. I heard the crack as his backbone shattered. His life ended almost instantly and it was though someone had sucked the life from him. His body collapsed in a bloody heap on the sand.

I was almost spent. My left arm could barely hold my shield but this was not over. "I have killed this traitor. Is there any other who wishes to fight me or dispute the right?" I could not fight another but I had to make the offer.

I saw them look at each other and then they shook their heads. I turned to look at the body of Jarl Harald. "There are those of you here who followed this treacherous jarl because you were oathsworn. Your oath is no longer required. If you wish to return to Man with us then you can do so, if you swear allegiance to me."

One man, whom I vaguely recognised, stepped forwards. "And if we do not?"

"Then you can stay here with the scum who followed Tadgh." I shrugged, "I care not which you choose but choose now." I had seen Rolf wave to Cnut and knew that our newly captured ship was heading towards us.

Twenty warriors knelt in the sand, "We will follow, Dragon Heart!"

I saw the black looks which the men I had insulted gave to me. I cared not. They would not do anything about it; they had no honour and if they did fight they would die. I let them live because they would never bother me again. I could see it in their faces. They had been defeated. They would rob and murder but they would never cross the waters to my home.

We boarded the captured ship and, as dawn broke I saw the survivors arguing amongst themselves over the armour and weapons of Tadgh and Harald. I shook my head; I had had the measure of those men. They were not men that I would choose to lead.

I went to the stern where Cnut steered and Prince Butar lay. "Thank you, my son. The day I made you free was the greatest day of my life. You will be a greater warrior than Ragnar or any of the old heroes."

"I am sorry we could not save your weapons or your armour."

He shrugged and Rolf said, "But we did save them. They were in Tadgh's hut along with a chest of jewels and precious metal. We took them in anticipation of your victory although, my lord, it might be considered a little risky by some, to insult warriors who outnumber you."

"In that case, let us go home. Steer a course for Jarl Erik. He will need men to row." I winced as I dropped my shield.

Scanlan came to my side, "My lord what is it?"

"My arm I am afraid." I suddenly remembered Jarl Harald. "And I owe my life to you and Snorri. Snorri, choose the best sword we have captured." His eyes lit up with gratitude. "And for you Scanlan, you and your family are free." His eyes filled and he grasped my hand. He had no words nor did he need them. He had saved my life.

The ship we had captured was a larger drekar than mine but I wanted to sail home on *'Wolf'*. The Ulfheonar transferred with me and we left Rolf and the newly recruited warriors to sail Prince Butar and the captives, home. We did not ask them what privations they had suffered; there would be time enough for that. I was just grateful that we had managed to save so many of them.

My arm became steadily worse on the way home. Cnut had to steer and Scanlan fretted over me like a mother hen. I did not know if it had broken again or if this was to be a weakness for the rest of my life. I had only had to take a few blows and I was surprised how quickly the pain had returned. Before I had been wounded I had been struck many times on the shield and it had never bothered me.

Scanlan examined it. It was not tender to the touch but every movement jarred it and send the pain coursing through my body. Scanlan was no doctor but he was good with animals. I was just an animal which could talk. "I think there is a slight break again. With your permission, master, I will put splints there again."

I nodded my agreement but said, "You forget, Scanlan, I am not your master any longer."

He shook his head as he broke the spear shaft in two. "You will always be my master. Being free will not change that. I am your oathsworn just as much as Haaken, Cnut and Snorri."

Once he had cut the wood to the correct length he gently bandaged it and then tightened it. The pain was momentary but as soon as he put the sling around my neck, the pain lessened. I actually smiled. "I have your calling when we get home; you can tend to the horses and the sick. You have a real skill." He nodded modestly and then sat with his arm around the sleeping Aiden.

Chapter 21

Ran did not give us an easy ride home. The seas were huge and we suffered wounds and injuries when oars sheared and rigging broke. The worst storms were around the savage rocks at the edge of the world. It was always a terrifying time for sailors. To the west lay death and the end of the world and to the east were the most savage rocks known to man. It took us two days to pass and enter the slightly more sheltered waters to the north. We lost no lives but we were all glad when we saw Mona to the east and knew that we were but hours away from our home. To us, the two voyages had seemed like naught but I knew the many days we had been away would seem like a lifetime to those waiting for us. For that reason, we headed to Duboglassio first. They would need to know who had survived and who would be mourned. I had no doubt that the sentry in the tower above my village would tell my wife that my ship was safe.

The damaged rigging and oars meant that it seemed to take forever to sail up the coast. It gave the people time to gather and watch the three drekar limp home. They would not recognise the third ship but Jarl Erik's and mine were well known to all. They would not fear an attack. The storms had not helped my weakened arm. I resolved to allow it to heal completely this time. It had nearly cost me my life.

When Prince Butar gave a wan smile and a wave from the ship the people erupted in a wave of emotion and cheering. He was a well-loved leader. During the voyage back I had watched him on his boat and he looked like a shell of his former self. I would need to speak with him; I owed it to my mother to help her husband regain his former power.

The women who waited for husbands were either relieved when the warriors fell into their arms or they were distraught when they saw how many had failed to return. My Ulfheonar and I were the last to land. Our people would be many miles away; it was more important for those with families to land first. I left Cnut and Rolf to finish seeing to the boat and I sent Scanlan and Aiden across the island to tell my wife of my safe return. Jarl Erik and I followed Prince Butar to his hall.

The hall had an empty and desolate feel. Eurwen and the slaves were with my family. The only occupant had been the old slave who had kept it clean. When we entered Prince Butar was slumped in his seat staring at the floor.

I approached and dropped to my knee. "Tell me father, what is it that ails you?"

When he looked at me I saw nothing but pain in his eyes. He shook his head, "I know now that I am old. I saw my death on the hillside in Frankia. There was no glory there. I watched as my warriors, my oathsworn, died one by one and I could do nothing. Tadgh was not a warrior; he was a pirate, a mercenary and yet he defeated me. My time is over."

I stood and I became angry. "I am glad that my mother is not here, to see someone she loved and respected, feeling so sorry for himself. Rid yourself of this self-pity! You are alive and you are back amongst your people. When Erika brings Eurwen she will not want to see a decrepit old man. She will want to see her loving father returned to her safe and sound."

I wondered if I had overstepped the mark. Jarl Erik took a step away as though to distance himself from my comments. It was only when my stepfather stood and gave a half smile that I knew I had spoken true. "You are right. Your mother would have given me the sharp edge of her tongue but, Dragon Heart, I tell you this, my days of raiding and trading are over. I stay here and I defend my land."

I nodded. "You have earned that right and there are others who can go trading for you." Even as I said it I was running through the oathsworn who remained. He had only returned with twelve of his warriors.

He put his arms around us. "Let us see if there is any ale left and we will drink and toast the dead."

The slave must have been listening, for he scurried off and returned, with three frothing beakers of ale. "Thank you for that. Now get us some food. I am hungry." He lifted his beaker, "To the dead. Enjoy Valhalla!"

After we had drunk I ventured another question. "What happened in Frankia?" I nodded to Jarl Erik, "Erik told me what he saw but you were there."

"It was my fault that we were so close to the coast but I did not expect there to be pirates there. The four drekar raced out so quickly that I had no time to escape. I knew that Erik was further out to sea. We could see that we were lost and we tried to fight them to aid their escape. We were rammed by one of the drekar. I think that was a mistake for that drekar also sank but we were thrown into the water. Luckily most of us did not have mail on or we would have been dragged to the bottom. They rescued us but it was a cruel rescue." He finished off his ale and shook his head. "We were led off like beasts about to be slaughtered. Our weapons were taken and we were stripped of anything of value. Erik the Bald tried to escape but he was caught and they impaled him on a stake. It took half a day for him to die but he never uttered a sound. He was a brave warrior. The rest of us were tethered as you saw. Each day they took one away to impale him too. It was a slow death for all of us. We had to watch our comrades suffer."

"I am just sorry that Tadgh died so quickly. I wish he had suffered."

"He will suffer in the afterlife. The dead will not forget his treachery. Tadgh has more enemies than enough."

I was just pleased that Sweyn had survived. He had been Ulfheonar and I knew that he would build up my stepfather's warriors to make them as good as they had been before the disaster. We spoke, as we waited for the food, of the trade goods they had lost.

"It is a setback, Dragon Heart. Perhaps we should trade close to home."

I had been thinking along those lines myself. "Perhaps with Gwynedd? They are our closest neighbours."

Jarl Erik looked distinctly worried. "Aren't they as bad as the Hibernians?"

I looked at Prince Butar and we smiled in the joint memory of my mother. "My mother's family came from there and perhaps, with the crowns of Rheged in our possession; it might be possible to talk with them. I will go in the spring when we have more trade goods and our warriors are in better shape. This has been a hard year for them and we have lost many fine warriors. We will have to look for the young to replace them."

After we had eaten I rejoined my ship and we sailed home to Hrams-a. We were all silent as we sailed home. Haaken would have more sagas to devise and we would all have to heal our wounds. There were good memories to take from the fight. Snorri and Scanlan had shown themselves to have warrior's hearts and we had captured much armour and many weapons. We would be better equipped in the spring.

Scanlan and Aiden had reached home before we had and we were expected. This was a more muted reception than the one in Duboglassio. The Ulfheonar had sailed and fought more than any others on the island. Even Cnut looked weary. Haaken looked on, sadly, as we disembarked. After I had hugged my family he came over to clasp my arm.

"I have fulfilled my oath and protected your family Dragon Heart but next time it is Cnut's turn. I yearn for the adventure which you always seem to attract."

I nodded, "Hopefully we will not need to do so."

"Tadgh and Jarl Harald?"

"Both dead. Scanlan and Snorri killed Jarl Harald with arrows and they saved my life." I turned to Erika, "I freed Scanlan and his family."

Her face broke into a smile. "And that is a bargain for saving your life. Besides, I think they will stay close by. Seara and Maewe are good friends and it matters not if they are free or slave."

I had been a slave and knew that what she said was true. We never mistreated our slaves and were rewarded by loyalty. As the autumn storms began we settled into a new life with freemen instead of slaves and with an added vigilance to protect our way of life.

Prince Butar, Olaf and Jarl Erik arrived with their oathsworn just a month after we returned. They came unannounced and dressed in their finest. Erika, Haaken and Cnut all had knowing smug looks but I had no idea what had prompted the visit. The fact that the warrior hall had been cleaned and a feast prepared should have told me of my wife's part in this conspiracy but I am a warrior and do not notice such things.

She and my children stood to one side as Prince Butar waved his hands for silence. "We are here today to reward a great warrior. All of us owe more than we can say to Dragon Heart. On this day, we are here to confer on him the title of Jarl. Jarl Garth will rule the lands and seas around Hrams-a and I name him now as my heir so that when I go to the Otherworld he will rule this island. He will be prince."

The cheering from all those around me was deafening. I was stunned. I bowed my head and Prince Butar placed the seal of my authority around my neck. I had refused the honour before but now I accepted, I had been a slave and a warrior, now I was a jarl. I looked upwards. I hoped my mother and Ragnar were watching. I closed my eyes and swore a private oath that I would never let any of them down. I would be a fair jarl and I would protect all of my people on this Island of Man.

The End

Glossary

Áed Oirdnide –King of Tara 797
Bebbanburgh- Bamburgh Castle, Northumbria
Byrnie- a mail shirt reaching down to the knees
Caerlleon- Welsh for Chester
Cymri- Welsh
Cymru- Wales
Drekar- a Dragon ship-a Viking warship
Duboglassio –Douglas, Isle of Man
Frankia- France and part of Germany
Garth- Dragon heart
Gaill- Irish for foreigners
Glaesum –amber
Hrams-a – Ramsey, Isle of Man
Jarl- Norse earl or lord
Joro-goddess of the earth
Lochlannach – Irish for Northerners (Vikings)
Legacaestir- Anglo Saxon for Chester
Manau – The Isle of Man
Midden- a place where they dumped human waste
Njoror- God of the sea
Nithing- A man without honour (Saxon)
Orkneyjar-Orkney
Ran- Goddess of the sea
Rinaz –The Rhine
Seax – short sword
Skeggox – an axe with a shorter beard on one side
Sigismund- Frankish trader living in Cologne
Sif- Goddess of battle and the name of Harald's ship
Tadgh- a former slave and renegade Viking
The Norns- Fate
Threttanessa- a drekar with 13 oars on each side.
Thrall- slave
Ullr-Norse God of Hunting
Ulfheonar-an elite warrior who wore a wolf skin over his armour
Wyrd- Fate

Historical note

The Viking raids began, according to records left by the monks, in the 790s when Lindisfarne was pillaged. However, there were many small settlements along the east coast and most were undefended. I have chosen a fictitious village on the Tees as the home of Garth who is enslaved and then, when he gains his freedom, becomes Dragon Heart. As buildings were all made of wood then any evidence would have long rotted save for a few post holes. My raiders represent the Norse warriors who wanted the plunder of the soft Saxon kingdom. There is a myth that the Vikings raided in large numbers but this is not so. It was only in the tenth and eleventh centuries that the numbers grew. They also did not have allegiances to kings. The Norse settlements were often isolated family groups. The term Viking was not used in what we now term the Viking age. Warriors went a-Viking which meant that they sailed for adventure or pirating. Their lives were hard. Slavery was commonplace. The Norse for slave is thrall and I have used both terms.

The length of the swords in this period was not the same as in the later medieval period. By the year 850 they were only 76cm long and in the eighth century, they were shorter still. The first sword Dragon Heart used, Ragnar's, was probably only 60-65cm long. This would only have been slightly longer than a Roman gladius. At this time the sword, not the axe was the main weapon. The best swords came from Frankia and were probably German in origin. A sword was considered a special weapon and a good one would be handed from father to son. A warrior with a famous blade would be sought out on the battlefield. There was little mail around at the time and warriors learned to be agile to avoid being struck.

Honey was used as an antiseptic in both ancient and modern times.
When writing about the raids I have tried to recreate those early days of the Viking raider. The Saxons had driven the native inhabitants to the extremes of Wales, Cornwall and Scotland. The Irish were always too busy fighting amongst themselves. It must have come as a real shock to be attacked in their own settlements. By the time of King Alfred almost sixty years later they were better prepared. This was also about the time that Saxon England converted completely to Christianity. The last place to do so was the Isle of Wight. There is no reason to believe that the Vikings would have had any sympathy for their religion and would, in

fact, have taken advantage of their ceremonies and rituals not to mention their riches.

Eardwulf was king of Northumbria twice: first from 796-806 and from 808-810. The king who deposed him was Elfwald II. This period was a turbulent one for the kings of Northumbria and marked a decline in their fortunes until it was taken over by the Danes in 867.

Slavery was far more common in the ancient world. When the Normans finally made England their own they showed that they understood the power of words and propaganda by making the slaves into serfs. This was a brilliant strategy as it forced their former slaves to provide their own food whilst still working for their lords and masters for nothing. Manumission was possible as Garth showed in the first book in this series. Scanlan's training is also a sign that not all of the slaves suffered. It was a hard and cruel time- it was ruled by the strong.

The Isle of Man is reputed to have the earliest surviving Parliament, the Tynwald although there is evidence that there were others amongst the Viking colonies on Orkney and in Iceland. I have used this idea for Prince Butar's meetings of Jarls.

The early ninth century saw Britain converted to Christianity and there were many monasteries which flourished. These were often mixed. These were not the huge stone edifices such as Whitby and Fountain's Abbey; these were wooden structures. As such their remains have disappeared, along with the bones of those early Christian priests. Hexham was a major monastery in the early Saxon period. I do not know it they had warriors to protect the priests but having given them a treasure to watch over I thought that some warriors might be useful too.

The fort where they ambush the Saxons is Housesteads and the one where they put Lars on the raft is Chesters. I walked the wall in 2004 and I remember that section very well. I just had a rucksack on my back and I would not have liked to attempt it with mail, helmet and a shield.

I used the Osprey book '*Saxon, Norman and Viking*' by Terence Wise as a reference book as well as the Ian Heath Book- '*The Vikings*'.
Griff Hosker March 2014

Other books
by
Griff Hosker

If you enjoyed reading this book, then why not read another one by the author?

Ancient History

The Sword of Cartimandua Series
(Germania and Britannia 50 A.D. – 128 A.D.)
Ulpius Felix- Roman Warrior (prequel)
Book 1 The Sword of Cartimandua
Book 2 The Horse Warriors
Book 3 Invasion Caledonia
Book 4 Roman Retreat
Book 5 Revolt of the Red Witch
Book 6 Druid's Gold
Book 7 Trajan's Hunters
Book 8 The Last Frontier
Book 9 Hero of Rome
Book 10 Roman Hawk
Book 11 Roman Treachery
Book 12 Roman Wall
Book 13 Roman Courage

The Aelfraed Series
(Britain and Byzantium 1050 A.D. - 1085 A.D.
Book 1 Housecarl
Book 2 Outlaw
Book 3 Varangian

The Wolf Warrior series (Britain in the late 6th Century)
Book 1 Saxon Dawn
Book 2 Saxon Revenge
Book 3 Saxon England
Book 4 Saxon Blood
Book 5 Saxon Slayer
Book 6 Saxon Slaughter
Book 7 Saxon Bane
Book 8 Saxon Fall: Rise of the Warlord

Book 9 Saxon Throne
Book 10 Saxon Sword

The Dragon Heart Series
Book 1 Viking Slave
Book 2 Viking Warrior
Book 3 Viking Jarl
Book 4 Viking Kingdom
Book 5 Viking Wolf
Book 6 Viking War
Book 7 Viking Sword
Book 8 Viking Wrath
Book 9 Viking Raid
Book 10 Viking Legend
Book 11 Viking Vengeance
Book 12 Viking Dragon
Book 13 Viking Treasure
Book 14 Viking Enemy
Book 15 Viking Witch
Book 16 Viking Blood
Book 17 Viking Weregeld
Book 18 Viking Storm
Book 19 Viking Warband
Book 20 Viking Shadow
Book 21 Viking Legacy
Book 22 Viking Clan

The Norman Genesis Series
Hrolf the Viking
Horseman
The Battle for a Home
Revenge of the Franks
The Land of the Northmen
Ragnvald Hrolfsson
Brothers in Blood
Lord of Rouen
Drekar in the Seine
Duke of Normandy
The Duke and the King

New World Series
Blood on the Blade

Across the Seas

The Anarchy Series
England 1120-1180
English Knight
Knight of the Empress
Northern Knight
Baron of the North
Earl
King Henry's Champion
The King is Dead
Warlord of the North
Enemy at the Gate
The Fallen Crown
Warlord's War
Kingmaker
Henry II
Crusader
The Welsh Marches
Irish War
Poisonous Plots
The Princes' Revolt
Earl Marshal

Border Knight 1182-1300
Sword for Hire
Return of the Knight
Baron's War
Magna Carta
Welsh Wars
Henry III

Lord Edward's Archer
Lord Edward's Archer

Struggle for a Crown 1360- 1485
Blood on the Crown
To Murder A King
The Throne

Modern History

The Napoleonic Horseman Series
Book 1 Chasseur a Cheval
Book 2 Napoleon's Guard
Book 3 British Light Dragoon
Book 4 Soldier Spy
Book 5 1808: The Road to A Coruña
Waterloo

The Lucky Jack American Civil War series
Rebel Raiders
Confederate Rangers
The Road to Gettysburg

The British Ace Series
1914
1915 Fokker Scourge
1916 Angels over the Somme
1917 Eagles Fall
1918 We will remember them
From Arctic Snow to Desert Sand
Wings over Persia

Combined Operations series 1940-1945
Commando
Raider
Behind Enemy Lines
Dieppe
Toehold in Europe
Sword Beach
Breakout
The Battle for Antwerp
King Tiger
Beyond the Rhine
Korea

Other Books
Carnage at Cannes (a thriller)
Great Granny's Ghost (Aimed at 9-14-year-old young people)
Adventure at 63-Backpacking to Istanbul

For more information on all of the books then please visit the author's web site at www.griffhosker.com where there is a link to contact him.